## About This Book

*25 Stories, 11 writers, 1 city.*

This collection of fairy tales for grown-ups contains dark moral tales, historical fiction, sci-fi, comedy, fantasy, crime, memoir and surreal fiction. All the stories have been freshly-written and all are set in and around the UK's only island city.

No chocolate box visions or soppy princesses in sight, the writers have used this magical genre to explore grown-up dilemmas, such as money problems, fear of rivalry in a relationship, floods, memories and changing bodies.

Find out why the real Guildhall clock is buried in an underground city to save time. Hear about the man who wished himself onto a ship in a whisky bottle. Discover why a Victorian detective joined forces with the circus to fight Spice Island's criminals. Embrace your bank statement or the ghost ship will get you.

Some stories delve into the city's rich island geography, others focus on rural Hampshire, its cow pats, mushrooms and breweries. Some have taken their favourite urban location and woven it into fantastical narratives that stretch back to Victorian times, or forward to a dystopian future.

Raw, mischievous, dark and yet familiar, these tales showcase a city bubbling with literary minds.

## By the authors
### Books
City of Devils – Diana Bretherick
The Devil's Daughters – Diana Bretherick
Lawless and the Devil of Euston Square - William Sutton
Lawless and the Flowers of Sin- William Sutton
Caught in the Web - Christine Lawrence
The Three Belles Star in 'We'll Meet Again'- Matt Wingett
Charlie and the Latex Factory – Tessa Ditner
The Bradt Guide to the Ivory Coast – Tom Sykes
Dune Tales: North African & Middle Eastern Travel Writing – Tom Sykes (ed.)
No Such Thing as a Free Ride? - Tom Sykes (ed.)
Rees Reads - Gareth Rees
### For Younger Readers
The Amber Room – Tom Harris
The Amber Antidote – Tom Harris
The Ten Rules of Skimming – Zella Compton
### Novellas
The Tourist- Matt Wingett
The Boiler Pool- Matt Wingett
The Tube Healer - Matt Wingett
Turn The Tides Gently - Matt Wingett
Heaven's Light Our Guide- Matt Wingett
The Song of Miss Tolstoy - Matt Wingett
### Contributions to Collections
Sini Sana – Sarah Cheverton
Spark Anthology – Lynne E Blackwood
Clickety Click , Closure Anthology – Lynne E Blackwood
Small Voices, Big Confessions – Tom Sykes
The Cambridge History of Literature and the Environment – Tom Sykes
### TV
The Bill (episodes) - Matt Wingett
### Plays / Performance
The Lesson in Dhansak - Lynne E Blackwood
Sing Sing Sing – Matt Wingett
London Life – Matt Wingett
If – Lynne E Blackwood
Beyond a Fairy Tale -Tessa Ditner
A Life in a Day - Tessa Ditner
### Poetry
All The Lonely People – Lynne E Blackwood

# PORTSMOUTH FAIRY TALES FOR GROWN-UPS

SARAH CHEVERTON
ZELLA COMPTON
LYNNE E BLACKWOOD
DIANA BRETHERICK
TESSA DITNER
TOM HARRIS
CHRISTINE LAWRENCE
GARETH REES
WILLIAM SUTTON
TOM SYKES
MATT WINGETT

*Life Is Amazing*

**A Life Is Amazing Paperback**
Portsmouth Fairy Tales For Grown-Ups
First published 2014 by Life Is Amazing
ISBN: 978-0-9572413-3-6
First Edition
*Collection and Introduction © Tessa Ditner, 2014*
*Cover Art and Design by Jon Everitt*
*All Rights Reserved*

*This book is dedicated to 10 Pompey diamonds.*

# Introduction

Angela Carter compared the writers of fairy tales to the inventors of the meatball: anonymous, genderless, stateless. She praised this story format for its flexibility, the way it could be told in any setting: a wedding, a pub, around a campfire, or re-packaged by Hollywood and turned into a multi-million movie.

J.F. Campbell, the Scottish fairy tale collector, would have called this Disneyfication 'putting tinsel on a dinosaur'; he believed you should only ever tell fables verbatim because they were locked into a time and place.

We're neither in the Carter nor the Campbell game, our fairy tales aren't tinsel-wearing Tyrannosauruses. They are new, have definite authors and yet, still retain a few whiskers of the originals. For instance, there are no frog princes to kiss, but a detective does sail to Spice Island to save a frog from a brothel. Rapunzel isn't a sultry seductress with fire exit hair, yet there are strands luring a stranger up a tower block. And a mermaid doesn't trade her tail for legs, but a man does purchase a tail to replace his missing leg.

I first discovered fairy tales, or rather 'Les Fables de la Fontaine', as a school girl in Paris. We read about a vain crow, with a whole camembert in her beak. She was tricked by a smooth-talking French fox into letting the cheese drop. In my class, pretty Parisian girls peppered their conversation with slaps; it was a standard form of punctuation. Paris was as pretty and unfriendly as my classmates were: warm waffles in the park with lawns you couldn't walk on, expensive flower shops and pavements strewn with dog poo, an equal obsession with patisseries and anti-cellulite cream.

I never imagined that I'd leave Paris and then London to live by the sea. I never imagined that it might be normal to hear foghorns instead of 'mind the gap'. The importance of living your life in an urban cityscape was my family's motto. My grandmother's saying was: 'I will retire in Oxford Street' and my mother's saying is: 'If you can survive in London...' My family believes capital cities apply the right amount of pressure, its caffeinated air propelling you forward.

And it wasn't just my family horrified, my London writing group were just as appalled: 'To Portsmouth? You're moving to Portsmouth? But what will you write about? What if you're happy there?'

'I won't be!' I swore. We all knew what 'happy' meant.

It meant bad writing.

But I was happy and it was frightening. What if I was so happy I wrote sonnets to Waitrose? What if all these years of building up London grit to stuff stories full of urban foxes counted for nothing? But I discovered that this city had its own sort of grit, its own marine-infused salty grit.

Portsmouth has ghosts of brothels, corset factories, asylums and especially ghosts of writers: Dickens, Rudyard Kipling, H.G.Wells, Arthur Conan Doyle had lived and written here. And of course Neil Gaiman had felt that grit growing up here and his first two graphic novels were, as he put it, a 'brain dump of his childhood in Portsmouth'.

As I spoke to others, I realised I wasn't the only one fascinated by this city. The wonderful Shirley Conran told me how much she had loved living here: 'particularly during storms when the seas used to crash over our house'. She remembers wearing a pink net ball gown and climbing through the dining room window to a waiting car, because the sea was crashing over her front door. Other writers had the same sensation: the combined effect of a city rich with past and its island geography meant you couldn't help but pick up characters, like gum stuck on the underside of your shoe. We joined forces, we collaborated, not just writers but artists too: Jon Everitt painted our cover, Port&Lemon created a map of the city with our fairy tale locations. 25 stories are contained in this collection. Some writers imagined a future Portsmouth, a city turned into a wave of concrete. Others chose to wind the city back to Victorian times. Others have collected pebbles, rain, pubs and starch and melted them into their own vision of life in this seaside city.

We hope you enjoy our collection.

Tessa Ditner, Portsmouth, 2014.

## The Bureau of Impossible Beasts
## Matt Wingett
*Map location: #18*

Let me explain, Officer. It all started when I read in this book about a curio shop down on The Hard, Pompey, in the 1830s. A long time back, yes I know, but the thing that jumped out at me was the unicorn horn.

Of course, some people said it wasn't a unicorn horn at all, but a narwhal's. But then, what did they know? - It didn't have a narwhal attached to it, did it?

I wanted one of those horns. I hunted through the antiques shops of Portsmouth - but no good. All snapped up long ago, I reckoned.

As for new ones – they've got to be illegal, right? I mean, there are thousands of elephants but you can't buy a tusk for love nor money. So how much more verboten is unicorn ivory?

Which means, when looked at logically, the only way to get a real, pukka, no-doubt-about-it unicorn horn is to go out and get one with a unicorn stuck on its blunt end.

That's what I decided to do.

Find a unicorn.

A real live unicorn.

Everywhere I looked I drew a blank. Marwell is the first zoo I've ever been where I was stared at so hard I thought I was the exhibit, and as for the Natural History Museum, well what a bunch of dinlos!

They had some nerve, though, I'll grant you. Saying there was no such thing as Curator of Cryptozoology. That proved it. Everybody knows the only reason someone's job gets covered up so there's notrace of it at all is it's deliberately being kept secret, see?

Think about it. All these sightings of mythical creatures over the years - yet not one scrap of physical evidence.

There's only one explanation. It's a conspiracy.

There's a team, right? Based in the Natural History Museum, they go out and they hoover up all unicorn bits, all centaur droppings and every last twist of yeti DNA. The big hole left at the core of every sighting of these fabulous creatures proves the team exists. They're the clear-up guys. The Bureau of Impossible Beasts.

I was shook up by my discovery. With the Bureau of Impossible Beasts ranged against me, how would I ever find a unicorn? I was about to jack it all in when finally I heard about one impossible beast that slipped through the net.

The Hayling Island Wildcat.

What, Officer? You haven't heard of the Hayling Island Wildcat?

Let me tell you – quickly mind – or the Bureau will get here and we'll never see the unicorn.

In the 1920s, rumours of a terrifying cat circulated around Hayling Island. It was fierce. A breed the likes of which had never been seen before. Terrifying burning eyes and teeth that could bite through sheet iron. 'The devil in feline form,' some called it.

Of course, there were doubters who said it was all made up. Just as these days they scoff at Sasquatches, laugh at the Loch Ness Monster and point fingers of fun at fairies. 'It's impossible,' they said. 'The Hayling Island Wildcat. Pah!'

But they were in league with the Bureau. Others of a more independent stripe said it did exist. So, did it or didn't it?

I refer you to the lofty subject of quantum mechanics. A gentleman very much at home in this field by the name of Schrödinger suggests the peculiar idea of burying a cat in a cage alongside a radioactive isotope. The isotope has a 50/50 chance of decaying. If it does decay it kills the cat. If it doesn't, moggy lives.

Schrödinger says that if you ensure there's no way to monitor its life signs, then logically speaking the cat is both alive and the cat is dead. As the wild fowl hunter once said, 'that's a pair o'ducks.' Get it, Officer? Pair o'ducks?

Okay. Maybe not. Moving on.

Now, with half saying the Hayling Island Wildcat existed and half saying it didn't, according to Schrödinger , that wildcat both existed - and didn't exist.

Let me be clear. Not finding something isn't proof it doesn't exist. It's proof you don't know how to look.

One day the Hayling Island Wildcat was minding its own business when it got a Bentley's tyre mark pressed into its fur. It ended up in a taxidermist's display case in Havant. After that, anyone could go and see it. The mystery cat that once both did and did not exist suddenly definitely did.

All because the Bureau didn't get to it in time.

Staring at the forlorn cat in its glass case, that's when I realised what I had to do. I had to roadkill a unicorn and nab it before the Bureau of Impossible Beasts got to it and disappeared it.

And so, Officer, that's why you find me here, searching among the bushes at the side of the motorway, next to a car with a very dented bonnet. You won't believe what I've knocked down and pulled out of these bushes in the past. Fairies? Oh yes, we all know we can find them in the bushes, *haha*. Werewolves? Most definitely. Vampires? You betcha.

But tonight Officer, tonight, I hit the jackpot. Literally. It jumped out in front of me and - smash! Look at that wrecked radiator grill if you want evidence! That's why I crashed, and that's why I'm in the bushes. Because I'm on its track, see? Definitely on its track.

Will I submit to a breath test? Well, officer, there's the matter of my asthma. Did I not mention the asthma? No? See, I can't breathe into it.

Yes, yes, I'll be very happy to go to the nick and submit to a blood test. But please don't take me just yet. We're so close.

Because they're coming - the Bureau of Impossible Beasts, to clear up the mess. There! Do you see that helicopter coming over, with its light on - over there?

Wait with me, Officer. The unicorn's in here somewhere. Dead or wounded. This is our only chance. If we don't find it, the Bureau will, for sure.

And does it really exist? And am I drunk?

Well let's just say, for the next few minutes, before I come with you, that I'm both drunk and not drunk.

And until that helicopter lands or doesn't land, that I definitely did and did not run over a unicorn.

### Day of the Clocks (Time-X Part 1)
### Tom Harris
*Map location: #3*

They won't tick anymore.

And they won't tock.

Of all the things to stop time, I never thought it would be us – the human race.

Looking out over my city, up here on the hill, the Guildhall Clock Tower is a speck on the landscape, but it's been so much more than that.

At high noon, the Pompey Chimes will ring out for the last time.

I am alone on Portsdown Hill, but surrounded by people. They have banners. They are here to get the best view. To watch the end. I am here to pay my respects and then I'm getting out of this place.

I feel inside my pocket for my father's watch. It's all I have to remember him by. I will not give it up to Time-X. No way.

I am a man of voting age. I have no family left alive. So I make my own decisions. I am saying NO to the abolishment of time.

Day of the Clocks – that's what they call it!

Today is the big day. The day they blow up all the clocks.

The chronometer at Greenwich Meantime was the most important clock in the world, setting time zones for the earth. So the UK went first. The BBC breakfast newsreader finished his shift with... 'Us Brits will still have our G&T, but no more GMT.' What an arsehole! He used to host the ten o'clock news, you'd think he'd show some remorse.

The Cosmo Clock 21, in Yokohama, Japan kicks off day two tomorrow. It's good to know it's not just our country that has lost the plot.

The Time-X agents in the crowd look bored. They start to frisk people at random. They are looking for the last of the smart phones and the watches. I edge away, my hand clutched around my father's pocket watch. I shuffle through the crowd, head down, till I reach the cordon. It's the worst view, but I have to get out.

The agents are all in black, which is appropriate, because today we should all be mourning. I don't know why they can't see it as clearly as I can. All these people, they seem happy that time will no longer exist. They can't have thought it through.

BBC, Sky and ITV are all covering it – live!

Every hour on the hour. They've set the destruction of time to a timetable! I would laugh, if I could remember how...

One by one they have fallen.

As the cameras roll, so our precious monuments crumble to dust. It started at midnight at Greenwich. They surprised everyone by not opening with Big Ben. *Size Doesn't Matter* was the headline grabber. I want to twat the idiot who came up with that.

They're going to finish with Ben of course. The UK has quite a line up: Wells Cathedral, Somerset, The Royal Liver Building in Liverpool, Eastgate Tower in Chester...

I've heard that when all the clocks are gone, they'll move on to destroying the sundials. Yep, they've thought of everything. The Samrat Yantra in Jaipur, India has star billing. I'd never heard of it until today.

The fuse has been lit. And like that, the beginning of the end of time is upon us.

The agents are restless, they're wading into the crowd.

I have to go.

For a moment I forget. It's so stupid, that I want to blow my head off. I reach into my pocket and I check the time. Can you believe it? It's a mistake that will cost me everything, because she sees me.

A girl. She looks out from under her black Time-X cap with that blazing red logo, her black hair bobs about her ears, her piercing blue eyes fixed on me.

She has seen the watch.

I glide it back into my pocket. We stare. It's too late...

Then she smiles. Maybe all is not lost. I smile back. It feels weird. Maybe there is hope...

I mime – Thank You!

She nods as I back away.

The crowd count down from ten. They are using numbers. An expression of time.

I hang my head. I turn and walk away.

An explosion fills the sky and the people cheer.

With tears bursting from my eyes, I run... My heartbeat racing out of time.

This is part 1 of THE TIME-X LEGACY – the story continues in The Last Watch.

**The Monster Beneath**
**Sarah Cheverton**
*Map location: #22*


*Morass* – *(noun) 1. An area of boggy or muddy ground; 2. A complicated or confused situation.*

Before Portsmouth there was the Great Morass, a swamp of mud and seawater fed by the Solent and shaped, so they say, like a huge hand, spreading its fingers from Southsea Castle across to Canoe Lake. In fact, for all the seaside charm found in its tidy flowerbeds and quaint pedalos, Canoe Lake is all that remains of the Great Morass today, the last water rising from that long sunken swamp into the modern city. Its middle finger, extending rudely into our present from the primordial sludge of our past, is a Pompey-esque reminder that something dark and ancient lies there.

If Canoe Lake is the last remaining imprint of the finger of that ancient beast, then running through the centre of Portsea island is its spine, and on its back, humans unwittingly play out their lives, cocksure and confident that the time of monsters is long since gone.

It is only children we tell of monsters, when darkness falls: tales of dragons, giants, trolls and ogres, and of princes and princesses that through valour overcome them. But who are we really comforting with such tales, the children, or us?

Life is deep and dark, complex and evolving, much like the Great Morass itself. And those monsters made for bedtime stories still sleeping in its depths? I don't believe they really exist, at least, not beneath the island city, but maybe in us. Such ancient beasts are found, I'm sure, beneath every dwelling, town and city that humans have ever made their home, but this is a Portsmouth story, and it is into the eyes of our beast I ask you to look today. But don't look too long. You never know what – or who – you might see staring back.

I learned of the monsters lurking beneath the surface from an early age, beasts that stared down from the branches of my family tree. Mine is a Portsmouth family: born, weaned and raised for generations in the city that rose up. Dark mud runs through us all - cut us and we are likely to ooze sludge and seawater blood.

My mother's roots extend deep into the sandbanks of the Little Morass of Portsea, the oldest part of the city, where soldiers and centuries raised the first walls that formed the city itself. My mother was raised by her grandmother, Violet, though my mother thought her only 'Mum' until a chance trip to the passport office revealed her adoption, long after Violet's death.

Violet's son, my mother's biological father, Fred, had six children of his own, though he barely seemed to notice. He was a petty thief, a drunk, a bully and, according to the whispers that hiss behind the raised hands of gossips, with a certain fondness for teenage girls. His tastes caught up with him in the end, as all sins do. When Fred was finally imprisoned, Violet was unable to save my mother's five older siblings from the Cottage Children's Homes to which they were finally sent, so she saved the babe in arms she could not bear to lose, my mother. She passed her off as her own and her second husband, no biological relation to my mother at all, as her father. My mother grew up adoring them both, never suspecting for a second the intricate fictions that lay beneath her names for them, and on the back of love – and lies - a family was made.

My mother's roots were buried in the oldest part of the city, but my father's roots roam Portsea island, buried deep beneath the neighbourhoods he and his siblings called home as children. His father was a bully, a man-monster who ruled his roost with fear, cruelty and arbitrary rules. Under his irrational temper, his wife, my grandmother, abandoned truth, living by lies and the scattered coins he occasionally threw her. She lent heavily on her children, involving them in her elaborate schemes to beg, borrow and steal food, while the neighbours looked on, muttering rumours that she would drop her knickers for a cigarette.

As a boy my father was afflicted with St Vitus Dance. St Vitus was a martyr who danced in a cauldron of boiling tar and lead, his punishment for driving out a demon from a man possessed. In medieval times, Vitus was blamed for the Dancing Plague, as men, women and children began to dance in their thousands across Europe, all unable to stop, until they danced themselves to death. My father's dance though was not fatal, only restless and reckless. When Father was only 10 years old, my grandfather removed the cover from the drain in the yard to carry out some repairs, and as he turned away, Father jumped from the wall into the darkness of the drain. Everyone blamed it on St Vitus, but perhaps it was something else inside him, struggling to be contained.

My parents' paths first crossed when they both got jobs in the same bank, counting notes and shiny coins in numbers they would never own. My father was a fast talking funny-man, a Romeo clown with bright blue eyes set firmly on my mother. The fact that she was engaged to another man meant nothing to him. He swept her off her feet and into his bed, and little more than a year had passed before her belly began to swell with the early germ of my brother's life. My father slipped a wedding ring onto her finger and my parents prepared for a life happily ever after. But monsters were waiting, as they often are, in the shadow of their short-lived happiness, and so was I.

Where Father and his siblings had been left to grow untamed, my mother had always been watched over. But Violet's 13th heart attack stole her breath clean out of her chest a quick year after their wedding day. My mother was left an orphan, alone with only her husband to protect her, unaware that in her fairy tale, my father was not the rescuing prince, but the sharp-clawed dragon that would leave her with scars no fairy godmother could heal.

By the time he was married, my father's dancing was over. As a grown man, the involuntary movements he made were more often punches than prances and it was us, his family, who danced for him. I could read my father's mood like music at a piano from the moment he entered a room, learned well the steps that pleased him. I was daddy's little girl, dainty, quiet and quick to please, but it seemed my brother was cursed with two left feet, every move awaking the beast that lived within our father's skin.

That there was a monster in him, I was certain, because the man that read me 'Winnie the Pooh' with a voice for each animal was not the beast that raged through the house for hours as we silently shivered behind barricaded doors. The man who raced and chased my brother and me around Eastney's beach houses until we screamed with laughter was not the man who ignored my mother's screams to stop as his fists came down upon her face. There was someone else there inside him, I had no doubt, and surely neither did my mother. Why else, I reasoned, would she stay so long imprisoned by a beast, if there was no hope her laughing prince could slay him?

Though the beast was often with him, I think there was a day my father tried to kill the monster that lived inside him, when I was a child.

It was a rare day at home for my brother and me. In the days before star-flung satellites and mobile phones sewn to every ear, my brother and I were always street-bound. We knew every short cut, back street and side alley from Fratton to Buckland, always making it home for tea from our trips to Portsmouth's forbidden playgrounds: the building sites and high rise roofs we secretly visited when our mother thought we were at the park. We needed no breadcrumbs to bring us home, we were seasoned explorers in a wide world that could offer us no terror like the one we lived in.

Our house on Jessie Road in Fratton was built not from gingerbread but from Victorian bricks. That day my brother and I were not outside, but like an early eighties Hansel and Gretel, were poised before the kitchen oven, cooking not witches but toast before an electric flame. Upstairs in our parents' room, my father's voice was rising with his temper, though we were barely aware of it. His anger was the backing track to our lives. My mother was silent, as she often was. There is no argument to give to a fury that does not respond to reason.

We were playing fools, waiting for the toast to brown. I reached for the grill handle.

'Stay away from that, it's hot,' my brother warned.

'You touched it,' I objected.

'Because I'm big.'

'I'm big!' I protested, tears stinging the backs of my eyes.

He took pity. 'Yes, you are.' He reached out to tickle me and I exploded into giggles.

For children so often afraid, we were always laughing, filled with mischief born of the solace we found in one another. My brother, with the soul of a lion, had crowned himself my protector on the day my parents brought me home and placed me in his arms. We grew as soldiers do, united by camaraderie and a common enemy.

Father came in behind us through the kitchen door. We didn't hear or see him at first. Reaching over my brother's head to the knife rack suspended on the wall, he picked the largest one. Perhaps my mother's carving knife was the closest we had to a sword and he knew it would take a large blade to slay a creature as fierce as the one inside him. He didn't say.

'I'm sorry,' is what he said instead, though I did not know what he was apologising for.

Perhaps he was sorry that the good father in him was not the only one we lived with. Perhaps he was sorry for the dances he led us to perform to keep the bad father at bay. Perhaps it was an apology for what we were about to receive, like a sad, bad grace before dinner. Or perhaps he apologised only for the battle that he was about to begin, for the chance that he might lose and the beast might win.

My father reached for the knife, took it and left. I was small, we both were, but four years my senior, the unfairness of sibling responsibility sat on my brother's shoulders for as long as I can remember.

I looked up at my brother for instructions on how to react to this strange turn in our day, but his eyes were not on me. They were first on the knife as our father hovered over us, and then on my father himself, as he retreated into the bathroom that led off our kitchen.

My eyes followed my brother's. We watched my father as he made first his curious apology, and then his way to the bathroom, a concrete cell he had helped to create, knocking through the separate bathroom and toilet to make one complete and improved model. The whole room was sealed in concrete, only a thin, cheap carpet covering a cold stone floor. Only months before, expelling fury from his lips in wild, incomprehensible incantations, my father had taken hold of my brother – a mere insect against a man's looming madness – as he kicked and thrashed against his grip. It was in this cold, concrete bathroom that my brother faced the most recent in a long line of punishments no child deserves: my father's fury, doled out in punches and slaps reserved exclusively for two of the people who loved him most, his wife and his son.

Perhaps Father took the largest knife to atone for this, his largest sin. Father's monster was in him that day but for the first time, the target was himself. Perhaps the beast that filled Father's eyes with fury when he looked at us finally turned his scarlet eyes inward. Or perhaps the one who held the knife was the Father who loved us, the Father who read to and played with us. Perhaps he took the knife and thought he could win.

Outside the closed door, the toast was only just starting to burn. My brother and I stared like baby owls, first at the door, then at each other.

'Get mum,' my brother whispered, 'Get mum or uncle. Now.'

I did not understand what was happening, but I obeyed. I did not know the threat inherent in a broken man taking a knife into a locked room with only his own darkness for company. But my brother, having offered himself up as protector of a family that failed to protect him, knew. With wisdom too heavy for a boy of only eleven summers, he knew that some punishments are too great for us to bear, even within the inverted moral universe of our home. He knew that worse than the many bad things that would likely continue to happen if Father came out of that room unscathed was the one bad thing that would mean Father never walked out at all.

It isn't fair that he knew this, but he did, and following my brother's compass as I always did, I ran.

It is true that we feared Father but he was our father and we loved him. We loved the man who escaped the shadow of the monster that lived inside him, loved his corny jokes and his overzealous ticklings. We loved his deep voice reading to us before sleep claimed us and we loved running, screaming, from his outstretched arms as we tore with him along the beach. Without the monster in his eyes, our father ran for hours with us through the park, taught us how to work our first computer, made us laugh until it hurt. We did not want him to leave, it was the monster we wanted gone. But we would not pay any price for its departure.

So I ran. Upstairs in his room, my uncle was reading.

'Uncle, you've got to come, Father has a knife and he's gone into the bathroom with it.'

Perhaps this is what I told him, I can't remember. Such panics were not unusual in our house and did not arouse confusion or inspire delay.

Whatever I said, Uncle came to the kitchen. He called to his brother through the plastic bathroom door, cajoling him to surrender the knife, encouraging the monster to release our father to the family that loved him through their fear.

Following the sound of panic - the anthem of my father's fury - my mother ran into the kitchen. Father had been bad-tempered with her all morning and she tracked his moods with the keen sense of a bloodhound, always trying to predict the violence that might come.

She reached for my brother and me with practised grace, ready to herd us out of danger, to place herself between us and harm.

And there, as if I fell asleep in the middle of a bedtime story, my memory ends.

My brother is frozen always at the oven, clutching his fingers for a moment before reaching out a hand to bring me to his side. My uncle stands, stone still, whispering words of hopeful, futile magic to his brother behind the bathroom door. My mother is in mid-stride, reaching to remove us from danger, still hopeful she can keep us safe. And I am as I always was, the tiniest subject in Father's kingdom, looking on with eyes wide enough to take in all the horrors of his madness, waiting for the time when my limbs would stretch me into a full grown writer.

For a long time before I knew the ending, I thought I had been taken away at exactly that moment, left with only the half-formed legacy of events that children so often inherit long after their protection has been made impossible.

Yet it turns out I was there all along, saw the ending play out in a Technicolor reality I deny myself in memory, or am somehow denied.

I wish I knew, I wish I understood how a memory becomes so impenetrable, so unyielding to the clutches of will. But all I know is that I never move past that moment: my brother at the oven, Uncle at the door, Mother with arms outstretched, and my father out of sight facing down his monster with the biggest knife he could find.

What I know of what happened next is a matter of someone else's record, shared with me in the spirit of regret in a whiskey-soaked whisper. I cannot say who told it to me, and that's fine. I know the language of secrets far better than what passes among humans as truth.

As it turns out, there were many there that day with cause to remember.

Despite the blood that tied them, no words that Uncle whispered to the monster in my father were enough for it to relinquish its hold. Uncle and my mother called the police, who duly and dutifully arrived to take over the siege. But no one in the bathroom that day had any fear of the law.

Perhaps fancying them as further demons, my father fought the two officers that came to save him. My brother and I were whisked outside to safety, where we stood with Uncle as the siege became a battle. Mother stayed inside, staying true to the promise she made in a princess gown never to leave my father's side. Perhaps she knew even then it would be a promise she could not keep, that one day she would be forced to choose between the children and the man she loved, forced to leave him to the monster he could not yet defeat.

Father fought them first in the bathroom and then in the kitchen, wielding the knife as a sword and a dustbin lid as a shield. He held the officers at bay, barricading himself behind the kitchen door. The police, as fearful of him in that moment as his family often were, called for reinforcements, a luxury we rarely found at our disposal at such times.

More police came and more. I am told it took several officers and a police dog to finally capture and restrain Father, proof perhaps of the monster that had him in its grasp, and the determination it possessed to possess him forever. Upon his capture, these huntsmen and their tamed wolf threw him in a van brought specifically to contain such madness and drove their struggling cargo to St James' Hospital, Portsmouth's own Bedlam for those still touched by the darkness beneath the Great Morass.

It is fitting that they chose Saint James' as the asylum's namesake. There are two Saint Jameses, distinguished by the church with the titles 'Greater' and 'Lesser'. I imagine many minds dragged through its doors found themselves similarly divided.

Uncle had been taken there too as a child. With a loss of memory that seems to run in our family, he cannot remember why, but they kept him within the walls of St James' for many months. My brother too, while still a child, would be sent through those gates for reasons named by adults as his loss of control. After locking a teacher in a cupboard, my brother was sent to a boarding school, the first time we were ever separated. His face, like my blood, would freeze when we left him there. My brother, the lionheart always in absolute command of the few small things in life he could control, never shed a tear.

I don't know how long they kept my father at St James', but the doctors believed they had silenced the beast in him long enough to send him back home. But was it Father that convinced them, or the monster inside him? All I know is that something else still stared at us from Father's eyes when he came home, sullen and silenced, though it would not stay quiet for long.

Eventually the monster's screaming would deafen us all to our father's suffering, would drive our mother to pack our bags and set off on the long road to survival. I was not sorry to leave the house on Jessie Road. My brother and I were as scared of that house as we often were of Father. We would never miss it, would remember nothing that happened there with fondness or joy. The only heaven we ever found in that house was in each other and our love is the closest I ever came to understanding what humans mean when they say 'God' – a holy, living light within and between us, untethered to the bricks and mortar where the religious go to worship. That light no monster of my father's could dim or extinguish, indeed its hatred only made it shine brighter. That so much light could penetrate my father's darkness is, perhaps, the happiest ending we could expect from our time in the house in Jessie Road.

Away from Father's monster, we all began to shine a little brighter, particularly our mother. I remember little of my mother in the shadows of our old home, but in the years that followed their separation, her laughter and wise-cracking tongue would pepper my days with smiles and wrap me in a safety missing from my early years. Having spent so many years living with fear, she dispensed of it when we left that house. I know my mother only as a warrior, the fierce protector who took over from my brother and who would never forgive herself for the past from which she could not protect either of us. I think each one of us carries that guilt towards each other, our own little monsters that whisper to us in the dark.

So who won between the monster and my father? Well in different ways, I think they both did.

The monster inside him stole from my father everyone he loved - my mother, my brother, me, another wife, another child. Some of us he lost only for a while, some forever. Perhaps in all that losing, my father realised the war could only ever be between the monster and himself. And that war, over many years and many battles, my father won.

This was a battle he fought alone, without any of us there to hold his hand, and no army to shout his valour when the beast lay defeated at his feet. It takes more bravery than most of us ever know to face the monster that lives within us, to step into the dark shadows of ourselves most of us so desperately hide. I was a grown woman fighting monsters of my own before I understood the profound courage and quiet dignity with which my father fought his. I will be long in the grave before the pride I feel for his victory fades away.

This is no happy ending, I don't believe in those. My father conquered his demon but he is no angel, just a man. Yet to me, he is and always will be a hero, a knight in blood-stained armour, standing over the dragon he fought for much of his life to kill.

As for me, growing up with a monster has its advantages. I learned to be ready, always, for whatever dark mischief it might awake. Thirty winters later, and my own demons grown full size, my response to danger always is watchful, calm. I am an old hand at fighting monsters now, especially my own.

Observation is the cornerstone of storytelling. If I had not grown up always watching for the monster in my father, I would not be a writer now. Memory itself is a fairytale, made of the stories we tell over and over, to ourselves and to each other. Our fairy tales are passed down in families, they grow, shift, and evolve with each telling. If I added each one of my family's stories of what happened that day to my own, there would be five different fairy tales, each one of them absolutely true to its teller.

28

Sometimes I wake in the night when memory's fairy tales stretch their fingers between dreams and reality. On such nights, I walk to Canoe Lake to stare a while at the water, all that remains in our civilised city of the Great Morass. On such nights I try to forget the monster in my father's eyes I knew as a girl, but sometimes, I see his scarlet fire shining there, in my own.

## The Mr Potato Parts Shop
### Tessa Ditner
*Map location: #5*


Henrietta printed out the Wightlink ferry ticket and handed it to Matt along with his credit card. She had booked the most expensive crossing time, even though things had been slow at the estate agents where he worked.

'Are you sure you don't want me to keep hold of it?' she asked.

'I want you to relax,' he said. One day without her enormous handbag that contained a thousand distractions from their marriage might help get them back on track, he thought.

'Have you got the tickets?' she reminded him as they locked the house. He rushed back in to pick them up from the kitchen table. She rolled her eyes and walked to the car. The postman stared at her, wondering: *wasn't she that girl from the magazines?*

As she strapped herself into the passenger seat, she added 'forgetfulness' to the list of cons. She knew that being married meant that *pros and cons* lists shouldn't matter anymore, but she'd never really stopped doing it. A year into the marriage, her husband was getting further and further from her perfect man. She had a fairly clear picture of Mr Perfect too: Brad Pitt's body, Russell Brand's cockiness, Colin Firth's manners, Joaquin Phoenix's top lip... She reached for her lipstick, reminding herself that in model years she was 73. Matt noticed how much gloss she was layering onto her lips. He shouldn't have told her to leave her handbag at home. He had wanted her to feel like he would take care of everything, especially today, but that ridiculously expensive bag was one of her shields.

'Check out that healthy breakfast,' she snorted as they waited to board the ferry. Matt turned to look at the couple in the car beside them.

'So unhealthy,' he mumbled, but secretly he wished he was in that sort of comfortable relationship. He wished Henrietta would eat peanut butter sandwiches and borrow bits of his newspaper as it rested against the steering wheel.

'I'm getting a coffee, do you want anything?' she asked, before remembering that she hadn't been allowed to bring her wallet. Matt handed his wallet over, realising the plan to make her feel looked-after had already backfired. He was coming across as controlling.

She came back clutching two Costa cups. She turned her L'Oreal face towards him. 'Matt, I've been thinking...' His stomach twisted, but the car in front moved and he had to focus on driving onto the ferry.

Henrietta softened as they found the steps down to Forelands Beach. The Beach Hut restaurant was where he went down on one knee. Matt watched the huts that gripped on to the side of the beach. He had promised her they would buy one and spend long passion-fuelled nights hidden away, only the sea banging at their door. Henrietta thought of the Isle of Wight festival where they'd met. She had been camping with friends, all modelling buddies. None of them liked each other but they hung out close together for maximum impact, especially when photographers were near. After two days of washing with wet wipes and shovelling *Confessions of a Concealerholic* on her face, she decided to use her looks to secure a shower. Matt had gone to the festival as a last minute thing. Henrietta was more thankful than she had thought, escaping with this stranger for a night of fluffy towels, shampoo and a springy bed. As the dust and flies drowned in his plumbing, she felt beautiful. The next morning, she refused to get out of the protective shell that was his duvet.

But Portsmouth hadn't been the permanent festival she'd imagined. No one spent the day in fairy wings or t-shirts that said: 'Sometimes I just want to dress in a bunny suit and scream'. Plus she had missed the opening of the new Louis Vuitton store where her friends had been papped, because she'd been in Waitrose wondering what fish to buy for dinner.

Matt ran his hand across the smooth pebble that had their table number written on it. Henrietta ordered crab and avocado and a large pot of coffee from the springy-legged owners of The Beach Hut. Matt chose the same and hoped this was a glamorous enough anniversary for her. Maybe he should have booked the other ferry, the one that went all the way to France. They could have driven to the Champagne region, the Chateau d'Etoges where they'd stayed for their honeymoon. Henrietta had been content there, sipping her morning coffee from Limoges porcelain.

A woman and her son walked past with rusty tools in a bucket. They wore matching Wellington boots and puffy, sleeveless jerkins. They must have been going to fix their hut which had been damaged by the recent storms. Matt felt his heart beat faster. What if he offered to buy it from them? Which one was it? How much storm damage were they going to fix? He told Henrietta his plan.

'You think I want to spend my old age wearing wellies?' she sneered, giving her sunglasses a wipe. Matt promised he'd be responsible for repairs. Besides, he was an estate agent - he knew plenty of handymen. Henrietta knew that if she said yes, he would buy her a beach hut as their anniversary gift. But at what price? Another year in Portsmouth?

When the crab arrived Henrietta was shocked to discover how subtle the taste of the crab was compared to the harshness of the coffee. Her taste buds were barely able to pick up the sea-drenched flesh lying on its bed of creamy avocado. She lifted the cup of coffee to her lips and washed all the softness away. 'I want a divorce,' she told Matt and watched the pain etch itself onto his features.

Matt didn't like the tinkling sound that filled the shop when he walked in. It had taken all his courage to come here. He had followed the instructions on the website: 'walk past The Groundlings Theatre, down the alleyway marked 'Artist Ironmonger', climb the fire exit steps to the first floor.' He felt like a thief, or a criminal, but if this could save his marriage... Lately Henrietta had taken to wearing La Perla under her clothes to 'pop to the supermarket'.

'Can I help you?' the shop assistant asked, smiling.

'Do you have The Brad?' Matt asked in a choked voice. The shop assistant walked him over to what looked like a wall of doorknobs: every size, every shape, floor to ceiling. Each had a name inscribed on the drawer but instead of sizes or styles, it featured the names of the rich and famous.

'We have it in skin or silver plated.' The man opened a drawer. He handed Matt a box lined with white velvet. Inside was The Brad, glistening, perfectly polished like a chunky Tiffany's jewel. Matt felt a lump in his throat. A small voice in his head told him that this wasn't going to make a difference.

'The skin-colour is more subtle,' the shop assistant explained. 'But if it's for a gift, the silver is more of a statement.'

'How much is the silver?' Matt asked thinking *Henrietta doesn't do subtle*.

'Three thousand pounds,' the shop assistant said. It was far more than Matt had expected to pay. Then again, Keith from accounts had boasted spending three grand on his last skiing holiday.

'Or,' the shop assistant suggested, seeing his customer hesitate, 'we offer part exchange. Our Real Man range is doing well at the moment. I can give you a quote, if you step into the changing room?'

Matt was astonished when the part exchange reduced the price of The Brad by seventy five percent. He handed over his credit card relieved (and a bit flattered). He left the shop with a lightness in his step, despite the clunky new purchase. That evening, he met Henrietta for dinner at Kitsch'n d'Or. He felt bulky and self-conscious, like he was carrying a whole load of keys in a front pocket. She checked her teeth in the polished surface of her fish knife and prepped herself for being odious. Why wouldn't he just sign the divorce papers? It's not like she wanted any of his cash. If anything, she was richer than him. He was too nervous to notice her snide remarks about every dish. 'This soup tastes of ashtray', 'the salmon is obese, check out the white lines in the flesh...' Why wasn't he reacting? Why wasn't he getting embarrassed by the way she talked down to the waiters? He usually hated that.

It was only later, as he undressed for bed, that she noticed there was something different about him. Maybe he was having an affair too? Not that it counted as an affair given their imminent divorce. She felt a pang of something as she thought of him with someone else. She felt her own affair was glamorous; an excuse to dress up and wear expensive underwear. But it wasn't so glamorous if he was doing it too. That's when she heard a clunk as something knocked their side table.

Then she saw it. The accessory Vogue had said was 'a must-have for spring', GQ had named 'bedroom buddy #1' and Cosmo had called the 'orgasm-guarantor'. She hadn't expected Matt to be into body modification. For the first time in a long time, she was intrigued by her husband. She pulled him towards her, eager to test his upgrade.

Matt chucked his wife around her favourite 800 thread count Egyptian cotton sheets. She felt like she was in bed with James Bond. She felt like it was their first night again: she was clean and beautiful. But every time he said 'I love you', Henrietta winced. By three in the morning, she blurted out that she was having an affair. Matt had been too shocked and frankly too exhausted to stop her from packing her bags.

'I'm sorry,' she said before leaving. But she wasn't looking at his face, she was apologising to the metal between his legs.

It only dawned on him the next morning, as he sat miserably at his desk, that changing had only made her leave faster. Keith from accounts dropped a lads mag on his desk with his usual sarcastic comment. But Matt didn't see big breasted beauties; he just saw half-naked, female versions of himself. They had changed their hair colour, their breasts, maybe even their mouths and noses. How much of himself would he have to change to keep Henrietta?

'I'd like to return this and go back to my own one,' Matt said the next day. He handed the shop assistant The Brad in its case.

The man looked apologetic as he said: 'We've actually sold your one.'

'Sold it?'

Matt was in shock. They had sold his penis? 'But I want it back!' he said stupidly, panicked and confused. It wasn't that he thought his one was any better than any of these famous, polished and sophisticated ones, it's just that it was... his. The shop assistant tried to tempt him with The Cruise and The DiCaprio but Matt didn't want a designer penis or a celebrity penis. He didn't care that his had been plain and not shiny.

A sound came from the changing room, followed by a soft voice calling out: 'Do you have anything else from yesterday's range?'

'Interested in selling any others?' the man asked Matt with an encouraging smile.

'Others?'

How many penises did he think he had?

'Hands fetch a great price,' he explained, 'and arms if you'll swap both. It's very rare.' Matt was too upset to tell the salesman the whole thing had been a horrible mistake, that even if David Beckham's butt was in the discount bin, it wouldn't be enough to keep his wife. It was best all round if he got back to his miserable desk and his miserable life with all his parts clicked back in place.

'The full package?' a woman beamed at him. She had been in the changing room but she hurried over to Matt and took his hand. She flipped his palm round like she was checking the size of a T-shirt in Gap. She unbuttoned his shirt and examined his chest which was neither firm nor flabby. He was too surprised to move. The shop assistant watched, intrigued by the growing popularity for Real Men ranges.

'You have a whole sample,' the woman said, 'and it matches the part I bought.' She was relieved. She thought she would have to buy him in parts and assemble him with a little screw driver. She was about to ask: 'How much?' but the shop assistant had vanished down the back room, to call his stockist and cancel the Jay-Z and the Vin Diesel range.

'Hello,' Matt smiled. He felt nervous, but not too nervous to ask to buy his penis back.

They braved the fire exit steps together and took a seat in the cafe of the nearby Groundlings Theatre. The place was busy with volunteers carrying costumes to the back room. A writing group were reading out each other's play in a chaos of laptops and coffee cups. A family were enjoying a Sunday roast. They sat at a quiet table beside a glass cabinet that contained a lion's head. The table had a teapot in the middle with a plastic flower sticking out of the sprout. Henrietta would never have chosen that table, Matt thought to himself. The more they chatted, the less Matt felt the need to own his penis in the same way he once had.

By the time he was back at his desk, he had agreed on a time share. Matt signed the divorce papers that night and posted them off. He called Henrietta in London and they chatted easily for ten minutes. When she put down the phone she felt uneasy, like she had lost something precious. Then she noticed she'd dropped an earring and figured it must be that.

Saturday morning was Matt's first date with the girl who owned his penis. She arrived at his with a bottle of wine and a box. Matt anxiously checked the box to make sure it was definitely his penis. It was. He was relieved. And it was shinier than when he had part exchanged it. She had polished it and looked after it.

'Do you need help with that?' she offered with a cheeky smile, as he clicked it back on.

## Heads and Tails
## Diana Bretherick
*Map location: #19*


### Spencer

Even now I wonder what might have happened if I could have warned her. But like all humans she did not speak dog. I tried my best with the tools at my disposal but paws and whimpers are no substitute for hands and words. Does this mean that I am to blame? It certainly feels that way. But let me tell you my story and you can be the judge.

Stones are inoffensive things as a rule – round, smooth, pleasant to touch, warmed by the sun perhaps and smelling of earth or, if they are beach pebbles, the salty old sea. But these stones... these stones were different. They had eyes.

I remember it so clearly. It was one of those strange days in early spring when the sun shines as if it's summer but the air is still cold. Meg decided to venture onto Southsea beach as part of our early morning walk. She sat and squinted, looking out to sea as I snuffled about in my usual way, more to fulfil expectations rather than anything else. Then I found them – three stones staring at me with those deep black eyes. I stared back; a mistake, as it turned out. They responded by...well, I know it sounds ridiculous – by biting me. I yelped in shock and pain. Meg came running over.

'What is it, Spencer?'

Yes that's me. Nice name, don't you think? Distinguished – a sort of elder statesman feel to it, which is just as well, as I'm getting on these days – almost 9. Funny really – I never felt my age – well not until recently.

I tried to tell her. 'It's those stones...no...no...don't touch them!' But it was no good. She couldn't hear me.

'Have you caught yourself on something sharp?' Then she found them. They were sharp...but not in the way she meant.

'How strange! Look Spencer...they're watching us!' she said. 'They're like heads.'

Then she gathered them up, peered at them for a moment and put them in her pocket. It was obvious to me that she shouldn't have done. Almost as soon as she had, the sea mist started rolling in from the island over the water, and soon we were surrounded by it. I couldn't see much. Even Meg was barely visible. It was as if we were suddenly enshrined in our own little world. I barked a warning but she took no notice. Instead of putting the stones back, Meg just grabbed me, put the lead back on and off we went.

When we got back, at first she seemed to have forgotten the stones altogether. She put out some food for me and then went into her study. I followed her in and sat by the fire while she worked. She's a freelance translator. Ironic really – if only dog had been one of her languages then things would have turned out very differently. But instead she was an expert in Mandarin. Fat lot of use that was in the end. Anyway there we were, in her study, which is also the living room... all was peaceful... but sadly that didn't last.

**Meg**

They were only stones... I don't even know why I picked them up really but I did, so I guess that makes the whole horrible thing my fault. Spencer trod on something when we were on the beach and made a bit of a fuss and that's when I saw them. They just looked a bit odd...sort of quirky...like three heads. They even seemed to have faces. I thought they might look nice as ornaments. Then this weird fog descended on us. It seemed to come from nowhere. I couldn't see more than a foot ahead of me so I decided we should head back to the house. I didn't even remember that I had the stones until it was time for a coffee. I fished them out of my pocket and put them on the mantelpiece in front of the mirror and went to put the kettle on.

I looked out of the kitchen window. The sea mist had thickened and was swirling about the garden in a very peculiar way. It was a sort of yellowish colour. I'd never seen that before. I poked my head out for a moment just out of curiosity. There was a slight whiff of rotten eggs and I started to wonder if there had been some kind of chemical spill or something. I turned the radio on and listened to the news but there was no mention of it so I assumed it was just a weather thing. We get some odd things happening here in Southsea. The place seems to attract the bizarre. Still I rolled a few old towels up and put them by the doors and windows, just to be on the safe side.

It wasn't until later that day that it started.

### Spencer

It seemed to get dark earlier than usual and the mist didn't clear at all. If anything it got worse as the day wore on. Usually I lie by the fire on days like these but somehow it didn't feel as welcoming. Every time I looked at it my eyes were drawn to those stones staring down at me from the mantelpiece. They were peculiar looking things. The first was grey but had large white patches, not unlike Rex, a dog friend of mine who lived nearby. But Rex didn't have the face of an owl etched into his side like the stone did.

The second was like a horse with flared nostrils but it had scales and one eye staring out at me.

But the last was the strangest of all. It was almost a human face but the head was misshapen. It had eyes like the other two but these were sort of narrowed as if they were full of hate... it seemed to be screaming.

In the end I settled down some way from the fire, between the stones and Meg. There was a layer of something in our house that day – a malevolence is the closest I can get to describing it. It sent a chill through me every now and then, as if it was reminding me that it was there. I had the feeling that Meg needed to be protected from it, whatever it was.

We had both dozed off. Meg had finished her work and was reading in her chair by the fire and I was lying at her feet when something woke us. I couldn't swear to it but I think that I saw, in the corner of my eye, something fluttering outside the window. I looked over to Meg who was stirring in her sleep. Then the sounds began.

### Meg

I had been asleep in my armchair when I heard it – first there was a rhythmic beating of the air – like the wings of something and then a thud... over and over again... as if a bird was flying into the window. That was where the noise seemed to be coming from. Spencer had heard it too. He was sitting up and staring at the mantelpiece, for some reason. When I went over to the window he howled. It was as if he was trying to warn me.

'Don't be silly Spencer, it's just a bird!' I said. But when I looked out into the garden with the mist still swirling round it, I couldn't see anything, even though the noise continued.

Then it started to get louder and louder. It sounded as if it had come into the house. I just had to back away from it. Somehow I knew that if I didn't, it would get hold of me... that it was coming after me. I grabbed Spencer and we ran upstairs to the only room without a window – the bathroom. We locked ourselves in but the noise had followed us... the beating of the invisible wings went on and on and there were repeated thuds against the door as if the creature, if that is what it was, was trying to get to us.

Eventually, after what seemed like hours the noise began to fade. We did not come out immediately, for fear of what we might find. Instead we sat on the bathroom floor and waited. After a while when we started to feel safe, we came out. If only we had realised that safe was the last thing we were. We didn't know that it was just the start.

### Spencer

Once we were brave enough to go downstairs, we crept along the landing and tiptoed down to the living room. All was still. I looked over to the mantelpiece. The owl stone was gone. I tried to alert Meg, nudging her and whining but she was not interested. She sat down in her chair and looked into the glowing embers of the fire. 'What was that?' she asked. I wish I could have told her. It would have saved her from all that came next. But instead all I could do was comfort her so I nuzzled her hand. 'We'd better take you out...' she said and looked nervously into the garden. Well I wasn't keen, in case the bird was still out there but when a dog's got to go, he's got to go...So we went.

### Meg

It was all right to start with. The mist was worse than ever but we had made a joint decision not to go further than a quick trot round the common that leads down to the sea. It was deserted, which wasn't surprising, given the weather and the time. There was a silence and a stillness that was unusual. I know it sounds odd but I remember that I found it strangely moving. The place looked eerily beautiful and for a while I was happy for Spencer and I to have it to ourselves. The tops of the trees were just about visible, like black lace emerging from a white fur cloak. I could see the lights from the street lamps glowing in the distance like eyes. But as we went on, the mist seemed to sink until it surrounded us completely, just as it had on the beach earlier. Spencer usually runs round a bit but not that night. He stuck by my side, determined for us not be separated. And he was right. For the second time we heard a noise but this was different. It was not the beating of wings, it was hooves.

### Spencer

The noise surrounded us, as if horses were circling, but getting closer each time, until they were so near I could hear them snorting and whinnying. But we could not see them. And the other thing was... I could not smell them. I pride myself on my olfactory prowess but that night it seemed to have failed me. It was almost as if the horses weren't there at all. Except... their sound was all too evident. The hooves beat on and on and got closer and closer, louder and louder, until they were almost on top of us... an invisible stampede.

### Meg

'Run!' I shouted. Well what else could we do? I couldn't see them but I couldn't be certain that they were not there. What if it had been something to do with the mist – an optical illusion? I could not take the risk. So run we did. At first they seemed to be following us but as we got closer to home the hoof beats faded into the distance and it seemed as if we were finally safe. Or at least that's what we thought.

### Spencer

Once we got home and Meg locked the door behind us we stood looking at each other. 'I just want this day to be over,' Meg said. 'I'm going up.' She went round the house first, making sure that everything was secure. The garden was still full of the fog and I watched her peer outside. But all was quiet...too quiet actually and that layer of something bad was still there. I knew that things had not returned to normal but what could I do? Meg went upstairs to get ready for bed whilst I did my own check. I couldn't find anything and I was about to join her when I noticed... the second stone was missing.

### Meg

I lay under the covers with Spencer at the foot of the bed. I didn't normally allow him to do that but that night was different. I needed him... well... the truth of it was, I think, we needed each other. The Pompey chimes sounded their final knell of the day. It was midnight. I felt my eyelids drooping. I started to descend into that nether land of dreams and reality where nothing quite makes sense and yet... in an odd way it does. Then I heard it... a kind of rustling. At first I thought it was just Spencer stirring in his sleep but then I realised it wasn't in the house at all. I went over to the window. There was a shape in the garden. It seemed to come out of the mist and yet somehow be part of it at the same time. The figure grew and grew until it was as tall as the house itself. I felt pulled towards it. I began to open the window.

### Spencer

I barked. It was all I could do. I wanted to stop her but she ignored me. She was staring straight ahead at the figure in the garden. It began as nothing more than a big mass of fog but then it seemed to take some kind of shape. It grew what looked like arms and they began to extend towards Meg. By the time it had reached her through the open window the arms had hands at the end of them and those hands had fingers, long feathery things that went to her throat and wrapped themselves around until I could hear her struggling to breathe...

### Meg

I tried to pull away but my hands just went straight through. I clutched at nothing. They tightened their grip around my throat. I could not even scream. Then I felt myself being lifted and pulled until I could sense that I was no longer in the house. I was surrounded by mist and I could not breathe. Then the mist cleared.

### Spencer

I saw her being taken and I could do nothing but bark. She seemed to diminish, bit by bit as it swallowed her until there was nothing left. I ran down to the living room to see if I could get into the garden. I looked up at the mantelpiece . The third stone had gone. I went to the window but Meg was not there. All I could see was something hanging in the air. It was a misshapen head. The face had narrowed eyes, full of hate. It seemed to be screaming.

### Meg

I can see Spencer sometimes, in the house, but I can't get to him. I'm trapped in this mist. I see his face at the window and I hear him crying. It breaks my heart.

**Spencer**

I can see her sometimes, in the garden, but I can't get to her. I'm trapped in this house. I see her face through the window and I hear her crying. It breaks my heart.

## The Flame Haired Girl and the Whale
## Zella Compton
*Map location: #13*

The first time I saw her, she was barefoot, digging her feet into the shingle trying to stay upright as the tide rushed in and out. The water cut at the bottom of her skirt and she laughed from her belly as she played with the sea. The sight of her filled me with a deep longing.

She had a camera strapped across her chest, and a bag of friendship behind her feet. Towel, scrunched up swimsuit, Frisbee, sun lotion from a day clouding over, worn favourite sandals.

I think it was her freedom that drew their attention. The sound of her laughter through the long-baked afternoon, echoing off the high hot walls back down to her. They were high up, looking down at the small figure.

'Hey, hey, little girl.'

And

'Why you ignoring me sweetie?'

And

'You want me to come and play with you?' Not local accents you understand, somewhere north of here, I'm not really sure, but not local.

'I can teach you a new game.'

And

'Answer me bitch.'

Then they started to build a rhythm, calling her a slut, and shouting about her flaming hair, and about the way she looked in general, and how they'd rather have a wank (but I knew that wasn't

45

true as I had eyes and I could see what they saw).

'I'll give you a lollipop to suck-on.'

That's when I walked up the beach, back from the water, past the tangled sticks in orange and blue string and the clumps of drying weed. I hid in the shadow made by the towering sea wall and poked at a broken green bottle with my foot.

She ignored the calls. Didn't turn once. I wondered if she knew it was about her? But, with the promise of a dark storm coming, and hot fat rain drops breaking ground, there was no one else on the beach except for me, and I was hiding in the darkest spot. So she had to know, right?

'Last chance to show some respect bitch.'

Nothing.

That made it worse.

Because as she laughed into the sea's black depths, totally oblivious, they came down from the walls, across the shingle with laughter slowing like their footsteps, until they stood behind her, and one grabbed her roughly by the shoulder, and pulled her around, and she slipped in the shingle, and cried out in fear, and shouted words which were dense in their sound, really full, big, because she couldn't quite pronounce them as you would.

'Get off me, get off me.' I didn't know it then, but she was deaf, and that's why her words were clogged. They thought she was a freak, her speech marked her, as their alcohol stench which I could practically taste as I scuttled away, marked them.

I was deaf to her pleading as I hurried to the shadows and through the gap. I made myself deaf to the screams of the seagulls, and the hot shriek of the buses and the children passing me by, acting like teenagers are supposed to, dropping litter and spit, and the older people hurrying because the storm was coming and they had to get home to stay dry. I was deaf to it all because if I listened, what else would I hear?

That evening the local news reported a whale had washed up on the beach. The storm had failed to happen, instead the whale appeared, no one knew where it had come from (how would they?) but it had beached itself, in the place where I'd seen the girl. Deep black in colour, deep shine in texture and with deep sorrow it lay on the beach. The radio, the television, and the internet played the soundtrack of its drawing breaths. I made a flask and headed back to the front.

The beach was mobbed. I could hardly see due to the crowds, but I pushed my way down the rushing shingle. Children were swimming out in the water trying to get a look at the creature from a different viewpoint, a couple of them were on brightly coloured rings. It didn't seem quite right to me, but what could I do? Tell their parents that the death of whale was a serious business?

Boats kept watch at a more respectful distance, some small and scudding with pert stiff white sails. Ferries passed by, calling out deep belches as holiday-makers in their hundreds hung over the side craning to get a good picture.

Near the beach there were three TV vans with tall aerials and young crowds hanging around their doors. Radio interviewers stalked among the people, plying overripe microphones under their noses, looking for a comment more than 'I've never seen anything like this'.

Most of the crowd watched from behind their lenses of phones and cameras while policemen patrolled their yellow tape and firemen shifted buckets of water up from the sea and poured and poured. Crackling radios gave tiny insights into a longer term plan of hoses and sea water.

My attention was drawn from the flip-flopped masses because, as the sun sunk over the island, the flame haired girl appeared, and made her way down towards the beast. The crowds fell silent and parted to let her through. She'd lost her sandals sometime that afternoon. Her shirt was open to her belly, knotted under her breasts, her hips hardly covered by her skirt. Her head was high, the bruises below her right eye clear for us all to witness.

The whale breathed out as she approached, which blew her hair out behind her in a spectacular firework. Even the police stepped back and allowed her access through the cordon; we all knew she was magic.

I could have bottled that silence on the beach, it was so thick, as the girl moved forward to lay her hands on the whale's head, just underneath one of its dark beady eyes.

Then she pressed her head against the beast, and the whale began to sing. The melody dried my heart to a crust of old leather. Children, adults, the very old sunk to their knees at the desperate sound, some dug their hands deeply in the shingle, bringing out dribbling handfuls of sand to plug their ears in despair. I closed my eyes, and shuddered my breaths in and out, focusing on the dry heat. If angels were to sing, this is how they would sound. How we would fall in front of them.

I don't know how much time passed like this.

When it was over, and we uncovered our faces, and uncovered our ears, and our mouths, the whale was dead. Its eyes were closed, and the girl wept openly. No one spoke. Then she moved running one hand along the whale's head, touching its glistening body as she circled the carcass. We bowed our heads in silence, this was a ritual we would witness but not participate in.

Eventually she stepped forward and turned to address the crowd in that strange half-light which some call dusk, but I now know to belong to her. Her light.

'He sang for me,' she said, in those thick round words that she used. 'His secret. He told me how to. . .'

It didn't sound as clear as I type it, the voice in your head probably heard all those words perfectly. But it wasn't like that, each word that she said was fat and a bit too long, and if you didn't know her secret, what would you think?

One child laughed, not at what she said, but how she said it, and was shushed by an anxious mother. But then another and another laughed and it was a river of contagious relief from the sorrow. The laughter rippled and spread, so it was only the front few people who heard the rest of her words.

'Everyone in the city must come to the beach, when we're all here I can tell. . .' She must have seen the people laughing, and as she continued to speak, the sea of silent laughing faces started to change, to turn sour and bitter, blaming her for the inappropriateness of the moment.

The first projectile that arced through the air stole away whatever magic she had left. An empty can of Coke sailed over her head, before bouncing off the whale's flesh. A half-eaten soggy bag of chips followed.

I left after that, a minute or so later, when a banana went skimming across the crowd. She was trying to shelter the whale's dead body, I turned away as rubbish hit her head and she stuttered backward. I got out of there as quickly as I could, the police were pushing people back and yelling for order as the cameras rolled on. I didn't want to be a part of that. I didn't even open my flask.

The next time I saw her was maybe three or four days later when the smell of rotting flesh drew me, as it had so many others. We were nasal voyeurs, intent on a journey into the realms of disbelief, but which we all sucked up nevertheless.

'What do you think of this?' a young mother said to me, while her young boys screwed up their noses.

I nodded. There's nothing like a massive carcass to bring people together. Strangers spoke to me. I acknowledged comments like:

'A fine mess.'

And

'Lucky the weather's turning, less flies.'

And

'Who's going to clear this up?'

And

'The council have just left it lying here, it's a disgrace.' But all the time I was nodding I was staring at the girl.

She crouched by the carcass, building decorations with shells and pebbles around its flesh, head down, lost to gazes and commentary.

She looked as if she could be blown away in the wind that drew cold breaths across the water and pulled at people's skimpy garments, warning them to get dressed, their summer was over.

I wondered if she had left this beach since the whale appeared, her clothes were the same, but someone had wrapped a faded blue towel around her thin shoulders. The tide was rising, as it must have done day after day; it felt like the sea was trying to reclaim its own.

A rude noise brought me around from my reverie, you know the type, when vehicles speak: reversing, reversing. A lorry, of immense proportions, could be spied through the arched gap. How anyone planned to squeeze the carcass through that hole and out the other side was anyone's guess. For sure this would involve heavy-duty chainsaws. The flame haired girl took one look at the vehicle through the gap and screeched.

'No, no, no,' she yelled, running up the beach. As she moved away from the tide line, the waters started to rise, inch by inch and then metre by metre, the crowd following her movement with fear, scrabbling through that small hole. I lost sight of her then, caught up in the melee, and actually I didn't care. I was suddenly very nervous of the too fast rising tide.

I'm alright at swimming, I swam the harbour entrance when I was in my late teens – it damn well near killed me. I was dragged a good half mile into the port's mouth before I managed to get out on the other side. I certainly didn't fancy the ugly belligerence of today's waters. Not one bit. Full they were, big and fat. I left the beach quickly, it was only later that I heard the whale's body floated away in 'the freak wave caused by a passing ferry' and was not seen again.

Thing was though, it wasn't a freak wave. We all believed the first one was, but then, when you get one bigger and bigger with every tide it becomes pretty normal after a month, especially when you are piling sandbags up against your door.

I was surprised to see her the next time, it stopped me in my tracks, as we weren't at the beach. I was on a side road, just round the corner from where I live. It's a street of houses which pretend to be identical but aren't. Like kids sometimes pretend to be twins but you can't help noticing one has blue accessories, the other red.

She was in the middle of the street – which itself was a few inches underwater you understand – circled by a group. I knew it was her for the colour of her hair and the strange cries that she made.

Every time I saw that kid she was in trouble of some kind. Was I witness to everything, or was her whole life like this?

'The secret,' one of the group demanded, raising his fist as she spat at his feet before watching the phlegm drift away in the water, 'tell me the whale's secret!'

I would have stayed, I would, only I was carrying a bag of fresh fruit from the market, sloshing through the water, and I wanted to get it back to my house, safe like, as no ships had made it into the harbour for a while on account of the too high tides, and the city had become a proper island again, what with all that water sucking away the roads. So who knew when I'd get grapes like these again?

It was about that time, when water in the roads got to waist height, that people stopped going out. We sat in our houses and waited for someone else to save us, but we all knew that only one person could.

Her.

It was written everywhere, graffiti about her and the secret that she wouldn't share. Pictures of her, riding the whale, laughing at us, appeared on dry walls, but she was given a demon's head, with too large eyes that seemed to follow you no matter where you stepped. Maybe that's the truth of why people stopped going out, because of those pictures. They were afraid that she would come surfing through the water on the back of a whale and... do what?

There's only so long that a city can be under siege before it fights back. It took us three months. And our weapon? The girl with the flaming hair of course. She'd been caught, and it was time to try her – we'd all seen the way she'd called the waters on us – that's why we'd thrown stuff – it was her fault for bringing the whale in the first place. She had to be taken back to the beach, and made to tell her secret, or, or, or. The alternative was simple.

'She must die,' a deep voice shouted from the back of the crowd that struggled to hold its footing on the moving shingle which was now, in fact, the moving sea bed. Ropes had been strung out from iron rungs in the wall to give the masses some kind of purchase in the malignant tides. One man had managed to wrap the rope around his belly fully, while others grabbed for handholds, and others held onto those with closeness to safety. Human seaweed.

'A sacrifice to the sea!' yelled another.

'Hold her head under!'

The girl stood alone in the waters, unfettered by the ropes, and looked from one end of the crowd to the other. She chose not to read the words on the lips of her tormentors, and instead called outwards desperately: 'Are you all here? You all have to be here.'

'She's mad,' a man called out, holding a baby tightly to his chest and a toddler, wrapped in a life jacket, to his thigh. 'Soft in the head.'

'Sing with me,' the girl pleaded, looking directly at the man, 'sing with me.' Then she started to hum a noise which may have sounded beautiful if issued from the lips of another, but from her? Some laughed, a couple threw stones – but they were quickly stopped by their neighbours – we needed dignity for this moment.

'Kill her, kill her, kill her.' A low chant started from in the crowd's bosom, keeping a rhythm for the girl's humming.

'I can save us!'

'She'll never tell the whale's secret!'

'Drown her!'

A hand stretched out from the rope and grasped a handful of her hair. A child was raised high to push down on her scalp. The girl fell to her knees, water swirling around her, tugging at her rags, surging into her mouth, eyes and ears. She spluttered, and tried to stand, but a man stood one side of her, holding down her arm, a woman the other and the child pushed her head under.

The crowd roared its approval as the skies darkened. Down she went again and again and again. They were really going to do it this time.

I moved cautiously along the rope towards her as her head rose from the depths, and she whipped her hair back and sucked long gasping breath deep into her belly as the water ran in torrents down her skin. Then her eyes locked with mine.

'Save me,' she said.

My foot slipped on the shingle, I was cold, I was one person, what could I do? I turned away, I couldn't witness this. I scrabbled to make my way through the water, back to the high safety of the hot walls. They were thronged with people, there would be no space for me, but I had to try, to find safety from the rising waters.

'Drown her, drown her, drown her.'

A hand grasped me by the shoulder as I squeezed through the archway, the incoming tide grasping at my waist.

'Where are you going?' a gruff voice from a wide spittle flecked mouth. The grip tightened.

'Answer me! What, you're too proud to speak to a stranger? Not to your liking am I? That's arrogant, that is! Seems to me like you're hiding something.' He shook me real hard, my foot slipped beneath me, I had to grab onto his shirt front to save myself from falling in the water. Its icy touch seeped high on my belly.

'Let me go, let me go,' I begged. The shouted words were dense in their sound, really full, big, because I couldn't quite pronounce them as you would.

'I've got another one,' the man roared. 'Skulking around, trying to escape.'

'I don't know her,' I said desperately trying to pronounce each word as he would, 'I don't know her.' But my desperate pleas fell on ears that only heard the difference in my voice as I was pushed, and pulled forward, through the human seaweed, to where the flame haired girl now floated face-down in the water.

A foot in the back of my knee brought me to my knees as my arms were grabbed and pulled out sideways. The hands on my head were small, with little strength, but they were soon joined with more force.

I didn't shut my mouth in time, or my eyes. Cruel salt puckered into me as the freezing waters devoured my skin.

I came up for air, but couldn't plead as I was spitting, and gasping, and then I was under again, this time for much longer, long enough to know that this was it, and to feel the furious strength of the fight ebb from my body, and for my mind to go limp.

The waters hadn't finished with me yet, I felt a great squeeze around my body, as if I were a stress ball, and I was suckered backwards, and spat to the surface, and dragged under, and spat out, and pulled and pulled and pulled away from the shore. Wiping my eyes, I looked back over my shoulder while furiously kicking to get as far away from the beach as possible. The water, with me in it, had receded so far that the people on the shore looked like gaudy skiers on top of a beige mountain staring into the distance. Had I wanted to go back to the beach I would never have managed to climb those shingle slopes. A few stepped forward and slipped down the new beach, falling, falling, but mostly it looked to me as if they were clinging onto the ropes in terror, looking beyond me into the sea. The lowest drop ever witnessed had happened in seconds.

No one was going to swim out and try to stop me leaving; that was clear.

Instead those on the beach stared at the disappearing waters of the sea while those on the walls cheered and celebrated. Their sacrifice had worked, the sea had gone. I wiped my eyes, still swimming outwards as best I could, crawl, doggy paddle, floating for a bit on my back while I thanked the universe that I was still alive.

Eventually I flipped to my front, I had to make headway to somewhere. And that's when I saw it. A deep grey gloomy wall of water, bellowing its way towards the island city, and me. It contained the whole of the tides in its belly. I looked around for something to hold onto, to give me a chance. There she was, her flame hair spread out around her like rays from the sun in a child's drawing. Face up, she drifted. Beyond her was a plank. I splashed my way towards them as quickly as I could, dragging her to the plank, cradling her in my arms. But I couldn't hold onto both. The wave was practically with me, I had precious few moments left. I heaved the girl onto the plank, splayed her across it. At the end, that's what I did for the flame haired girl. I put her onto a plank.

The last time I saw her, she was drifting, like she was asleep. I hoped she was going to find another whale as I turned and swam to meet the wave.

## Hampshire Boy
## Gareth Rees
*Map location: #16*

'Hampshire Boy', yes, I suppose I am. I've been in the county most of my life. Childhood was in the country and roaming the lanes, woodlands and fields that lay between Horndean and Rowlands Castle. And how was the morning air scented as we dodged between cow pats looking for mushrooms? It was the smell rising from Gales' Brewery in the village down the hill. Well, I'm still connecting with my childhood because here, in The Barley Mow tavern, my tipple is Horndean Special Brew.

It's amazing the freedom we had as children to wander. It wasn't that it was safe because we were always clawing ourselves up the banks of sunken lanes to avoid delivery vans or farm tractors. Sometimes though we rode on the tractors which in those days had no cabs. We'd sit bouncing on the mudguards and if we'd slipped off backwards we would have been sliced to pieces by the blades of the plough.

Sometimes I'd ride in my father's 1938 Morris into Portsmouth, still heavily bomb-damaged. I feared the hugeness of the city and the density of the population. How could people breathe when so closely-packed together? Where was there to play?

Years later, and myself living the urban life, I composed a ditty for the children at Bridgemary School. I also wrote it for myself to express the sadness that childhood was gone: 'I was born with fields around my home. I learnt to watch the changes all around me. I will be back there.'

Despite the eventual transition to urban life, the connection with the country was never broken and just yesterday I took the train to Rowlands Castle. Amongst the trees in Stansted Park I straight away felt a lightness of being and a lessening of anxiety. The natural beauty of the countryside hasn't changed but the sociology has. The little terrace of houses in Finchdean, for example, is, I suspect, a dormitory for well-off, car-dependent metropolitans rather than the meagrely-paid agricultural labourers of my childhood.

On a bend on a steep hill that takes you down to Finchdean, there used to be the great girth of an oak tree. It induced awe in us when we were children because our parents told us it was hundreds of years old and was mentioned in something called the Domesday Book. It's no longer there, burnt down, I think.

Near that old tree was Idsworth House. It's given over to offices now but was the residence of Major Clarke-Jervoise when we were children. He had all the aristocratic appurtenances like a long, tree-lined drive for his chauffeur-driven Rolls Royce and a uniformed footman to ease him through the portals and a butler to take his black cape. The children of the neighbourhood were entertained to a party there at Christmas. I remember the huge paintings on the walls which my father said were Canaletto's.

Not quite so grand but grand enough to have a Victorian walled garden and a meadow with a couple of Jersey cows was Cadlington House. The local children were allowed to use the tennis court. The court was pitted and the net had holes in it and that reflected an air of faded grandeur. There were no servants and the cows were milked by the lady of the house, a patrician but kindly lady.

Bordered by a farm, a churchyard and a road was our two-room school. The day began with the teacher playing the piano with great gusto and the children singing with equal gusto 'All Things Bright and Beautiful' or 'The Raggle Taggle Gypsies'. The music went when, aged eight, I was sent to an all-boys school an hour away by bus. Bullies were disguised as teachers and they regularly beat bottoms with a long, smooth-bottomed gym shoe known as Mr. Seaton's Slipper. One day, the music teacher left this instrument of torture on top of the piano and I stole it and burnt it in our garden when I got home.

I was very unhappy at that school and therefore euphoric when, aged eleven, my parents announced we were going to the United States. The Americans were folksy and didn't look down on children. There was no corporal punishment in the schools. There was lots of chocolate sauce and wonderful ice-cream which wasn't Walls. When it snowed, there was central heating and when it was hot there was Dr. Pepper in the fridge and a swimming pool to jump into. I started to read 'Newsweek' magazine instead of comics and I suppose childhood was beginning to slip away.

Americans were annoying in their ignorance of the outside world and their 'Mary Poppins' idea of England. It was like they'd run away from the English class system and yet were nostalgic about it at the same time.

Returned to England, it did feel as though we'd walked back into the Edwardian era. I stood in the study of the headmaster of Churchers College in Petersfield. I remember looking through the ancient glass of the window which distorted the view of the boys playing cricket outside. I wasn't long in that school and the childhood home in the country was no more when we moved to suburban Alverstoke.

I was a teenager now and the Sixties were underway. Suddenly, instead of being old-fashioned, England felt like the hippest place in the world. Our school by Stokes Bay originally served the Prince of Wales as a place of escape from his austere mother across the Solent in Osborne House. Austere times were over for us as well as we rocked to the bands playing in Thorngate Hall. Manfred Mann played regularly and I saw Cream play there to an audience of about a dozen. I was mesmerised by Eric Clapton for about twenty five minutes, but then got bored and went home. Well, there was school the next day.

And then, eventually you fly the nest although it's always worth remembering you always take yourself with you. You can change the geography but you don't change yourself necessarily. I went back to America and I was glad, but never so glad that I wouldn't return to my Hampshire rambles. When you're seeing new places, maybe subconsciously, you're beginning to see the old places in a different way. When I returned to England after nearly a year, my parents drove me to a pub in the Meon Valley, 'The Shoe Inn' I think it was in Cheriton. How perfect. But it wasn't. My much-cherished Hampshire countryside on this occasion looked twee and overly-manicured. I was shocked and my comforting certainty was shaken. But I was over-reacting, a bit deranged. The edginess which I felt in America made me long for the serenity of the English countryside. When I got that peaceableness back I wanted the edge again!

The child remains in the country perhaps. The adult is in the city. And here we are in Southsea, a cosmopolitan village in the city. There's no need for a car. The shops and restaurants are walking distance. The train station too is walking distance and if I want the woods of my childhood I can be there in twenty minutes. But in the meantime, there's the Common for an amble and of course the Solent and the interest of the maritime traffic. It's a great place.

**Lawless and the Three Pompey Piglets**
**William Sutton**
*Map location: #6*

*A short story featuring Victorian detective, Sergeant Campbell
Lawless, known as Watchman because he was formerly a
watchmaker's apprentice.*

> 'One of the most disgraceful, horrible and revolting
> practices carried on by Europeans is the importation of
> girls into England from foreign countries to swell the
> ranks of prostitution.'
> > - Henry Mayhew, 'Traffic in Foreign Women'
> > - London Labour and the London Poor, 1862.

*Rana's letter*

Dear Sergeant Lawless,

I throw myself upon your mercy. I am an honourable woman,
fallen into ignominy, through no fault of my own. Where once I
travelled the fine cities of the Grand Tour with my wealthy family,
now I live days of disrepute and nights of shame. I have read in Mr
Dickens' paper of your prosecutions of the London netherworld; I
humbly beg that you turn your detective abilities on the ignoble
practices perpetrated here, in Portsmouth, where many a shapely
vessel is shipwrecked and sunken in the mire.

I grew up in Bombay, but my father's mercantile dealings brought us to Amsterdam, where we enjoyed a social life of the highest order among the broad-minded Dutch. We travelled often, and luxuriously. Summering in the resort of Le Touquet, I so delighted in walking by the seafront that my family allowed me to promenade unaccompanied. Among the civilised holidayers, my father had little fear for my safety, thinking me still a girl, while I thought myself a woman and ready for adventure. How misguided we were.

A fine madame engaged me in conversation in a cafe. After some manoeuvring and bush-beating, she asked me if I knew London. She happened to be scouting for tutors and governesses on behalf of certain reputable houses. My father had kept us from England, demonising it as a pit of immorality, where revolutionaries and assassins consorted with philanderers and home-wreckers. I longed to see England, and told her so, though London sounded foggy and dark, and I should miss the sea. What good fortune, said she, that she also knew of a house in Portsmouth. The salary was high, the house comfortable.

'Just be good enough to sign this agreement, ma chère. Merely a matter of form. Sign without fear or trembling.'

The coffee and sea air had me in high spirits. Without reading the half sheet of foolscap, for I had no wish to offend her, I wrote my name. We arranged to meet at the dock the next day. I knew my parents would never allow me to go, but when I returned a year hence, with my purse full of gold and my heart of new experiences, I hoped they would forgive me. Father always said we learn most by seeing how others live.

Aboard the steamer, I got to know two others of the madame's coterie bound for Portsmouth: Flea, a housemaid from the Basque country, and a Walloon cook, named Ladybird. We should all be working in different parts of the madame's establishment. They, poor things, were as deluded as I.

We were transferred to a vessel anchored at a buoy in the middle of the Solent. A fearsome naval officer named Wolfe oversaw us aboard a rowboat. As we entered the harbour, I wept, for it put me in mind of my childhood home, Bombay. One of the sailors told me the city was nicknamed Pompey for that very reason; he hoped he might tell me more in his visits to Madame Rosabella's; he dropped us on Spice Island, giving a peculiar wink to the madame.

The house was roomy and elegant; my bedroom compact, comfortable, and better furnished than I expected: red curtains, clean linen, a marble wash-stand and a bidet, a big four-post bed with handsome hangings of red damask; and a large cheval-glass.

I thanked the madame for her consideration. She began to laugh.

'Did I not say you would be well-treated?'

Need I expatiate, sir, on the horrors that ensued? After bitter struggles, I was soon enough conquered. Ruined, I was inconsolable. I begged to be sent home. My writing desk is filled with letters I composed to beg their help, but never sent, for I knew my father would revile me in this pitiable state.

Fool that I am, I had signed my life away. My friends, Flea and Ladybird, endured the same fate, but are kept in different houses, so as to demoralise us. Some customers are kind; but sailors have filthy appetites, even officers. If we behave, we are allowed the privilege of walking the walls, to attract trade; I ask the gods that I shall not end among those syphilitic veterans of Venus, embracing hurriedly in the shadowy arches. We are always watched, and warned that, should we flee, the big bad Wolfe will catch us, who governs the whole operation, and huffs and puffs at Madame Rosabella, threatening to blow down all our houses.

Help us, Sergeant. Liberate us.

Rana Cawnpoor (here known as Frog)

POST SCRIPTUM.

By all the gods, show this letter to nobody, unless you wish my swift extinction.

*Narrative of Sergeant Lawless*

The waters glittered beneath the rickety platform, as I stepped from the train at Portsmouth Harbour, come in search of a Frog, a Flea and a Ladybird.

The quality from first class stepped on toward the waiting ferry, but many a well-to-do child in Little Lord Fauntleroy garb tugged a father's arm, begging a farthing to throw from the precarious platform. In the mud below, knee-deep in the grime, waited a legion of urchins. These mudlarks, with acrobatic tumbles, scooped up the coins with a genteel bow, doubtless trumping my income as detective sergeant of £58 per annum.

It was low tide, and the smell eclipsed the town's aromas of biscuits and breweries. I screwed up my nose, tugging down my borrowed sailor's cap, as I espied a boatload of women being rowed ashore.

The stationmaster noted my curiosity. 'Seeking aught, Sir? There's fresh piglets ashore. Fine ham on Spice Island, if that's your taste.'

I glanced at the boat, and regarded him. 'I like an exotic dish.'

'Madame Rosabella's, then,' he winked. 'She cooks a wild boar, she does.'

Through narrow streets, I followed his directions into Portsea. A stroll past the fish market, fishwives braying and dockworkers catcalling. Over drawbridges, past the Ordnance wall, into back alleys where venality and fleshy indulgence were offered me from every window. The brass plaque of a Philosophical Institution was tarnished by time, but the bill alongside was fresh, offering prize money for slave-captures, if only fiddlers, midshipmen and quartermasters would sign up for HMS Procrastination:

*GLORIOUS NEWS*
*for the Gallant British Lads.*

*Increase of the Royal Marines, Portsmouth Division.*
*The Standard is Lowered and the Bounty Increased.*
*They serve both by Land and Sea. 40 to 50 POUNDS per man to*
*spend as they like.*
*Many return from abroad to receive £100 in Pay and Prize*
*Money and may purchase their discharge with plenty left to enjoy*
*themselves.*

It did not take long to understand that Spice Island was not merely named after import goods. Down every alleyway stood girls painted for action.

One raised her brows, addressing me drunkenly. 'Is the ship in?'

'I have no idea,' I replied.

'I'd say the ship's in.' She glanced unapologetically at my breeches. 'But needs work, in the dock, as you might say.' She pronounced these innuendoes without moistening her lips or showing her ankle, or any of the wiles I had seen in London's Haymarket.

I found Madame Rosabella's, on Bateman Alley, besieged by Russian sailors. 'Rom! Rom!' A Cossack monk, in bearskin cap, long velvet gown and top boots, bolted his rum as a juggler swallows fire. 'Madame! Rom, rom!'

My careful demand for an exotic piglet led to the room of Letitia. This blonde Belgian beauty, still rejoicing in the plumpness of youth, also had hangings of red damask around her bed; between bidet and wash-stand stood a large inviting tub; the cheval-glass, which could be turned in any direction, stood just at the level of the bed, so that sitting or lying you might see yourself reflected in it.

In broken French, I established that I preferred to try her storytelling rather than her horizontal talents. Overcoming a certain incredulity, Letitia told of her enticement to Madame Rosabella's. Undoubtedly, she was the Ladybird mentioned in the letter.

I paid and, without risking mention of Rana (here known as

Frog), left town by the next train.

I drew up my Guernsey frock collar, and pushed my way into The Benbow's Head, where Commissioner Fox of the Portsmouth Police was to meet me. On this, my second visit, the Portsmouth docks were still thronging with Russians: big ugly men of a burnt hue and a faithful look, a mix of swarthy, Scandinavian and Tartar, their ship's name on the ribbon of their hat, knives dangling at their sides.

Armed with a pint of Long's Southsea Stout, I lurked outside, eyeing the waters that seemed to insinuate themselves beneath the very streets of the town. The tide was high, and it looked as if the buildings were floating, like islands, upon the shimmering harbour. I had brought along Molly, an urchin associate in my occasional employ. Versed in all manner of underworld argot, she would be better placed than I to dig out secrets from the harbour grime; I could see her, at work already, exchanging quips beneath the Dockyard walls, winning the confidence of the mudlarks.

Nobody asked who I was or where I was headed. This was a place where men of all stations gathered, without question, for their last taste of English beer.

Twenty minutes late, up rolled a rickety chaise in the latest style. The Commissioner, like a Persian Emperor, declined to descend until his constable had opened the door and brushed straw on to the pavement. Down he swept and into the pub, nodding and waving to all assembled; and I had requested a quiet meeting. I kept my head down, and gave no greeting; for there could be no swifter way to be known by the city's debauched and criminal element. I needed my anonymity. Instead, I observed the Commissioner lapping up the benefits of his position: attentive barmaids, bigwigs and braggarts paying their respects and, in at least two cases, giving moneys.

This, then, was the way of the police. The Customs House and the Navy Police had equally assured me that there could be no trafficking of women in such a well-monitored port. And yet, stood between The Fortitude Tap and The Receiving House for the Drowned, I saw with the naked eye rowboats plying to and from the Spit Sand buoy, with cargoes of women, just as Rana's letter had described.

This time, I asked Madame Rosabella for a swarthier girl. She escorted me to the next door house, where I was presented to the Basque, by name Felicia, or Flea; a fetching figure of a woman, but I was disappointed that she spoke not a word of English, nor even of French.

'If it's talk you're wanting,' said Madame Rosabella, 'you're in the wrong house. My specialism is foreigners and gypsies, and not one of them speaks the Queen's English.'

I did not need to accentuate my Scots brogue. 'No more do I.' I fingered in my pocket Rana's strange letter, looking around the opulent brothel: the tired grandfather clock, the new range blacked with lead polish; everywhere trinkets, green glass, an ornamental cat, the harmonium at which a spindly girl sang Thomas Adams' Burlesque Quadrille.

The madame followed my inquisitive eye suspiciously. 'Are you a mutton shunter?'

'What if I were? Don't policemen have desires too?' I laughed. 'You need have no fear. And if I repair your clock mechanism, will you not find me a more outlandish girl? Have you no Persians? Or a Hindoo, perhaps?'

And that is how, for an increased fee, I gained my introduction to Rana Cawnpoor (here known as Frog), the maharajah's princess of Madame Rosabella's third house. Well-groomed, simply dressed, a satin saree draping her sylphan shape and comely kettledrums; bright gold garters, three quarters of an inch broad, holding up black silk stockings; her hair was black, her eyes dark hazel. It was easy to see how she made men rampant with desire, though she was barely eighteen. Of the anguish apparent in her letter, I saw little trace, as she retold her tale cheerfully enough.

I confess I was a little in love with all of them, the blonde Belgian, the full-bosomed Basque and this Hindoo sorceress. Any red-blooded man would have been, though he might not readily admit it, competing in his daydreams as to whose favour he would prefer to win.

I produced from my pocket the fateful envelope and held up her letter as a talisman.

'You? The Johnny Darby?' Blinking rapidly, she swooned, rather deliberately, into my arms. 'But where is your bulls-eye?'

'Detectives carry no lantern,' I said setting her delicately on the leather chair. 'I have my billy, if you need convincing.'

At the sight of my police truncheon, she became most attentive. 'You may need it, if they have rumbled you.' She leaned close to me and whispered. 'If they should summon Wolfe.'

Continually listening at the door, to see if we were overheard, she fitfully apprised me of the details she had omitted from her letter. How were girls smuggled in here, circumventing the efficient customs house? Why, Madame Rosabella had a deal with a commodore or two. Navy ships could not carry women, or rather, not officially. Officers' wives, however, had the right to come aboard in harbour. In return for certain favours, captains ferried women to and fro, with the remit of the customs and the harbour police, endorsing a modern servitude beneath the very noses of the naval police. The point of transfer was HMS So-and-So, anchored at Spit Sand buoy, supposedly, to plumb the waters; for one of Palmerston's 'Follies' was to sink its foundations there (that mighty ring of forts encircling the Dockyard to ward off Napoleonic pilfering and pummelling, an excessive deterrent for which the nation is still paying).

I promised Rana I would return, soon, and with the force to see the thing through. Making good my debt to Madame Rosabella—the grandfather clock needed the slightest adjustment to the pendulum arm—I left, and precipitously, for I felt the madame's eyes upon me.

What did the beguiling Rana want? She wanted to be liberated from Madame Rosabella, the bawd responsible for her slavery; and she wanted the madame punished with the full fury of the law. Stop one of the boats sent out into the harbour, check the credentials of these naval wives, and my job would be done. That was her plan. But such an intervention might prove little, with so many palms so very greasy; I must prevent Madame Rosabella denying her culpability.

I am tall, and broad enough as policemen go. Rarely in my rounds of London do I feel physically intimidated, even south of the river. But within five minutes of leaving Madame Rosabella's, I was ill-at-ease. Down every alley flooded brutes and animals, stoutly booted, shouldering leather bags, every doorway disgorging wives and children to welcome their master. I fled, under the shadows of the old city wall; but as the stampede continued, I took the chance to ask an old washerwoman what was afoot.

'Home.' She drew her sleeve across her face. If her intention was to clear it of mucus, this had rather the opposite effect. 'From work.'

'All at the same time?'

She looked at me as if I were mad. 'Dockyard, in't it, you dinlow.'

Too late did I notice I had fled in quite the wrong direction.

My mind was taken up with Rana's tale. I believed her. Yet something disconcerted me. It was no surprise that she had turned up the heat of her anguish, once she realised I was her knight in shining armour; but I knew several Indians, and her accents sounded more Hibernian than Hindoo.

Not until I reached a stretch of barren beach did I stop. Grand vessels alongside Spit Sands buoy glimmered on their sides, canvasses flying in the wind; boats flittered between them, butterflies among sea-eagles. The mist was descending; the Isle of Wight was already obscured; a foghorn sonata sounded.

I walked on, thinking of Molly, amid that stampede. In such streets, a young girl all alone was in danger, even one as savvy as Molly; among these dockers and sailors, her boyish garb would give her little protection. I regretted involving her in this. How relieved I was to see her strolling across the Common toward me.

'I scarpered, Watchman,' she said, 'I don't mind telling you, lest they shopped me in as a spy. Them mudlarks down The Hard, and them dirty Gunwharf grubbers, they took my queries quite amiss. I reckon as the whole city's in cahoots.' She tugged at my coat, her eyes wide. 'But fear not, I've found you someone with a sharp eye. Someone who's not in colluding with this city's fearful masonic leagues. Look.'

I blinked at the shoreline ahead, unable to credit my eyes.

Two sea-monsters were emerging from the waves. They squirted playful jets of water over the fearless man who led them ashore.

'Sanger's Circus,' Molly grinned. The red and white marquees dotted Southsea Common. 'Elephants' bath time.'

Mr Sanger, a gentle, dapper circus man, clearly fond of his beasts, confirmed what the Hindoo girl had told me; but his version darkened the waters. The girls were coerced from abroad, redistributed at Spit Sands, to outwit the customs; then not only dispatched to local brothels, but sold to the highest bidders in a secret nefarious auction house on the hill. He urged me to catch the blackguard kidnappers and throw them in the Tower of London. Why should he wish to inform on these practices? The web of secrecy was tight. Had he no fear of reprisals?

Because those blackguard villains had stolen his own little daughter. Back when she was only a child and wandered too far from her caravan, as every little gypsy girl is wont to. They had stolen his little Frog.

At Portsmouth Harbour station, the fine matrons battered aside sea salts to get to the Isle of Wight ferry.

I caught the stationmaster's eye.

'Find yourself some good crackling, did ye?'

'I did.' I moved closer, speaking softly. 'But if I wanted to buy a piglet of my own? A lovely fresh piglet.'

He eyed my sailor's cap appraisingly. 'Come into some prize

money, have we?'

I touched my cap. 'Her Majesty's been generous.'

'You'll want to go up the hill. Fort Nelson. Ask to see their piglets.'

Fort Nelson was the most complete of Palmerston's Follies upon the hill overlooking the city. It took several weeks of planning, and negotiating with admirals, through the Prince of Wales, to have the harbour watched, to follow the women freshly arrived from the continent and herded up to the fort, to demand an instantaneous inspection. We unearthed an auction room in the tunnels beneath the fort: a luxuriously furnished bordello, with adjoining dormitories, where the girls had their halfway house. There they were paraded before assorted bawd madames and wealthy gentlemen, come from as far afield as London and Liverpool to make their sordid purchases.

Several officers were reprimanded, though none was ever gaoled. Which galled me.

We turned our attention to the houses of Spice Island. At every turn, I expected the wrath of the police Commissioner; instead Fox sought a transfer to Hartlepool. At every turn, I expected the mysterious Wolfe to materialise and defy us. By the time we arrested Madame Rosabella, I had armed myself with pistols to be ready for him. We closed the bordello down without a shot. I began to believe that Wolfe was an invention, to scare the little piglets into conformity. Who authorised and organised the trade remains unclear.

From our intervention, little changed. The police Commissioner used his naval contacts to set up a new trafficking line in Hartlepool. The Portsmouth traffic doubtless continues through other more clandestine routes. This is the normal state of affairs in harbour towns; two Inspectors at the Yard wondered why I wasted my time on it.

I went to liberate the women; but my three beauties had vanished. I drew it out of the madame, rather roughly.

The three girls had misbehaved, and been dispatched to a private asylum, between Fratton station and the Canal. I went forthwith, bringing representatives of the Society for the Prevention of Cruelty to Women.

Letitia the Walloon was traumatised; but she recovered. She returned to Wallonia, where her friends were reluctant to believe the tale she told them. Thrown on her own resources, without a character, and her mind disturbed, she found it impossible to secure reputable employ, and had at last recourse to prostitution; so hard it is to return to the right, when once we stray upon the path of dalliance.

Felicia the Basque resisted with imaginative violence, she had to be sedated and restrained. The nurses would not hear of her being freed from her straightjacket; and with her papers in order, we had no jurisdiction.

Rana, the Frog, had been prey to the caprices of the energetic surgeon who owned the asylum. He reported, quite at ease, his experiments upon her. Following the latest theorems, he had run electrical currents through her cerebellum, aiming to expunge her tendencies toward vice and immorality. He had success at first. She wept, and spoke lovingly of her family, alongside incoherent accounts of acrobats and elephants. I said nothing. The picture was clear enough. Rana was no Hindoo princess, but rather the lost itinerant circus girl, Frog, whose family had no idea their lost darling was so nearby. Whether coerced, or simply run away, from the circus into a more debased trade, she had invented for herself a past to rival her glamorous colleagues. Given to reading sensational news and detective stories, she had written to me in a fit of romanticism. How she basked in the role of dispossessed damsel, just as she thrived as a courtesan. Having fallen into the trade so young, she was innocent of the gravity of great affairs. She had no intention of overthrowing the whole trade. She just wished to free herself, and her friends, from the tyranny of Madame Rosabella's; perhaps they hoped to take over the bawd house, or to run away, and invent new characters for themselves. Instead, she was brought to this pass.

The doctor blinked. 'Sadly, after the third treatment, you see, she became depressed, and somehow squeezed through the bars of her window. Astonishing, really. As if she were a trained acrobat. Straight into the canal, poor thing.'

### The Last Watch (Time-X Part 2)
### Tom Harris

*This is part 2 of THE TIME-X LEGACY – the story begins in Day of the Clocks.*
*Map location: #8*

105 metres above the ground, inside the Spinnaker Tower, he stared out at the remains of his world through the salt-stained glass.

Memories, once cherished but now too painful to recall, scarred his heart. The beautiful, imperfect world he loved was gone forever. But he'd held on to what he could, and inside his clenched palm, the last watch on earth ticked perfect time.

In these final days, he'd questioned if time mattered, and so today he was standing in line. He knew they would return here. That was why he'd come back to the place of his birth – Portsmouth.

It was time to stop running.

The sailboat on the horizon, bore no pirate banner. It did not approach to the sound of guns or Wagner's Ride of the Valkyries, but it was them. Time-X were coming.

Ruined with oil, the black waters of the Solent burned. The high rise towers of Gosport now just mountains of rubble. Portsmouth had survived war before and had come back strong, but this was different. It was uninhabited, like many cities of his England. The proud people of Pompey had deserted their island. He was the last man standing. The last of his kind; fighting the apocalypse of time... but all that was about to change.

He returned from the window to the battered, leather chair in the middle of the room. He closed his eyes, lost in his past...

Born in the middle of the blackouts, his first sights and sounds were from inside this very room. View Deck 1. Delivered by the famous Moonlight Midwives, he was a testimony to the courage and resolve of the island. They didn't know it then, but those days marked the beginning of the end of time.

That was eighteen years before he turned his back on his decaying city. The day they blew up the Guildhall clock.

He'd tracked time ever since. He knew he was thirty six. He knew the vernal equinox had triggered spring two weeks ago. It was April. It was the year... What did it matter? Time would soon be irrelevant.

That was the way the President of Earth wanted it. So they could all start again. Some embraced it, but not everyone followed the master plan. There were others who stood against the President. A resistance formed.

He had no family or friends left alive and they wanted to take the memory of his father from him. He could not let them have the watch. And so, submerged in shadow, forced outside of society, he became a defender of time.

The sailboat approached through the flames.

Soon it would be over. He was glad. He stroked the watch in his palm. Of all the people he'd met, of all the watches in the world – his was the last. Yet, however far and hard he ran, time was against him. His years ticked by relentlessly. This was no life. Time had become his enemy. It had left him lonely and isolated. There was no choice.

It was time to stop.


The sailboat moored at Gunwharf and two men in suits made their way along the broken jetty, glancing up at the tower. He returned to the chair and faced the staircase as the last watch recorded the final seconds of time.

Their boots echoed through the building as they climbed the stairs. It had just gone quarter to eleven.

'Mr Tick. Mr Tock,' he said as the two men appeared.

'You're funny – Mr?' one of them spoke.

'My name's not important. I'm not important. I know what you've come for. You can have it.'

'Tired of running?'

He nodded. 'You could say that.'

'Give us the watch.'

'Does Mr Tick speak?'

The man who had not spoken shook his head and opened his mouth.

'No tongue,' said Mr Tock.

'I'm sorry.'

Tick shrugged.

'Well then...' said Tock.

'Here it is. Come and get it...' The men in suits approached and he held out the watch in his palm; the chain slipping through his fingers. 'I heard your broadcasts. The serial numbers on the back. I hold the last watch?'

Tock nodded.

'So what will you do with it?'

'Mr Tick will take care of it. May we?'

'Be my guest.' It ticked as it left his palm. He closed his eyes as the heartbeat of the watch faded along with the agents' footsteps.

The end of time.

Just like that.


He peeled his eyes from the burning horizon as the sailboat blurred in the distance. Stepping through the rubble of Gunwharf, a melancholy washed over him. The shops, restaurants, pubs and people, all now just echoes in the dust.

Beyond Gunwharf, the naval sports fields of HMS Temeraire were wild with weeds and grasses; punctured by huge craters in the ground. The fences around the old United Services sports ground had been strangled by bindweed and ivy. Tree roots had burst right through the middle of Park Road. The place was unrecognisable.

Only a handful of the University buildings that once dominated this area, had survived the storms that had hit the South Coast. He'd heard the news, sitting in a patisserie in Calais. The storms hit France two days later.

Without time, the government were unable to predict, plan and communicate. The storms were unrelenting. Tsunamis, tornadoes and twisters. It was not the anticipated revolutionary time wars that destroyed the world, but nature.

It was annihilation.

The human race was not prepared.

They took for granted the things that mattered and that was why Guildhall Square no longer had a clock tower. Once the proud voice of the city, chiming out for all to hear, all that was left was ash and rubble and the bones of the dead.

Had everyone known what would happen, those people he'd stood with on Portsdown Hill might not have cheered so loudly.

The council buildings. Central Library. The Theatre Royal. All gone.

'Mortar and dust, Maximus, mortar and dust...' he mumbled as he sat amongst the boulders and bricks. And that was when he saw her.

'This is all new to you?' She hid behind a baseball cap, pulled over her eyes, but her accent was strong and local.

'You stayed here?' he stuttered, staring as if she were the first of her species.

'You're proper clever, you,' she said. 'You came back then?'

'Guess I did. But now I'm here and I've done what I've done, I can't quite believe it...' his voice trailed off as he sat with his head in hands. 'After all this time, I just handed it over,' he said, eyes boring into the rubble.

'You held on longer than anyone else.' Her voice was calm, but she kept her distance. Her hands clasped tight around a metal pole at her side.

'Do you know me somehow?' he asked.

She nodded. 'We do, but what we don't know is why you gave up the watch.'

'We?'

'Yes, I'm not alone here... So?'

'I came here to stop running. They knew I'd come back. I just stopped fighting. I'm so tired...'

'Who did they send?'

'Time-X. The formidable *agents of time*... They were just two men in suits, like the ones at the conference at the Guildhall.'

'I remember. I was there,' she said, turning the faded cap on her head, revealing her face. She was beautiful. All women were. It had taken such devastation for him to realise they all were and always had been.

'I was too young to vote,' he remembered, 'by a bloody day!'

'The Vote on Time,' she whispered. 'I couldn't vote either.' The memory made her shudder.

'Would we have made a difference?' The words barely escaped his lips. 'We all know what happened to those that voted against the abolishment order. Then after everything, I just hand it to them – just – like – that. I thought they'd...'

'Kill you?' she nodded knowingly.

'My way out. And now... I don't know what I've done, what I'm going to do, or how I even feel about anything...'

'I understand,' she said. The pipe clattered in the rubble. It seemed to ring out forever. 'I have friends. I'll take you to them. Looks like you might need us now...'

'How do you know about me?'

'You held the last watch. You kept time when we all gave up. If it wasn't for you time wouldn't exist.'

'You listened to the broadcasts?'

'We all did,' she nodded. 'Every day when they tried to reach you. For years you were my favourite part of the day. We'd gather round the radio when they appealed for you to come in. We left the radio on always. We couldn't risk losing the frequency. We took it in turns to guard it.' She laughed. 'I remember them asking you to give yourself up and every time you'd reply...'

'I've No Time For You!' Their voices overlapped perfectly.

'Then you'd tell us the time and we'd all cheer!'

He blushed as red as fire. 'I'd no idea anyone was listening. I had hoped, but I...'

'I know, it sounds a bit gimp now, but having that hope was everything. Time kept us going. You kept us going. You were never alone.'

'Can I see the radio?'

She shook her head. 'A week or so ago they sent agents on one final sweep. They took it. It's our own fault, we were playing music way too loud – like bloody kids! Laptops, smart phones and the devices that people had cobbled together were all taken. It's freaky hearing your voice. You sound different on the radio.'

'Like the speaking clock, I bet,' he laughed.

'Don't do that,' she scolded. 'You alone did what no-one else could. You held on. You kept going. You told the time and... well you'll see soon enough, all is not lost. Come with me.'

She held out her hand.

'Who are you?' he asked, as she adjusted her cap again.

'No-one special,' she smiled.


The sticky comfort of her sweat was intoxicating. The sensation of skin against skin after all this... time. His body curled and quivered in ways it had not for so long. Every tiny hair sprang to attention, aroused by the touch of her hand in his.

'Where are you taking me?' he asked, hypnotized by her eyes, blue, yet dulled with grey, as if the dust of the city had settled there.

'King Street,' she said. 'Once home of Hide's Drapery Emporium, inhabited by the great H.G Wells,' she smiled. 'Impressed?'

He nodded. 'Wells saw this coming.'

The girl removed her cap and folded it into her back pocket. She looked ashamed, revealing her closely shaved head. 'Not my best look, but I got fed up being a Travelodge for lice. Can't get decent shampoo here any more. We make do with what's left of the soap.'

He nodded, suddenly conscious of the grime clinging to his skin. 'Why here?'

'Irony or some shit. We thought it was funny once upon a time. Come on...' This time she almost pulled his arm out of its socket, dragging him along, like they were a couple of kids on a first date.

He held on tight as she led him through a doorway and down a narrow flight of stairs. Together, they journeyed into the bowels of the old factory building, beyond basements and cellars and down mountains of rubble.

'I forget how far down this place is,' she laughed, pausing to catch her breath, her hands on her knees. 'I'm not as out of shape as I look, honest,' she said as a *toc, toc, toc* echoed around them.

The sound of shifting concrete drew him to the candlelight, flickering through the floorboards. The plank creaked and a man's head popped up by their feet.

'Look who I found,' she said.

The man in the floor flashed a toothless grin. 'Welcome to the New World,' he said and disappeared beneath the boards.

Down a rickety, wooden staircase they followed the candle man.

In the quiet, voices chimed out below, like the echoes of a thousand clocks.

'Your friends?' he asked the girl.

She nodded. 'What we have down here is simple.'

'What do you have?'

'Life. Here, this will do. Gappy, you go on, I want to show him...'

The man winked in the candlelight and chuckled, leaving them alone in the dark. She led him through an opening onto to a small balcony. There was light.

'Is it safe?' he asked, testing the boards.

'Six fell through last month, but we've had a good week... Course it is you idiot! It's safer down here than up there. There's something you need to see. Go on,' she smiled. 'Take a closer look.'

Edging further along the balcony, the darkness dissipated. The light of new life pumped through him like oxygen. Gas lamps illuminated an underground world, formed in the image of Victorian England. Cobbled streets and stone houses. Hidden in dust. There was no sky. No sun. But something greater gave light to this world.

'It's like going back in time,' he said.

'Who knows, we may even meet Wells himself, down here?' The girl sighed. Proud. She squeezed his hand. 'You like it?'

'It's what I've been dreaming of.'

'Ah, but you haven't seen the best bit! Here, look.'

He shuffled by, so close he could smell her. No perfume. Just human sweat. He'd missed that and breathed it in, just in case he never got the chance again.

'Time still exists because of you. We still exist, because of you.' She didn't need to point, because he'd already seen it.

In the distance, within nameless streets, was the most amazing sight his weary eyes had ever seen.

'But you said... I thought I had the last watch.'

'The people of this city saw it coming. The greatest cover up of our time,' she sniggered. 'Time-X blew up a replica. This is the original. We beat them. The people of Portsmouth did the one thing Time-X could not. They took time to save time.'

Under the light of a circle of gas lamps and a million candles, the original Guildhall clock ticked on towards midday.

'It's almost twelve. The time. It's accurate.' Tears rolled down his face as he reached for her hand.

'Bloody hell! You don't listen too well, do you? This is all down to you. We took the clock, but it was damaged. It was months before we got it working. You told us the time. You made all this possible.'

'I didn't have the last watch?'

'Of course you did. This is an f'in clock!' As she laughed, the clock chimed. She shouted but he could not hear, so together they waited, chuckling until the final chime rang out.

'It's loud isn't it?' he smiled. 'So what were you saying?'

She slapped him playfully, dislodging the cap from her back

pocket. 'I said. It's a clock not a watch.' He smiled and picked up the cap. When it caught the light she noticed the faded red Time-X logo.

'You?' he said. The Time-X agent from Portsdown Hill. The one he'd met all those years ago. The one who'd let him go. Her eyes were scarred and barely blue and her black bob shaved to an inch from her scalp, but this was the girl. No doubt.

'I'm Hope,' she nodded, offering him her hand. 'Come with me.'

## Zell and the Golden Thread
## Lynne E Blackwood
*Map location: #1*

Could you ever believe such a drab building would hold a terrible secret? Zell couldn't when he stepped out of his small council flat that afternoon.

Manoeuvring Baby La's pushchair through the narrow fire door into the main hall with young Ciprian in tow was his main preoccupation. It was his week to take the children to nursery and Zell was late for his afternoon taxi shift.

'Remember to buy some milk and nappies for tonight,' Anca called from behind the half-closed front door. Zell noticed his wife's tired appearance and decided they should discuss affording some kind of a holiday this year. Working alternating shifts respectively as taxi driver and nurse was hard. Anca came home to a few hours in bed before looking after the children when Zell went out to work, assuming the same duties on his return. The past few years, they had swapped this routine cycle. They were saving up for the deposit on a house of their own. Two young ones and saving on babysitting fees was worth all the effort, but Anca's eyes were circled with dark shadows and Zell realised they both needed a break. Cramped living in a one-bedroom council flat with two small children was taking its toll, despite being on the ground floor and with a small garden. Zell's mind was half-attentive when four year-old Ciprian saw it.

'Daddy, look. A golden spider has spun a silk.'

Then Baby La's chubby finger pointed, the little girl shrieking with delight from her pushchair. Zell was in a hurry but glanced up the stairs. In the light streaming into the building from the stairwell window above, was a golden thread that snaked down over the steps to his front door. It shimmered. It glimmered.

'You're right. But probably not a golden spider. It's the sun that makes it shine like that.'

'A money spider, then, Daddy?'

'I wish it were. Then we could move to a house where you and Baby La had a bedroom each.'

'And a garden so I can play outside?'

'Of course. But Mummy and Daddy have to work hard before that happens. One day, Son. One day when you're older. Come on, enough talk, Daddy's late for work.' Zell dismissed what he saw as a trick of the light.

'Daddy look! The spider's still there.' Ciprian pointed to the stairs on the second afternoon. Two intertwined golden threads this time. Zell stared, puzzled and bent down for a closer look. Two, yes, two, no figment of his imagination. He touched the silks gently. They shrank and recoiled back up the stairwell. He stepped back in surprise.

'Daddy!'

'Sorry, Ciprian. Did I step on your toes?'

'No. The spider says you mustn't touch.'

'And how do you know that?'

'Because I know. The spider says it won't be happy.'

'I'm not sure it is a spider...'

'It is. It's a spider and she lives upstairs. She told me.' His son's imagination never ceased to surprise him. 'Bunica says spiders talk. You have to put your ear close to the silk and listen.'

Ciprian's Romanian grandmother, Bunica, came to visit them regularly, bringing her Carpathian traditions and superstitions into his children's education. Anca and Zell were glad of his mother's thrice annual visits and the efforts she made to preserve his children's heritage and language. It was impossible for them to visit

Romania as a family. Buying their own home was their absolute priority and additional expense was out of the question. Bunica made the trip religiously and with great pleasure. Since their birth she had sung them Romanian lullabies, taught them Romanian nursery rhymes. Zell had been a promising engineering student under the dictator Ceaucescu. He had also known secret police, raids and threats as an activist. It didn't matter if he was British and had been in the country for over twenty years. His heart still beat strongly to Romanian rhythms and with the desire to transmit his heritage to Ciprian and Baby La. *Never forget your roots never forget who you are and your place in the world. Never ever forget others around you,* his mother often said.

Was the spider silk a sign, a call for help? He rarely met the neighbours in his seven story stairwell. Brief encounters at the lift outside his front door. Mostly silent, some disapproving glances at his evidently foreign looks and accent. Zell however, continued to say hellos cheerfully, refusing to forget neighbourly gestures. *Never forget others around you. No man stands alone in this world.* Zell squinted up through the sunny stairwell and resolved to investigate later.

The next day, the two silk threads had been joined by another. Three intertwined threads waiting for him as he opened his front door, a fine golden skein shimmering, reaching along the narrow entry corridor to under the fire door and outside to the stairs.

'Anca. Come and take a look.'

Anca peered through her dishevelled curls. 'Look at what?'

'That.' Zell pointed to the doormat.

'I can't see anything.'

'The spider threads, along the floor. Don't you see them?'

'Zell,' Anca stared at her husband, 'you are working too hard. I don't see anything.'

'Ciprian can see them,' he whispered. His wife frowned.

'If a child sees it, then it must be. What do you think it means?'

'The boy says I mustn't touch because the spider upstairs won't be happy.' The whispered conversation hadn't escaped their son's ears.

'She says you must visit soon. She wants to talk to you Daddy.'

'Go later and see who lives upstairs, Zell. I have to go to bed now,' Anca pecked her husband on the cheek and returned indoors.

Fourth day and four strands. Zell took the children to nursery earlier than usual and returned to the growing golden skein that snaked upwards over the linoleum-covered treads. He mounted the stairs to the first floor where two flats faced each other, a set-up repeated on each landing. The threads continued their shimmering journey further up the stairwell. Zell followed. Second, third, fourth... on the seventh floor landing they disappeared under the entrance to the top flat. Zell pushed the heavy fire door that cut off the narrow corridor leading to the front door. He knocked. Nothing stirred. Zell put his ear to the wood and listened. He couldn't hear any human presence. The corridor was dusty. No treads marked the grainy linoleum flooring.

'Anyone there?' Zell knocked louder. Thumped with his fist. 'Do you need help?' The skein at his feet trembled, came alive, reached out towards his feet. Sweat ran from Zell's armpits. Turning away rapidly as the four golden threads began to dance in the half-light around his ankles, he raced through the fire door out onto the landing.

Zell propped his body against the wall next to the lift and looked back at the flat allowing the hairs on the back of his neck subside. Number forty-five. He would ask the wardens who lived there. Zell took the stairs three by three, his sturdy frame leaping down the seven floors, and ran along the hall towards the main entrance. The two wardens were fixed to the computer screens, biscuits and tea on desk.

'How about this one...' they were shopping on Ebay.

'Hello.' Zell said to them. The older warden, Tony, peered over the edge of the screen at him.

'Yes?'

It was always like that. No first names. Reserved uniquely for the older residents who had lived in the building for over forty years since construction in the nineteen-sixties. No *good morning Mr Gregoria*. A Romanian surname that was surely easy enough to pronounce. He was the outsider.

'Does someone live in number forty-five, Tony?'

'Why?'

'Just wondering...' Zell scrambled his brain for a reason. 'If it's empty and bigger, I'd be interested in a swap.'

'It's not a council flat. Belongs to a family, never see them. Never rented out either. But owned flats aren't my business.'

'Can you find out who owns it?'

'Not my job. Ask the housing office, or why not Harry? He's lived here since the sixties. Old guy with the scooter.'

'Where does Harry live?' Zell knew the conversation was going nowhere. Better ask Harry.

'Number twenty-eight.' Tony's head disappeared behind the computer screen. 'Did you put in a bid?' he asked his colleague who grunted in reply.

Fifth day, five threads intertwined. They were of an intense gold. They formed a distinct skein that wound from Zell's front door and up the stairwell to number forty-five. Ciprian was at the bottom of the stairs, on his knees, head cocked, whispering.

'Get up, Ciprian. The floor is dirty.'

'I'm talking to the spider. She wants to speak to you soon.'

'What if I talk to her here?'

'No. You have to go to hers. She has to see you up there.' Ciprian raised his head and pointed a finger. 'That's where she lives.'

'No one lives up there, son. I've tried knocking on the door.'

'She says you haven't tried hard enough.' With that, Zell's son stood and walked towards the main hall. 'Come on Daddy, we'll be late.' Zell stood perplexed. *I haven't tried hard enough?* Anca and

Zell's weekly shifts changed tomorrow. He would have time to talk to Harry in the evening. Zell raced the pushchair along the entrance hall, Baby La laughing with excitement at the sudden acceleration.

'Harry is elderly so go before teatime,' Anca told her husband when he came home that night. 'You won't want to disturb him too late.' She was also disturbed by Ciprian's incessant chatter about his conversations with *the spider upstairs*. 'There is a meaning to all this and you have to find out. Perhaps someone needs our help?'

'Hmm,' Zell placed the mug on the small dining table. Anca had, as she did each week, replaced the vase with fresh flowers from Commercial Road market. *A clean house should always have the scent of flowers to bring it alive,* was house proud Anca's mantra. This week, freesias and dahlias. The freesias' heady scent had met him at the front door. 'I'll chat with Harry tomorrow. In the meantime, we have to discuss taking a break.'

'No holidays. Not yet. Buying our home is more important, you know that. We must think of our babies and their future.'

'You are tired. Working full-time and then coming home to two little ones. We have to manage a holiday with the children this year. It will be their first and ours together. Just think how much fun it will be? We can go out of season. Ciprian will be starting school next year and we won't be able to afford a holiday after that. What do you think?'

'But the deposit for the house? We are so far off from what we need to obtain a mortgage. My salary is the only stable income. We need a large deposit, then there's the moving and decorating ... I'm not sure. Our dream home seems so far away.' Anca stared intently into her coffee dregs as if her whole future was held amidst the dark-brown mud. 'I wonder what answer your mother would find if she read these coffee dregs tonight.'

'Well, she's coming next week. You can ask her yourself. But I guess she would probably say you needed a holiday.' Zell squeezed his wife's hand. 'Come on. Off to bed with you, beautiful woman.'

We'll work something out tomorrow.'

Five in the morning and early light filtered down the stairwell, illuminating the six strands of a thicker golden skein. Checking no one was in the vicinity, Zell knelt and whispered. 'I'm coming for you, I promise.' The threads remained still. He gingerly outstretched one finger and touched. No quiver, no tremble, no retracting and coiling suddenly up the stairs, as on the first day. 'Are you dead?' he whispered. The threads quivered and twisted in response. He touched them again. This time they moved in a concerted caress over his fingers and hand. Zell gazed on in wonderment as their warmth made his skin tingle. 'I have to work, Spider upstairs. I'll be back later.' Although he heard nothing, he believed his son. The skein was growing in luminosity and strength... it was alive.

'Good evening. I'm Zell from number thirty-one on the ground floor. You're Harry, aren't you?'

Harry stood tottering on the doorstep. 'Yes I am. I have seen you in the main entrance several times. Lovely children you have and what a beautiful wife. You are both so polite and always ask me if I need help. Not like the others in this building. What can I do for you, Zell? Is that Romanian?'

'Yes, it is. I'm surprised you know that.'

'Second World War, lad. Quite a few Romanians came here. Jewish they were. Most left for London, but a couple of families stayed in Portsmouth.'

'Really? My mother is Jewish Romanian. But there aren't many left in the country now. The last sixty years has been very harsh for them. The country has a history of intolerance towards Jews. My mother married a goy so remaining in Romania was easier for her. In theory, that makes me Jewish - through the mother's blood, you know...'

'Intolerance. Oh yes, I suffer intolerance because I'm elderly, as if I'm good for the rubbish heap. You, well, I doubt whether many people in this building display civil behaviour towards you and your family.'

'Outside the building too,' Zell smiled.

'People are selfish and ill-mannered these days, Zell. Come on in. I suppose you want a chat about something and I'd be better seated. Into my eighties now and my old pins don't hold as well as they did.'

Zell gazed at the wall covered in framed photos, some colour, but most black and white.

'You were in the Navy?' he asked the old man.

'Yep. A Navy lad I was. Good times. Sailed all over the world. Just made a pot of brew. Do you want one? The cups are in the sideboard. Get yourself one, will you?'

'Allow me to help you,' Zell poured the steaming tea. 'This is an unusual teapot...'

'Ah yes, a present from a dear friend. Zelda. She lived at number forty-five.'

'What a coincidence. I was going to ask you about the flat. A friend of yours?' Zell saw Harry's eyes brim with moisture. From old age, or were they tears?

'A very dear friend. Such a stunner but not for the likes of me. Knew her as a young girl when her family first came to Portsmouth. They opposed it when we began seeing each other, so I joined the Navy. Zelda was Jewish Romanian. Not many relatives left, she told me. They first lived where those new houses have been built in Buckland. Most of the streets had been bombed out, but her father still had his jewellery shop standing after the war. He had a good business, quite well-off they were. Then the houses were pulled down and they were given one of these flats. Her father died and her mother was, well, not quite right. Zelda told me about how all her family had gone during the war and it had affected her mother. She bought the flat later under Thatcher. Said she needed a place to call home.'

'Number forty-five.'

'Yes,' Harry put the empty cup onto the dining room table. 'I was ill and sent to a nursing home for a couple of months. When I came back, her daughter told me she had put Zelda into a residential home. I never married, always hoped I could be with her one day, and she was gone. Her daughter wouldn't say where. Didn't even have her address to write.'

'When was that Harry? Her daughter, you say?'

'A few years back. Probably around the time you moved here.'

'And she has a daughter? Why isn't the flat sold, then?'

'Yes. But Zelda never married, and she kept quiet about the father. Some kind of scandal. I was away at sea and came back to find her pregnant. Offered to marry her, but she refused. I don't know why her daughter has kept the flat. Probably waiting for Zelda to pass away before claiming the inheritance. A right one, I can tell you. Nasty piece of work. Never treated her mother properly and was up and out of there as soon as she could. Lives somewhere up north. No kids, selfish witch. I see her sometimes. Just pops in occasionally then leaves. I had a right ruckus with her once. Wanted me to give back the key to Zelda's flat. I was the only one who visited her, nearly every day when she became frail. Not that ungrateful daughter of hers.'

'A key?'

'I still have it,' Harry winked at Zell. 'That witch daughter couldn't get it off me.' Harry gazed at a framed painting. 'She gave me that too. Said it was important.'

Zell had been too absorbed with Harry's tale of Zelda from number forty-five to notice the painting. But when he did he gasped in surprise. 'But that's a view of Iasi? It's my hometown!'

Harry's eyes squinted into Zell's. 'That's what she meant,' he murmured. Then a laugh broke his mouth wide open. 'You old gal. So that's what you wanted me to do,' and he stood unsteadily, moved towards the sideboard and pulled at one of the drawers. 'Here it is. Just as you said it would happen, beautiful Zelda.'

'What is it?'

'Ha!' Harry chuckled, he couldn't contain his mirth. 'Here, look at this,' and he thrust a small brown envelope towards him. There was a set of keys inside. Zell's heart raced trying to fit the pieces together: the spider, the skein of golden threads that wove a shimmering path from Zelda's flat to his own front door, the painting, his son's insistence *she wants to talk to you.*

'Are you alright, lad? You look a little pale,' Harry's voice brought Zell back to reality. 'She gave me this the last time I saw her. Said I should keep it for the first person who showed her some kindness. Always was a dark horse, knew things, read cards, you know.'

'But if Zelda's been in a home for a few years, the threads...' Zell murmured.

'What threads, lad?'

'My son keeps saying he can see golden threads.' He wasn't going to admit he saw them as well. 'Like golden hair...'

'Oh yes!' Harry said, 'Golden blond hair, a real beauty. Not the kind from a bottle, believe me. She had never cut it since coming to England. Said it was to remind her of the past when people were good and kind. Why do you ask?'

'It's nothing.' But the image of quivering golden strands remained with him. 'So what do I do now?'

'Zelda was a very smart woman. She always knew what to do.' They both looked at the key in Zell's hand.

'I'll go and have a look I suppose. Would you like to come?'

Harry hesitated, then spoke softly, 'I loved her from the first time I saw her. It breaks my heart not being in touch, to think of her all alone somewhere. Perhaps we can find a clue to her whereabouts?'

'We will, I promise.'

'Then let's go. I would like that. You are a good man. Zelda was right in doing things this way...'

Harry and Zell stood outside the lift. Harry supported by his walking frame, with Zell's arm under one elbow. 'Are you sure you'll be alright?'

'I'll be fine. Just a few good memories coming to mind.'

They took the central staircase lift to the ground floor and made their way slowly to the end of the long entrance hall and the lift outside Zell's flat. He could see the golden threads quivering so hard they coiled and twisted in an excited dance up the stairwell. *I'm coming Zelda*, he whispered.

The shimmering skein coming from under Zelda's front door entwined threads around Zell's ankles, tugging him inside. It danced along the hall and into another room. *Follow the threads*, Zell walked into the bedroom where they were surprised to see a large freezer. Electricity was still on, he noticed. *The daughter must have taken over Zelda's bank account and is still paying the bills. But why?* The skein of gold came from the freezer. Harry stood behind him.

'That's new. Wasn't here the last time I visited. Odd...'

'I'm going to open it,' Zell saw the golden threads agitating wildly, he could almost hear them hum they were vibrating so rapidly. He placed his hands either side of the skein which wrapped itself around his fingers. He couldn't let go even if he wanted to. They were compelling him to open the freezer. Zell lifted the heavy lid and cried out.

Zelda lay perfectly frozen, eyes wide open looking at him. A thick skein of golden hair grew from a gaping wound in her skull. As Zell stood transfixed, Zelda's jaw fell open. He could have sworn he heard her whisper, *thank you.* Then the dark eyes glazed over and the strands fell limp and grey. Zell could hear Harry sobbing at his shoulder.

'That witch. She did it. Her own daughter killed my beloved Zelda. She knew it would happen this way. How could a daughter...' Harry sobbed and lost his balance as emotion shook his body. Zell caught the frail man as he fell.

'Come Harry. Let's sit you down. I'll phone the police.'

Shaking, one from lost love and the other from stupor at the gruesome find, both men made their way to the small living room, the walls of which were covered in framed black and white photos of family portraits and groups. Zelda's lost family. Zell stared at a photo dated from before the war. A little girl attending a large family wedding. He recognised the photograph, his mother had the exact same one. *Oh good God. Is it possible?* Bunica had told him the little girl was her second cousin. He unhooked the photograph from the wall to examine it more closely. A wad of papers fell to the floor. Zell picked it up. *It read: The Last Will and Testament of Zelda Salomonivic.* 'My mother's maiden name is Salomonovic,' Zell told Harry handing him the pages.

'So that's where it went!' Harry sniffed. 'I'd forgotten about that. She told me to put the person's name in the will. See? There's no designated inheritor, just a blank space. She tried to tell me once, about the keys... it's you, Zell.'

'I suppose it's possible. But I...'

'Sign! It's all yours.' Harry fumbled around his pockets for a pen. 'Take the papers to the solicitor and register them so that daughter of hers can't claim a penny. I bet she's been looking for this all this time.'

'I can't believe this is happening.'

'That daughter won't get a penny. Well done Zelda, my lovely. You are such a smart woman.'


'Harry should take what he wants from the flat,' Anca shook her head in disbelief. 'I can't wait for your mother to come and find out what has happened. Her second cousin was living upstairs all this time. I still don't understand it all. Ciprian and his '*golden spider threads*', Zelda calling you both. Incredible! Are you alright, Zell? Still getting flashbacks of the freezer?'

'Yes. But that daughter has been locked up now and Zelda is in peace. I agree about Harry and what we discussed about selling the flat and putting some money aside for his nursing home fees. He was Zelda's friend to the end.'

'There won't be enough money to buy a large house otherwise he could live with us. I can't give up my work to take care of him.'

'Harry knows that, Anca, He understands. But we will come and see him every other day and bring him home for lunch as much as we can. I have to go upstairs and fetch him so he can choose what he wants. I'll see you later.' Zell kissed his wife gently and went to the front door. Tony hailed him as he passed the wardens' office. 'Good afternoon, Mr Gregoria.' Zell smiled. So that was what money did for you? His status in the building had suddenly elevated to respectable. All the occupants greeted him now. 'Hello Tony. Yes, a lovely afternoon, thank you,' and he sped on to Harry's flat.

They both stared at the freezer contents. Half-filled bags of frozen peas, potatoes, and other vegetables that had lain underneath Zelda's body. 'It has to be done, Zell. Do you want me to help you?' Harry queried.

'No, I'm fine Harry. You go and choose some things you want to take and I'll put all of this in binbags.' Zell reached down for the first bag, stopped, weighed it in his hand, squeezed the contents with his fingers, then stopped again, puzzled. Gingerly, he opened it up and looked inside. His jaw clicked open so suddenly it hurt. Zell feverishly opened the others then emptied each one's contents onto the bed. He was still gaping open-mouthed as Harry entered the room.

'Well I never. So that's what she did with it all,' Harry chuckled. 'Good old Zelda. Her daughter looking everywhere and all the time, my Zelda was lying on it.' Harry grinned then laughed heartily. 'Well, you are certainly a rich man now, Zell!'

The bed was strewn with jewellery, collector gold coins, loose gems. A fortune.

'So that's where her father's stash went,' Harry laughed.

Amongst the glittering jewels was a large envelope bound with tape to keep the contents dry.

'What are these?' Zell unravelled the tape carefully. 'Letters addressed to you, Harry,' as he handed them to the old man.

Harry sat next to the strewn gems and, fingers trembling, opened the letters one-by-one. Zell put a comforting arm around the frail shoulders. Harry was crying as he opened each one and read them.

'Letters from Zelda?'

'Yes.' Then more sobs. 'Letters she wasn't allowed to send to a goy. The first one from when we met as teenagers. This one... it explains they married her off to a Jew, who emigrated to Israel a few months after the wedding, abandoning her. No news of him since, so she remained legally married all her life.' Harry lifted his face wet with tears yet glowing with happiness. 'Every single one says how she'd always loved me.'

Zell smiled then laughed. 'So you are coming to live with us in our new big house, uncle Harry?'

'Of course I am. That's what Zelda wanted. What a smart beauty.' Harry gazed at him through his tears, 'I saw her hair, her beautiful golden hair one last time.'

## After Show Party
## Christine Lawrence
*Map location: #20*

The auditorium was quiet now, the after show party had fizzled out, the last few stragglers long gone home and Amy was left alone. She sat on the edge of the stage and looked up towards the back of the theatre, red plush seats like rows of soldiers standing to attention, gazing blankly back at her.

Playing Lady Macbeth had been amazing - demanding the depths of feelings - anger, madness, passion - and she'd never felt so close to a leading man before. Tom's Macbeth was stunning and between them they'd caused a sensation. Still elated from the final applause and the congratulations from other cast members, Amy could also sense the grief which seeps in gradually at the end of a run. She knew what to expect. Within three days a black despair would descend and she'd be trapped, doubting herself, unable to see any future.

The voices of the cast echoed to her: 'Here's to the next one!' 'Will miss you darling!' 'We must keep in touch!' 'You were marvellous!' Their voices faded as Amy brought herself to her feet.

Wondering where Tom was, she walked into the wings. As she passed the small props table she noticed that it hadn't been cleared properly. The dagger was there in its place, as if set for the next show. 'Well there won't be any more of those,' she thought as she took up the blade, planning to leave it with the night-watchman on her way out. Then as she turned away towards the stage door she saw them. Tom and the Third Witch. And they were kissing. More than kissing - his hands were all over her and she was obviously enjoying it. Amy was shocked and let out a short gasp. The couple stopped and Tom looked across at Amy.

It was the way he smiled at her that made her do it - a smug, winning kind of smile - but his eyes were hard and cold.

The dagger slid in so easily. It was as if it were one of those toy daggers that retracted into its handle whilst looking as though it were sinking into flesh. Tom stopped smiling after the fifth plunge. As he sank to the wooden floor, Amy watched the river of blood running across the raked stage and wondered fleetingly where the Third Witch had gone. Then she turned to the auditorium and took a bow. The red plush soldiers gazed blankly back at her as she sat on the edge of the stage to wait.

**Crescent Fall**
**Tom Sykes**
*Map location: #2*

Abel pushed his cap over his sore and sweating brow. Broken over his knee, the barrel of the shotgun warmed the skin beneath his jeans. The aluminium pin of the 'Ali-Doon Industries' badge on his left breast was so hot now that it stung his chest. 'Not *cushty*,' he sighed, getting up from the stool. He was no scientist but he wondered if this latest brume of smog that had drifted over from the Chinese Concession to the MERU Concession was acting like a magnifying glass, increasing the severity of the sun's rays. Either way, it was going to be another thirty-five-degree summer. That's what the radio had said this morning just before the power cut.

Abel snapped the shotgun straight and walked to the eastern edge of the roof terrace. He looked down onto St Thomas's Road, the unofficial border between the MERU and the Hindustani Concessions. The tin roofs of the slum spread out far and wide, rough-hewn squares like a jagged chessboard. But rather than black and white, the roofs were grey, made out of paint-stripped road signs and weathered corrugated iron.

Further south, autorickshaws trickled down Begum Road. Abel's eyes watered as they followed the exhaust fumes' journey up above the white-bearded vagrant sleeping on the steps of the Co-op Relief Centre, up above the children searching for plastic bottles on the mountain of litter that blocked the junction with Pervez Plaza, and up above the windowless tenement blocks, to feed into the smog that was fast shading the sky black.

Abel wiped his eyes with a damp handkerchief. He crossed the terrace, passing the chrome hatch with the WARNING – DO NOT ENTER sign. It was protected by three bombproof walls and twenty different combination locks. Beside it stood a flag with the crescent moon insignia of the great harbour city of Nu-Port-Zi. At the northern end of the roof there was nothing to concern him. Making its way up Geeta Basra Avenue was a jeep with mirrorshade windows, flanked by two trucks carrying armed goons. They'd come in from Poshtown to take care of one kind of business or another. From this side of the Ali-Doon Building, Abel could hear – but not see – one of Nu-Port-Zi's most valuable assets. Less than a mile away, the dockyard banged, crashed, droned and scraped. It would go on like this all day and it would go on like this all night. The radio often said that the docks were busier now than in their heyday three centuries ago, and that the foreign investors had made it possible.

Dr Yombashak had instructed Abel to check over the entire roof on an hourly basis, but Abel felt that three checks a day were quite enough. No-one would dare try to break in anyway, he was sure of that. Even if they somehow got past the electrified razor wire *and* the forty-millimetre-thick steel doors *and* him *and* his shotgun, Yombashak had assured Abel that it was physically impossible for strangers to access the silo itself.

Abel returned to the penthouse where his radio, gas stove and sleeping bag were. As he heated up another tin of noodle soup, he glanced around the penthouse, doubting the rumour that the Ali-Doon Building had once been a university. He tried to imagine students hunched over desks working hard on such luxuries as tablets and personal computers. But he could only see what was here now: a crate of ammunition, a rusty ceiling fan and a sinewy rat nibbling at the fungi stippled across the skirting board.

Night came and cooled the city. As usual he didn't sleep properly. He started to doze off and dreamed that a ferocious dog with orange scales was hurtling towards him. The image shocked him awake and he found that he was unable to move or breathe. The paralysis wore off after a few seconds. He turned the radio on. Muzak to keep the public serene during curfew. Soft Chinese gongs, Arabesque harp melodies, a bossa nova rhythm, a sitar line – a collaboration between all the ruling nations of Nu-Port-Zi. A power cut killed the music and he dozed again.

He awoke to the sound of footsteps. He clipped a torch onto his shotgun and crept out onto the roof terrace. Two pre-teens were crouched over the chrome hatch. 'What are you *dinlos* up to?' he shouted.

The boys turned round slowly. Rather than scared they smiled mischievously. Under the torchlight their faces were gaunt from hunger and luminous from jaundice. Abel guessed that they had nothing to lose and nothing to be scared of.

'You won't finds no *sparsy* up here,' said Abel.

'We's only lookin' for *scran*,' whined one of the boys. 'We's bloody famished.'

'You don't wants to be snooping here,' said Abel. 'Here's an important *eastny* operation.'

'He's right,' said one boy to the other. '*He* looks like an *eastny* too. And he's got a shooter. Let's leg it.'

'Naah,' the other boy said. He looked at Abel in defiance. 'Give us some *scran* and we'll clear off.'

Abel closed one eye and took aim. 'You's in no place to bargain, *lairy nipper*. I's orders to blow down anyone who comes up here.'

'Then why don't ya?'

'I will if you wants me to,' Abel fired a shot just above their heads. The boys sprinted to the guardrail, swung their legs over it and disappeared.

In the morning, Abel noticed that his warning shot had broken open a cupboard set into the skylight on the far side of the roof terrace. Inside the cupboard was a stack of old books so dusty that they looked like they were covered in cinders. There were a number of science textbooks and a paperback called *Pure and True: The Fight for England's Survival* by John 'Bull' Fledgeby. Fledgeby. He'd heard the name before, in shanty school. The teacher had called Fledgeby an evil man. He embodied everything wrong with the *skate* culture. He had been in a position of power once, before the Concessions, and had betrayed his people. His ideas had been discredited and his writings banned. Abel hesitated before bringing the book back to the penthouse.

At dawn Abel phoned Yombashak's office in Poshtown and told him to come to the building. After wrestling with the locking system of the outer steel door for twenty minutes, Yombashak and his goon, a fellow African, climbed out of the skylight and onto the roof terrace. Yombashak loped over to Abel, huge hands clasped together in urgency, the sun ricocheting off his globular bald head. '*Mjinga mkundu*, Abel,' he groaned. 'What is going on?'

'Lets me explain, sir,' said Abel. 'No needs to *have a mare*.'

'My boy, I cannot understand this pidgin English.' Yombashak pinched Abel on the cheek with sovereign-ringed fingers. 'Speak *pukka* please. You know how to because you are half-*eastny*, after all. Luckily it is the top half of you that is *eastny*, where your brain is located.' He let go of Abel's face and strode to the guardrail. 'You see him?' He pointed to the steps where the vagrant with the white beard was waking up with a coughing fit. 'He is 100% *skate*. Little better than a monkey. It is a law of nature that people like him will be lazy and poor unless they are brought under control, disciplined. That fool Fledgeby-'

Abel started when he heard the name. He was glad he'd stashed the book under his sleeping bag.

'That *paagal* fool Fledgeby,' continued Yombashak, 'thought he could organise the *skates*. Why did he fail? Because he was a dirty *skate* too.'

Abel and the goon traded bored glances. Yombashak never missed the opportunity to deliver a lecture.

'Shall I tells you what happened last night then, sir?' asked Abel.

'Yes, my boy, you better had.'

'These *nippers*-'

'*Nippers*? You mean *qingshaonian*?'

'They comes up here looking for *scran* – food – and I tells them no. Then they runs off.'

'So how did they get up here, past the security measures that Ali-Doon has spent a fortune on?'

'Don't know, sir.'

'How old were they?' asked Yombashak, moving towards him. The goon was closing in too, knuckles resting on the grip of his holstered pistol.

'Eighteen or twenty,' Abel lied.

Yombashak gripped Abel's shoulders and said to him carefully, 'Are you sure that's what you saw, my boy?'

'Yes sir.'

'It's just that none of this makes sense. How did the boys get up here? How did they escape? Is everything all right, Abel? Perhaps you are feeling a little stressed, not quite *raha*. You haven't been drinking the purple water in Tiffin's Laguna, have you?'

'No sir, I's fine.'

Yombashak grinned at the goon. 'Maybe his brain is in the *skate* half of his body after all, eh?'

The goon laughed, a single dulcet 'Hah!'

Yombashak's gaze fell back onto Abel. 'But it would be unfair to say that. While only in shanty school Abel won a scholarship to the Doon School in Delhi, no less.' The goon whistled, impressed. 'He gets his intellect from his *eastny* father, you understand. Sadly Fledgeby's 59 Resistance broke out and it wasn't possible for Abel to take up his place at the Doon. That is *zhengque*, isn't it Abel?'

'Yes sir.'

'So instead here you still are in Nu-Port-Zi on fifty MERUs a month. You could be worse off. You could be like those badmashes down there, knifing each other for *pag-pag*.'

'Yes sir.'

His expression turning sour, Yombashak pinched Abel's cheek

again, this time harder. 'I don't know what happened up here on the *çati* last night. What I do know is that I cannot tell our Head Office in Abu Dhabi that we may have a security breach. That would do me no good. No good at all. We must manage this problem locally and discreetly.'

'I understand, sir.'

'So let's put this foolishness behind us, shall we? From now on you must either refrain from eating the paneer powder before bedtime or, if you see any *kumbafus* for real, you need to put bullets in them. *Comprende?*'

'Yes sir,' said Abel.

That night, Abel felt truly lonely for the first time since taking this job. His mood was aggravated by the fact that he could always see so many people in the streets below, talking and laughing and having a good time despite their woes. That was the way of the native *skate*. He watched the veterans drinking hooch around the bonfires of plastic packaging, the flames making silhouettes out of the *pag-pag* women as they stole bin bags from the backs of restaurants and tenements. Some would pick out the waste food and eat it there and then. Others took it home, cooked it up in a stew, fed some of it to their families and sold the rest on. He wanted so badly to speak to one of these people, speak to anyone on friendly, equal terms, anyone who wasn't a bully like Yombashak.

His headache came back and he drank as much water as he could spare, pinching his nose to ease the bitter taste of the iodine purifier. Getting into his sleeping bag, he listened to a radio report on the last pockets of resistance to what the pundits called 'The Eastern Consensus'. While the Concession system had now pacified Western Europe, North America was another story. 'Survivalist savages' living in 'trees and mountains' were defying 'the rule of law' and waging a guerrilla war against the private standing armies of Brazilian, Chinese and Argentine corporations.

The *Comandante* of the Brazilian Concession in Seattle was

interviewed. 'These escória are nothing but terrorists, stealing land that belongs to every decent, hard-working Americanadian. Our intelligence suggests that their base is at Crescent Falls, Alberta. We'll be coming for them before the summer's out.'

It all seemed so abstract to Abel. Although he'd done well in school he didn't remember being taught much recent history, how Nu-Port-Zi and the Concession system and the whole modern world came to be. The radio wasn't much better. Most *skates* he knew thought it all propaganda to make the *eastnies* look good. After last night's events, he doubted whether he could even trust his own eyes and ears to relay the truth to him. He shuddered when he thought back to what Yombashak had told him: *'Are you sure that's what you saw, my boy?'* Perhaps he *was* under a lot of stress.

Early next morning the orange dog appeared again. Abel came out of his doze with a sore throat and chest. He nibbled some noodles and went outside to find that the smog had covered the roof terrace like a black cloak. He had to lean right over the guardrail before he could make out anything on the ground. The vagrant was now lying on his side on the steps of the Co-Op, concerned people crouched over him, a relief worker dabbing his forehead with a sponge. The scene worried Abel yet reassured him at the same time. Most *skates* had little in the way of money or possessions, but if your luck ran out they'd rally round and help you. They still had a sense of community.

Abel watched as the relief worker disposed of the sponge by squeezing it into a crack in the step she was kneeling on. *A crack.* Abel hadn't noticed that before. He looked up and down the steps and saw more cracks, none of them bigger than a fist, but they were cracks nonetheless. He saw too that the khaki paint of the façade had faded significantly and the dullness of the concrete beneath was showing through. Only last month, ten-year-olds in boiler suits came and gave the Co-Op a fresh coat of paint, right under the nose of some *eastny* charity worker who'd been questioning locals about the scandal of child labour in the Concessions.

Abel rushed over to the north side and found that perhaps fifty of the slum-dwellers were working on the roofs of their shacks, reinforcing the metal with scavenged bricks, lumps of wood, paving stones. You usually only saw this kind of reconstruction work after there'd been a flood or a fire.

*Fire.* The sun swelled and brightened until Abel had to cover his eyes with his hands. But even with his eyes closed he could see a firework display of orange. Arcs, sparks and volleys of orange. Amidst it all he saw the dog, bounding along and barking, outlined in spiky orange.

He staggered into the penthouse and slept until he was woken in the night by human howling. He went on to the roof terrace and peered through the darkness at the vagrant who was now lying on his back yelling 'FLEDGEBY SAVE US!' over and over again.

There was that name again. Abel went to his sleeping bag and took the book out. On the first page was a vintage photograph of a middle-aged man with an obstinate gaze. He wore a bow tie and a green gilet, and was toasting the camera with a pint of dark and stodgy-looking beer that was unfamiliar to Abel.

'Fellow Englanders,' the introduction stated, 'our sovereignty and freedom are under serious threat. Over the last ten years we have seen great nations – Germany, France, the United States – cut into little pieces not unlike the way my village butcher might chop up a side of beef. These pieces have been shared out between the new behemoths of the East – China, Hindustan, Turk-Ottoman, this worrying new entity called the 'Middle Eastern Resource Union' – and their allies in Africa and Latin America. Now the same process of neo-colonisation is happening in our country, in our beloved England. These foreign imperialists are coming over here to exploit our economy, which was permanently weakened by the Great Fall of 2008. They thieve our resources and they exploit and underpay our workers. They repatriate 95% of their profits while we are forced onto the streets to die of hunger and preventable diseases. In short, it's a bloody outrage.'

Abel put the book aside and thought about what he'd just read. It was bold stuff that contradicted everything he'd heard on the radio and the views of everyone he'd ever met – *skate* or *eastny*.

'Worse than the threat to our freedom,' continued Fledgeby, 'is the threat to our way of life. Of course English society has changed over the years, no-one can deny that. But there is something about England that doesn't change, an *eternal essence* that is impossible to define in rational terms precisely because it is all about instinct, feeling and emotion. It is the pride we feel when we see the George Cross billowing in a light summer breeze above the pavilion of a village cricket ground. It is the joy that bubbles up through us when we share a bawdy joke with our best mate over a pint of real ale in our local. It is our in-built politeness and our hard-wired sense of justice and fair play.'

Abel's headache was returning. He didn't like Fledgeby's arguments. They sounded like the flipside of Yombashak's sermons about the innate superiority of *eastnies*. Abel was mixed race anyway, he had no loyalties to either side. But then most pureblood *skates* he knew didn't either. They felt let down by the men in charge, whatever colour the men in charge were, wherever in the world they came from.

At sunlight Abel went out onto the roof terrace. The vagrant was lying face-down, blood leaking from his mouth and down the step like a waterfall. A security guard in a Levantine Banking puffer jacket looked on from the safe distance of Begum Road, hands over his mouth in case what had done for the vagrant was contagious. Abel thought about calling a public ambulance and thought again. Ambulances rarely came to this part of town because the traffic between here and Santa Maria Hospice was so dense. If you were an important enough *eastny* they'd send you a helicopter. If you were a homeless *skate*, they didn't care.

To Abel, the Co-Op Relief Centre itself looked almost as sickly as the vagrant. The cracks had become gaping holes through which the Centre's trays of medicines and food parcels could be seen. Large sections of its flat concrete roof were missing. Worse still, the buildings around it were in a similar state of decay, their flimsy plywood façades chipped and warped.

Abel's attention was diverted by a creaking noise. His eyes zipped along Begum Road to the mountain of litter which was swaying to its side like some big game animal that had been shot by a tranquiliser dart. It collapsed, taking with it several kids who'd been foraging in its upper reaches. Abel watched the little bodies sink deep into the tipped-over stew of tyres, wires, rags, broken glass and plastic bags. The security guard left the vagrant and ran over to the scene of the disaster.

'Them poor *nippers!*' gasped Abel. He rushed to the skylight, but halted. '*If you leave your post for even a nanosecond,*' Mr Yombashak hissed in his mind's ear, '*you will forfeit your job. You will also be held liable for any damage done to the Ali-Doon Building in your absence.*'

Instead, Abel sloped into the penthouse where he couldn't hear the cries for help. He continued reading the Fledgeby book.

'True, we are threatened by foreign imperialists, but we cannot wholly blame them for the mess we are in. Why does the East rise while we fall? Let me quote something my father liked to say: 'we got soft.' Instead of we Englanders pulling together for the national interest, we grew selfish and lazy. We demanded higher wages, fewer working hours and far too many luxuries. We kept borrowing money we could never pay back. On the other hand – or rather on the other side of the world – Chinese and Hindustanis were prepared to work eighteen hour days for a pittance. How could we compete with that?

'The imperialists beat us at our own game, the game of capitalism that we created three centuries ago, but no longer understand the rules of. The world our grandfathers knew and loved has now been turned upside down. Now we are the slaves and they are the masters. And not only that, they have to rub our noses in the fact, don't they? They re-name our streets, monuments and landmarks. As if to taunt us they speak this appalling 'Glenglish', a kind of bastardised dialect that dilutes our pure and true English language with Hindi, Urdu,

Turkish, Mandarin – even Portuguese!'

Though much of this was new to Abel and gripped him, he disliked the hysterical tone. He skipped forward to a chapter called 'The Ultimate Sacrifice'.

'Exactly a year ago today, on a chilly April morning, Kirsty, a forty-five-year-old secretary from West London, got into her car with her two children, eight-year-old Victor and six-year-old Liza. As soon as Kirsty put her foot down on the accelerator she detonated a thousand pounds' worth of high explosive. She and her children were killed, along with thirty bystanders.

'The perpetrators have never been caught, but I have a good idea who they are. The attack happened just a day after I, as the last Protector of the United Kingdom of England, refused to sign into existence a number of laws that would have turned us into a *de facto* slave state. The imperialists had put me under incredible pressure to do so. At first they offered me a generous cut of all the profits they'd make from all their business ventures here: manufacturing, property and, most importantly of all, mining. If I was worried about betraying my country and the recriminations that would surely follow, they would help me relocate to China or Brazil for a safer life. But I refused all of that and they got angry. The President of MERU took to phoning me in the middle of the night and abusing me. More than once did that scoundrel call me a 'backward *skate* bastard'. Finally, the imperialists did something that was worse than killing me – they killed my family.' Abel threw the book down and rubbed his head. He cried and cried and kept crying until he fell into real sleep for the first time in months. His dream was sharper, more vivid than reality itself.

*The goon drops the lighter and jumps back. The flames quickly coat the dog's body. The goon hurls a stone at the slum in the distance and the dog, rasping and screeching with pain, chases loyally after it. The orange beast enters the first alleyway which is itself surrounded by little fires. Smouldering refuse. Dustbin barbecues. Glowing crocks of vegetable oil. Gas stoves quivering behind greasy drapes.*

Before anyone can scream 'fire!' the dog is already zigzagging frantically, infecting everything it touches. Flames dash along curtains and radiate across chipboard walls. A gas canister blushes with a bassy thump. Bright, hot ash sprays from the roof of the meeting hut, dislodging a steel lintel that crashes onto the heads of the two children. 'Abel!' they cry. 'Abel! Abel! Abel!'

'Abel?' said a female voice. He jolted awake, but found himself paralysed again. He came out of it and was able to register the woman. She had a russet complexion and an abrupt frown. Dreadlocks dangled from under a black Homberg hat. A black leather jacket hugged her athletic frame. She was holding an old-fashioned service revolver at her side. 'Abel?'

He sat up in his sleeping bag. 'Bloody hell it's Rosa Spinnaker. What are you doing here? Been *yonks* since I sees you...'

'About ten years,' she smiled. 'How are you?'

'I's alive. I's got a job. I's can eat.'

'Good for you,' said Rosa, squatting down. 'And we both got out of Craneswater.' Abel thought of the dog and shook his head a little.

'Remember when we used to sneak into the *priddy's* garden and *scav* apples?'

'Yeah, you was always the best at that.'

'And when we first met? The other kids at shanty school was coming *lairy* about my surname and you stuck up for me.'

'Then the next day the tower was demolished.'

Rosa lowered her grin a little. 'Well, that was the official line...'

'Look Rosa,' Abel said and took a deep breath. 'What do you wants? It ain't safe for you to be here.'

'What's safe ain't important in the grand scheme of things.'

'How did you get inside?'

'This place ain't as impregnable as the imperialists think. They's got so greedy and lax that they don't any longer knows how to do a job proper or efficient.'

Abel laughed and folded his arms. 'I's sussed you. You's in the

Opposition, ain't you?'

'*Boffish* as always, Abel. What I wants is in that silo.'

'Is you a *lost-it case?* Nobody can get in there. And anyway, if you got past the steel door and the razorwire, why can't you gets inside the silo?'

'We knows that Ali-Doon did at least do a good job of securing the silo, if not the rest of the building.' Rosa gestured to the copy of *Pure and True* next to Abel's sleeping bag. 'Reading that are you?'

'Not sure if I likes the angle the *mush* takes. But I-'

'But you don't likes his racial and cultural essentialism?'

'You could says that.'

'We're not all like him in the Opposition, you know. Most of us don't hates the imperialists just because they's foreign. We hates them for treating our communities so badly.'

'Do you knows what happened to Fledgeby?'

'The imperialists put it about that he *squinnied* off and got himself killed during the '89 Revolt...'

'He's still alive, isn't he?'

Rosa swivelled her eyes.

'You was always *pants* at poker,' Abel said. 'So what's inside the silo? Why do you lot need it so bad?'

'You don't know?'

'I's just work here.'

'It's better that I don't tells you some things.'

Abel raised his palms. 'Well I's can't open that silo for you either. Nobody's told me the combo, see.'

'I knows that,' said Rosa. 'So I's got a failsafe plan, but I needs your help.' She put her arm around Abel. It made him feel warm and safe. He couldn't recall the last time he'd been this close to anyone. 'The imperialists treat you all like *dockyard oysters* stuck on their shoes,' she whispered. 'Why don't you gets away from this hell while you still can? Start a new life with us in Crescent Falls?'

Abel thought about his options. He wasn't sure what his options even were. Rosa cleared her throat. 'You know what my favourite game was back at Craneswater?'

'Making kites out of bin bags and flying them around Tiffin's Laguna. You loved every second of that.'

Rosa bowed her head and looked up at Abel. 'We was playing kites when *it* happened. Remember?'

'Course I bloody remember,' Abel said in a voice squeaky with emotion. 'Am I a *dinlo* or what?'

'I'm sorry,' Rosa said quickly.

'One morning you and me goes to Tiffin's,' he said. 'We play all day, miss our *scran*. When we gets back the whole township is burned to the ground. My whole bloody family,' he broke into sobbing and Rosa took his head in her arms.

'Chin up,' she said, kissing him on the brow. 'That bastard *priddy* what sent that dog in, eh? How many had to die so's that he could get some *sparsy* off the insurance company? A hundred? Two hundred? That's what the imperialists has done to our community. Profit come before people. It's wrong.'

Abel withdrew from her grip and wiped his eyes.

'You know why I joined the Opposition?' Rosa continued. 'Because something happened to me that I never even tells you or any of my friends about. I always says that my dad died of a heart attack but actually he was *puggled* to death by a gang of MERU soldiers. They found out he was playing around with my mum, who was a military nurse up at the cantonment in Poshtown. When the army found out about it she was sacked by a panel of male *eastny* officers. Hypocrites. They loved *skate birds* and went up the *skate* brothels on Nightingale Road. They wouldn't even lets her go home to Sudan so she ended up in Craneswater living amongst the poorest.'

'But that's all in the past,' Abel said. 'What's to do about it now? What's to do?'

'There *is* something we can dos. We can try not to end up like them and we can try to makes the future better for our community.'

Abel and Rosa waited in the penthouse until the sun rose and they could hear chanting outside. Abel grabbed his gun and checked the four corners of the roof terrace. The Ali-Doon Building was encircled by angry locals punching the air. Many of them looked ill: they were coughing or limping or had bandages round their heads.

Beyond the crowd, the built environment looked as if it were in a process of disintegration, like a field of crops being eaten away by locusts. The shacks of Begum Road were now little more than waist-high piles of rubble. The collapsed mound of rubbish had turned to ash. As Abel turned away from the guardrail he understood what they were chanting: 'WHAT'S INSIDE?'

Rosa followed him on to the terrace. 'You needs to call your boss.'

'What's this?' said Abel, pointing down at the protest. 'Rent-a-mob?'

'They didn't takes much persuading. Can't you hear them? They's worried about whatever's inside this imperialist-owned silo. All the buildings are falling down. Everyone's getting the *lurgy*. Now call your boss.'

Abel took out his mobile phone. 'Sir, we's got a problem here.'

'Not seeing things again are you, my boy?' said Yombashak.

'No sir, this is real. A load of *lairy mushes* is *having a mare* outside.'

'You mean a number of *badmashes* are causing *destruição* outside the building?'

Soon enough, Yombashak and his goon pulled up in their jeep. The goon fired his pistol in the air three times and the crowd dispersed.

'They's coming,' Abel said. The moment Yombashak and the goon stepped out of the skylight, Rosa and Abel aimed their weapons at them. Rosa yelled, 'Hands on your heads, you pair of imperialist *dinlos!*'

The goon did as he was told. Abel took the pistol off him and tied his hands behind his back. Yombashak didn't comply – instead he rubbed his hands together and chuckled. 'Now, now my dear lady what's all this *gila* hullabaloo?'

'Do as she says,' said Abel.

Rosa strolled over to the hatch and kicked the crescent flag so hard that its pole snapped and it flew ten metres across the terrace.

Yombashak's eyes flicked between Abel and Rosa. 'What is this, an intervention by the Half-Breed Liberation Movement? Armed, it seems, with weapons dating back to long before Nu-Port-Zi became Europe's greatest city?'

'Want to find out if they're *cushty*?' growled Rosa.

'I don't suppose you even know how to operate them, given that you talk like a damn savage!'

Rosa cocked the pistol. 'Only thing's we got to be proud of now is our *Skateish* dialect what's come about as a rejection of that awful Glenglish you imperialists have forced on us. Now you opens that hatch what leads to the silo.'

Yombashak chuckled again, this time deeper and louder. 'You... you... you cannot be *pukka*. You cannot just spoon that *huaxue* into a carrier bag and toddle off with it. Do you know what you're dealing with here?'

'Yes we do,' sighed Rosa. 'I's going to count to three.'

Yombashak glared at Abel. 'You are making a mistake, my boy. These people are nothing but *escória* and traitors.'

Abel raised his shotgun at his boss. 'One.'

'Two,' said Rosa.

'*Mjinga mkundu*,' said Yombashak. 'I'll do it. But you could kill us all, you do realise that?' As he moved towards the hatch, shaking his head, his mobile rang. He drew it from his pocket and answered. 'Yes, yes right away,' he said quickly.

'Drop it or I'll shoot!' shouted Rosa. 'I said drop it!' She pulled the trigger and a bullet ripped through Yombashak's phone and the palm of his hand. He fell to the floor screaming. Rosa tied a handkerchief around his hand to stem the blood. 'Now you tell me the combo,' she said to Yombashak, 'or the next hole will be in your face.'

Down in Begum Road trucks of goons were arriving. Rosa told

Abel to stand at the guardrail and take aim at them. 'The razorwire ain't electrified,' she said, 'and them bastards'll be climbing up here in no time.'

After muttering the final combination code, Yombashak slumped into shock. Rosa tapped the last buttons on the last lock and the hatch sprung open. She turned to Abel. 'Stay here and hold the imperialists at bay until I's grabbed the stuff.' She pulled out a book-sized metal cylinder from her pocket and climbed down the hatch.

Abel fired his shotgun down at the goons who had taken cover behind their trucks. He dodged a reply bullet and it pinged off the guardrail. A utility helicopter materialised from the band of blue smog a hundred feet above the goons' heads. The goons fired potshots in the air, but the chopper weaved safely past them and was soon hovering above the roof terrace. Abel fell back from the guardrail as Rosa was climbing out of the hatch. 'You goes first,' she shouted to Abel over the din of the rotor blades.

'Shouldn't you takes that stuff first?' said Abel, pointing at the cylinder in her hand. 'It was the point of your mission, weren't it?'

'No,' insisted Rosa. 'You's a civilian and a friend and you got mixed up in this *mudlark* through no fault of your own. So you goes first.'

Abel stood on his tip-toes and grabbed hold of the landing skids. Once he'd hauled himself up into the cockpit, he leaned down to offer his hand to Rosa. She stretched to pass the cylinder to him, but just as he was within a fingernail's distance of it, she paused suddenly. 'Rosa?' yelled Abel. 'Quick as you like.' She fell forward, blood jetting from a fissure in her back. The cylinder smashed against the ground.

An almighty flash of light consumed everything in Abel's vision. He could see nothing, but he was aware of an intense heat against the soles of his shoes and his nose filled with a melange of all the worst smells he'd ever known: the putrid yet syrupy stench of dead bodies, the fishy tang of fertiliser leaking from a factory, the bad-egg reek of raw sewage gushing down alleyways. The chopper lurched into the air and Abel blindly clung to the transmission box inside the cockpit.

As the helicopter ascended, the atrocious smell abated. 'S'all right, *mush*,' said a man's voice. 'You can opens your eyes now. Just don't you be looking down.'

Abel saw that the voice belonged to the pilot, a chubby *skate* in overalls and wearing headphones. 'We was right bloody lucky, we was,' said the pilot.

'What about the others?' asked Abel.

'I doubt they's gonna make it. That vinasium – I means, nobody really knew what it could do once it was unleashed.'

'What did you say?'

'Nobody knew what it could-'

'No, I means before that. What did you calls the stuff?'

'Vinasium.' The pilot looked at Abel with one eye closed. 'You not an agent then?'

'No. I's just a civilian.'

'Well vinasium is one of the main reasons we's got the Concessions in the first place. The imperialists wanted their dirty *mits* on it from the start.' The pilot paused. 'They ain't tells you any of that over this side, right?'

'Was never on the radio.'

'Of course,' said the pilot. 'And you'd never finds it online 'cos a computer costs a year's *sparsy* for most *skates* this side eh? Anyway, I don't knows the ins and outs, but I do knows that you only needs to refine a tiny little bit and you's got the harshest weapon since nukes. The imperialists was getting ready to use it on Crescent Falls, that's what our spies told us. They's been mining it round here, in the South Down Paraha.'

'So what's that little bit done to my city?' asked Abel tensely.

'Takes a peek for yourself, *mush*.'

Abel thought he was looking at a tempestuous ocean of hooked and twisted waves. But then he realised it was terra firma rather than water, and that the waves were in fact solid formations of colourless rock. He could see no sign of the people, architecture or natural features that had once defined Nu-Port-Zi.

115

'Don't look *cushty* to me,' Abel shouted. 'Looks like everyone been *puggled* by this. How far you thinks it's spread?'

The pilot shrugged. 'How should I knows? I's just a pilot and my orders is to re-fuel in Nu-Port-Wales then get back to Crescent Falls.'

'What if there's no Crescent Falls now?' said Abel. 'What if there's no anywhere now?'

'All right, don't have a *barney*. We's two safe ain't we? Must be to do with altitude 'cos the seagulls is OK too.'

Half an hour later, the wasteland started to peter out and Abel recognised the outskirts of Nu-Port-Zi. The jagged colourlessness of the wasteland morphed into the flat colourlessness of shanty town roofs.

'Phew,' said the pilot.

'What do you means 'phew', you *dinlo*?' said Abel. 'Most of my city's *decked*! Millions are dead!'

'I just means that at least the damage ain't spread too far, that's all. Look *mush*, where do you want to go? With me back to Crescent Falls or... here... or where?'

'I'll comes with you to Americanada,' said Abel.

'*Cushty*,' said the pilot. 'Although *bagsy* not being the one to explain to Fledgeby that his most trusted lieutenant dropped the vinasium and caused all this destruction...' Recent memories flashed unwanted into Abel's brain. Finding that book of Fledgeby's in the secret cupboard. Yombashak collapsing on the roof terrace. Rosa kicking the crescent flag down. People and their causes, their crusades, the sacrifices they were prepared to make. Rosa, he had seen her again. He would be forever grateful to her for saving his life. But she was gone, his only real friend was gone. Had she survived and they'd escaped, would he have joined her cause? Unlikely – it was just as repellent to him as Fledgeby's or Yombashak's or any other cause.

'No I don't wants to come as far as Crescent Falls,' Abel told the pilot. 'I wants you to drop me somewhere on the way.'

'But where, *mush*?'

'Somewhere green and remote and far from anybody else. I wants to be alone from now on.'

*

*A brief glossary of Skateish:*

*Barney / Benny / Mare: to become irritated or upset.*
*Dinlo: idiot, fool.*
*Dockyard oyster: spit, phlegm.*
*Eastny: colloquial term for foreigner hailing from one of the nations ruling the Concessions.*
*Mudlark: joke, ruse, trouble.*
*Mush: friend, chum.*
*Priddy: slum landlord, landowner.*
*Puggle: see deck.*
*Scav: scavenge, steal.*
*Scran: food.*
*Skate: colloquial term for a Nu-Port-Zi local and, more latterly, an Englishman or woman.*
*Sparsy: money.*
*Squinny: coward, to behave in a cowardly fashion.*

## A Whiff of Sulphur
## Diana Bretherick
*Map location: #23*

'Did I ever tell you about the Southsea Satanists?' Grace said. Her eyebrows arched as they always did when she was about to tell me one of her stories.

It was a game we played whenever we met. Grace would try to shock me and I would do my best to sound blasé.

'No' I replied.

Grace settled back into her seat with a satisfied smile on her face. 'I thought not.'

It was a dark October night in Portsmouth, our home city. It wasn't a glamorous place, bruised as it was by the attention of the Nazis in the Second World War, and then the town planners in the decades that followed. But what it lacked in glitz it more than made up for in character. Its history cloaked the buildings and inhabitants like a vast security blanket – shabby and worn, slightly unhygienic in places but something to cling to. Southsea was its genteel seaside sister, a bit faded in the glamour department but still hanging on valiantly to the memory of its prime.

We were in a pub near Grace's house not far from the sea. A gale blew outside and the flames from the candles on the tables and the log fire flickered, as if in response to her words. I was glad that we were tucked into a discreet corner. The clientele was mixed, just like the city's population, and it was hard to predict how they might react to one of Grace's tales.

'It may take a while,' she smiled and held out her empty glass.

As I waited at the bar, I looked over at her small round figure and steel-grey hair cut in a neat bob, scraped back from her face with an incongruously girly Alice band. She sat content in the tatty leather armchair reserved for her exclusive use. Grace and I had met at a storytelling festival in midsummer. I and other local writers were reading short pieces we had written in celebration of the fairy tale. Grace had approached me at the end and complimented me on my contribution – a rather lurid serial killer story about a woman who killed in order to avenge the villains in the fairy tales of her youth.

'Inventive,' she had nodded appreciatively, 'if somewhat inaccurate.'

'It's fiction,' I had protested. 'Does it matter?'

'It always matters.'

Infuriatingly she had refused to be drawn any further, leaving me wondering... well all kinds of things. She had a talent for uncertainty.

Grace, until recently, had taught history at the university, specifically the history of crime and criminals, but retired having, she claimed, become tired of her own lectures. I wrote crime novels, with varying success and Grace had promised to inspire me with some of her knowledge. It would be a change, she said, to tell her stories to people who listened.

I came back with a bottle of house red and pork scratchings, Grace's customary fee. The supernatural was a popular genre of crime fiction and I hoped that Grace's story might allow me to capitalise on that. My agent was hungry for something commercial to sell and so, to an extent, was I.

I filled Grace's glass as she opened the scratchings. Having crunched her way through a handful she picked up her wine, sniffed it, took a long slow sip and stared into the firelight as if issuing a challenge. Then she began.

'Our story starts in a graveyard, of course.'

'Highland Road Cemetery?' It had to be there, Thomas Ellis Owen, Southsea's favourite architect, had sold the land to the Burial Board in the nineteenth century and had even designed the cemetery for them when the original architect failed to supply plans. The end result was full of grandiose statues of angels and saints with its own chapel and a mausoleum at the centre. It could have been the set of a Hammer horror film.

Grace peered at me over her wire-framed glasses.

'Sorry,' I said, 'Do carry on... no wait. Did you say, of course?'

'I did. We are talking of an episode where death and life are blurred beyond recognition so naturally that is where we would begin... Now may I go on?'

I nodded.

'As I said we begin in a graveyard, one day in October as the light is failing. Try to imagine it. Close your eyes and see it through mine.'

Grace took my hand in hers. It was cool, despite the heat of the open fire. Her eyes closed and her wrinkled apple face seemed to glow. I shut my eyes.

'There is sea mist rolling in from the Solent, so visibility is very poor. We are walking through the cemetery now. What can you smell?

I breathed in and took in the air. It was not the stale beer and wood smoke scent that I was expecting. Instead I could smell damp leaves and a kind of underlying sweetness that reminded me of death. Ah yes and just a whiff of sulphur.

'It is quiet now, isn't it,' Grace said, her voice was almost a whisper but not quite. It caressed me somehow. I can't explain more clearly than that. It was if her cool fingers brushed the back of my neck.

'The solitude is not frightening. The company of the dead is quite innocuous. After all they cannot harm us now, can they?' she said.

I walked with her, hand in hand, through that imagined landscape of stone angels and sad, sad stories of people who had passed on from this world to the next, the sea mist gradually building until it enveloped us entirely although I could just see yellow lights flickering in the distance. And then...

'Last orders ladies and gents, please... last orders at the bar!'

I opened my eyes to see Grace peering at me. 'That's a shame. You were doing so well,' she said.

'Can't you just tell me what happened?'

'I like to show you the story. You know that. But this time we can do better than that. Finish your drink.'

I drained the last drops of claret from my glass. Grace put the re-corked remainder of our bottle of wine into her large bag. 'Waste not, want not,' she said as she pushed energetically through the large swing doors.

Opposite us, in all its glory was Highland Road Cemetery. The wind had dropped and a sea mist rolled in from the Solent creating an eerie vista. I felt as if I was paying a visit to someone else's nightmare.

'I thought we should visit the locus,' Grace said as we crossed the road and made our way towards the large iron gates.

'Won't it be shut to the public at this time of night?' I asked.

Grace shook her head impatiently as she fished about in her bag and brought out a large brass key which she waved at me in triumph. 'I am a friend of the cemetery,' she announced with pride.

In a moment we were walking along one of the paths towards Thomas Ellis Owen's famous chapel and I was reliving once again, the beginning of Grace's story.

'So these Satanists...tell me more,' I said.

'You see the mausoleum over there?' she pointed at a squat square building complete with arches and statuary. It was like a mini Roman temple – ostentatious and slightly vulgar. 'Ugly isn't it? But not as ugly as what lay within.' Grace said as we sat down on a bench. As she spoke she produced the wine and two glasses from her capacious handbag and poured us some.

'The Southsea Satanists were part of a long and not particularly distinguished occult history here on the South coast. Interest had ebbed and flowed over the years with the flames fanned in particular by the newspapers and horror films. In the 1960s it tied in with a film called *The Devil Rides Out* from Dennis Wheatley's novel.'

'Oh yes, I know it – it's one of my absolute favourites.'

'Really,' Grace said her upper lip curling. 'Well I suppose someone in your position needs to expose themselves to low culture from time to time.' She hesitated for a moment as if calculating how offended I might be, then she continued. 'There were also a number of vampire films following on from it – all as bad as each other – technicolour tosh.'

'Really? I rather enjoy them.' I said, not wanting her to have it all her own way.

'Each to their own, I suppose,' she said cuttingly. 'Anyway the Southsea Satanists were a ragbag of the mildly curious, the eccentric and the downright sexually odd who, in the late 1960s banded together under the leadership of a man rejoicing in the name of Keith Cantata.'

'Keith Cantata? You're making it up!'

Grace shook her head. 'Sadly I don't have to. Mr Cantata was only too real. He was a strange man in many ways – a small, wiry character with a penchant for wearing a cloak and an obsession with devil worship. He was absolutely intent on holding a black mass here. There had been a few instances of supposed desecration in other cemeteries in the South – feathers and blood scattered about from some kind of sacrifice (I think that may have been down to students), a few candles lit outside the chapel – that kind of thing. But then some graves were actually opened up and the bones left in the shape of what looked to be a pentagram.'

'Didn't the police get involved?'

'There was the usual hoo-ha but no proper evidence. This was way before CCTV and no one was going to be talking to the police. So the long and short of it was that Cantata and his merry band decided to go ahead with their mass.'

'What were they trying to achieve?'

'Oh the usual – the summoning of Satan, that sort of thing,' Grace said casually.

'So what happened?'

'I remember it as if was yesterday...'

'You were there?'

'Of course, hadn't you guessed?'

I hesitated, trying to decide which category of Cantata's followers Grace came into...mildly curious - perhaps, eccentric – almost certainly, but sexually odd... who knew?

She looked at me. 'I was one of the mildly curious... just to be clear.' Then she paused for a moment and rummaged about in her handbag. With a triumphant flourish she produced a second bag of pork scratchings and a packet of smoky bacon crisps. She always favoured pig products for some reason. We crunched on them in a companionable silence for a while.

'We waited in the pub until closing time,' she went on, 'and then we came over here and started our preparations. Predictably, Cantata tried to persuade us that nudity was necessary, but it was November and chilly with it, so that wasn't going to happen.'

I closed my eyes and, just as I had in the pub, I felt that I was there. I could see in the distance the shadowy figures of Grace and her friends busily preparing to conjure up the Devil. There was Keith Cantata in a black polo neck and a pointy beard trying to channel his inner Christopher Lee by chalking up a pentagram; and Grace and her friends giggling quietly as they lit candles and so on.

'Finally we were ready, so Keith started the incantation and one of his henchmen brought a cockerel out of a sack. It was then I thought – we're really going to do it!'

'You were going to kill the bird... just for a ritual?'

Grace looked at me suspiciously. 'Yes we were. Are you some kind of vegetarian?'

I shrugged. 'It just seems cruel, that's all.'

'Well as it happened we didn't get that far. Keith was chanting away and we were intoning the appropriate responses when out of the corner of my eye I saw a movement.'

She stopped, presumably to give me time to absorb this... Somewhere, something screeched, breaking into the silence like a pickaxe into granite.

Grace looked into the distance and sipped her wine thoughtfully. 'At first I thought it was an animal... a fox perhaps... but then I realised that it was a man. He stood by one of the graves, that one with the angel. Can you see?'

I nodded. The statue that she had pointed at was one I had always found rather disturbing. If you looked at it for long enough it almost seemed to move.

'It was weird,' Grace said. 'It was as if he had appeared from nowhere... like an apparition... a ghost.'

'What did he look like?'

'He looked like Christopher Lee,' Grace said matter-of-factly.

'Really?'

'Yes, really. He was wearing a top hat and a coat with a cape – an opera cape with silk lining.'

'Are you sure it wasn't Christopher Lee, on location for one of his Dracula films?'

Grace gave me a withering stare. 'In Southsea?'

'So not an actor,' I said.

'Correct,' Grace said. 'The man, if that is what he was, pointed over towards Keith who stopped and turned, like an automaton, and began to walk towards him until he was standing opposite - face to face. Then with one hand the man picked Keith up by the throat. He held him up there for what seemed like an eternity before pushing him down onto a tomb. Then he leaned over him and seemed to whisper in his ear for a moment or two before disappearing.'

'Disappearing?'

'Yes... he sort of melted away into the sea mist.'

I looked into the darkness and imagined the man looming

menacingly over his victim. 'How was Keith?'

'Changed.'

'In what way?'

'In a doesn't go out during the day, can't see his reflection in the mirror and likes the taste of blood sort of way.'

'He became a vampire!'

'Well that was what he claimed.'

'So what happened to him?' I asked. 'Where did he go?'

'He re-invented himself. You could do that in the 60s and 70s,' Grace sighed almost wistfully. 'He started to call himself Count Cantata and went off to London. I think he became a DJ.'

'And now?'

'Still there, as far as I know. I think he's got a website - CountCantata.com - 'still groovin'...'

'Catchy.'

Grace poured us some more wine. 'You're not too tired I hope. There is more to tell.'

I shook my head. I was used to working at night. It was when I did most of my writing. Darkness got the creative juices flowing.

'After that night no one seemed very keen on continuing with the black mass.' Grace said. 'After all when you've already conjured up some kind of demon then where is there to go?'

'So it was a demon then?'

'A demon vampire is what Keith said. The king of somewhere or other... I forget where. Anyway the point was that after that there were a number of... events. A few people went missing and then re-appeared but changed like Keith. Others performed rituals. There was some desecration of graves and so on. The police got involved. It was all very unpleasant. But everyone said the same thing.'

'What?'

'That a man who looked like Christopher Lee was there. The newspapers had a field day. There was even a TV documentary - The *Demon of Southsea*, I think it was called.'

'What happened then?'

125

'We decided, the rest of the original Southsea Satanists and I, to put an end to it. We did some research. Well we read *Dracula*, the Bram Stoker original. And it became clear that we had to summon up the vampire king and get rid of him. I think we felt it was a kind of duty.'

'How did you plan to do that?'

'Oh the usual,' Grace said breezily. 'A wooden stake through the heart. We met up in the pub as before and then made our way here. We did the same ritual as we had with Keith and before you know it there he was. Only this time he walked out of the Mausoleum, bold as brass.'

'As I recall, the stake through the heart bit only works if they're still in the coffin.'

'Spot on,' Grace said. 'In our defence, we were amateurs but it was a fairly fundamental error. The king of whatnot beckoned to me and I felt compelled to obey. He put his hands round my throat and I thought that I was a goner.'

'And?'

Grace smiled. 'Yes and then again no,' she edged a little closer to me. 'I'm thirsty...'

'Have some more wine then,' I said.

She laughed. 'Don't worry. He didn't get me. I'm no vampire. What he got was a wooden stake round the head from one of the girls. He staggered round a bit and then collapsed and we all ran off.'

'Was he a real vampire?'

'I don't know. There were one or two more sightings and a couple of successful prosecutions for the desecration of the graves but after that, interest died down. The Southsea Satanists disbanded and we never saw each other again.'

'So it could all have been a set up by Keith Cantata?'

'Well perhaps...' Grace said. 'But the photo on his website is interesting. He looks remarkably well preserved for a man in his 60s. In fact he doesn't seem to have changed at all.'

'Maybe he's had botox.'

'Botox or blood... one of the two. But I suppose we'll never know for sure.'

'Well there is one way of finding out,' I said nodding in the direction of the mausoleum. Grace grinned. 'It so happens that I have come equipped.' She reached into her handbag and pulled out a crucifix.

'I'm not sure how effective that will be,' I said.

'Well let's see.'

We drained the last of the wine and walked over to the mausoleum, squatting in the centre of the cemetery. When we got there Grace pulled out a piece of chalk and started to mark out a pentagram, whilst I lit some candles.

'Are you sure about this?' she asked.

'Absolutely,' I said. We'd come this far. I wasn't going to back down now. She started the incantations. The air grew chillier and I heard creaking. The doors to the mausoleum opened slowly. A tall dark figure came out and moved towards Grace. She turned and gasped as he reached out to her, took her by the shoulders and bit into her neck. She collapsed onto the ground apparently unconscious. Then the figure turned his attention to me. It walked over, took me by the shoulders and kissed me on the cheek.

'Hello Daddy,' I said. 'I'm home.'

**Bearskin**
**Christine Lawrence**
*Map location: #25*


It was white in the land and cold. The forest was dark and all the
gentle animals either hid in caves, or deep under the ground, where
all God-fearing creatures should be. In the village of Milton, the
people also stayed hidden, warm and safe beside their fires. They
only ever scurried out to the edge of the treacherous forest when
there was no choice, to find more wood, or to hunt for a morsel of
meat to fill their hollow bellies.

It was the boy's turn to do his duty by his Grandfather, who lived
alone in the deepest part of the forest. The forest was only ventured
into in spring and summer, unless the bitter months drew out as they
did this long, long winter. The wind howled around the chimneys as
the boy wound his bear-skin cloak around his lithe and innocent
form. He carefully wrapped the still-warm, freshly baked loaves of
bread in the blood red cloth his mother had given him. He placed the
parcel in his satchel, together with the small cask of wine, essential
foodstuff to ward off the bitter chill.

Before he began his journey, the boy's mother handed him the
long bladed knife once used for skinning the great Black Bear whose
hide he wore. The boy slipped the knife into its sheath and,
embracing her, left the cottage to begin his journey through the pure
white landscape to his Grandfather's house.

The forest grew quiet as he trudged. No sound, not even his
footsteps broke the virginal membrane in his ears. He had walked for
perhaps an hour when he saw the girl. She came from nowhere. He

looked up from the snow in front of his feet and she was there. There were no footprints around her, just the eternally smooth, white blanket covering the land.

The girl was naked, her jet black hair fell in seductive ripples the length of her mottled blue and white-skinned back. She turned to look at him, he caught a glimpse of her nipple, erect with the cold. A flood of emotions rushed through the boy's body. He had never seen a woman naked before. It didn't occur to him how cold she must be as he felt the heat of desire pump through his veins. She walked off, ahead of him, her body swaying with the rhythm of her stride. He called out and she turned again and smiled. How red were her lips, full of the promise he had never experienced. He had to touch her skin, to caress her hair, to feel her nakedness against his own young body. But she was moving too fast as he broke into a run, realising fleetingly that the familiar part of the forest was long ago left behind.

In a clearing she stopped and turned, opening her arms with a welcoming look in her eye. He was entranced with the beauty of her nakedness, the curves of her breasts, her nipples the same blood red as her lips in such sharp contrast to the whiteness of her skin. He drank in the sight greedily. As he took a step towards her, other women appeared, all blinding him with their voluptuous bodies. They danced around the clearing. He longed to touch them, to feel and taste them, but they were all tantalizingly just beyond his reach. At times he was close enough to smell the muskiness of their bodies and he knew they desired him just as much as he wanted them.

In the frantic dance, I notice the bread tumble from my satchel, still half wrapped in the blood red cloth. As it lands in the snow, some of the women break away, rip at the cloth, devour the bread in a frenzy of hunger. The wine cask crashes to the ground. The stopper bursts and the wine bleeds into the soft snow, a stain spreading ever outwards.

The first girl takes my hand, guiding me to the centre of the clearing. I see nothing now but her perfect body, knowing that I will soon be fulfilled. I feel hands gently undress me, caress me into a state of full arousal as she lies down on the altar, her hair flowing like black water into the snow-covered ground. Her legs are long and inviting, her thighs white and firm as she wills me to lie with her. They lift me up to the altar, I can wait no longer, the others women seem to blur.

A knife flashes and a roar fills my ears. The pure skin of the girl becomes mottled. Hair - no! Rough fur grows across her perfect breasts. Her face is changing, blurring. Her seductive lips draw back to reveal drooling teeth and tongue, her tiny nose thrust forth into a wet, black snout. The arms around me grow stronger now, her claws tear into my back. As I arch in pain and ecstasy the bear-skin cloak which was so carefully taken from me earlier, is once again wrapped around my form. As I reach the inevitable climax and my seed bursts forth into the willing belly of the Beauty, I realise I am fusing with a Great Black Bear. Part of my mind fights against this, recoiling in horror, but I know deep inside that I am fulfilling a terrible destiny.

Still, I try to break away. Wildly looking around the clearing, I see the women have all gone. It is just me and my terrible bride.

I raise myself up on my rear legs and roar from the depths of my soul.

## The Toy Maker's Son
## Tom Harris
*Map location: #4*


My father is a serial killer.

I've only just found out. It's completely fucked up, there's no way else to say it. My dad, small business owner, a killer? He owns a toy shop on Albert Road. I wouldn't believe it, if it wasn't for my best mate, Jim, oh and the fairy. She told me to go straight to The New Theatre Royal, so I could witness it with my own sea-blue eyes. So here we are. Me and my best mate Jim.

I'm not sure what we're watching – some modern opera bollocks, but the music is proper intense. It would make the hairs on my neck stand on end, if I had any.

Dad is on the back row, across from us. The boy on the seat in front is his target. From out of Dad's sleeve shoots a huge needle. It's wafer thin, I mean you wouldn't know it was there unless you were looking for it. As it pricks and injects the serum into the skin, the boy flinches and slaps his hand against his neck; as if he'd been bitten by a massive bee. The needle pulls back and disappears up Dad's sleeve. The boy is as good as dead. Dad would say this was a toy, but believe me this is no toy. This is an instrument of death.

The boy gets up and makes his way out.

The kid beside him shouts. 'Oi, Mowgli! Where you off to?'

He doesn't reply. He's probably feeling pretty crap, all woozy and stuff. As the door closes behind him, Dad follows.

'Come on, Jim, this is our chance,' I say, and we follow Dad out of the door.

In the corridor outside the theatre, the music is muffled. The staff at the bar stare at me – it's no biggie. I ignore them. He has the boy by the arm and the receptionist smiles at Dad and his victim as they waltz out the main door into the fresh air. Then the receptionist glares at me. That look. No-one understands. No-one knows what I am. But what I am to Mowgli tonight is life.

I leave the theatre and head out onto the crowded streets of Guildhall Walk.

Jim is with me as we move through the heckling drunks, wading into the abuse.

'Freak!'

'Muppet!'

I've heard it all before. I hear them on the streets at night, when I'm alone in the workshop. It's how I've picked up their language.

'What have you come as, mush?'

'He looks like a fucking puppet!'

I stay focused. I never take my eyes off my father. What do they know? They're just a bunch of twats!

The boy is slumped on his arm, but the serum, whatever it is, hasn't worked. There might be a chance for this Mowgli-character. But Dad is at his location now.

This is it.

The Guildhall clock tower rises into the bruised sky. Night is coming, but there is still time.

It's my destiny to stop my dad.

It's why I was brought to life.

The fairy told me all this. I'm not lying. I'll explain, but I'm a bit busy at the moment. Give us a minute, will ya!

It's a glorious summer's evening, but death looms like an axe before me. Murder swamps what little there is of my mind. I am not normal – you should know that by now, but I do know right from wrong. Jim makes sure of that.

The Guildhall doors are closed. I duck behind some students, who giggle at me, but they serve their purpose. Dad checks the square. He cannot see me. Oh, but I see him.

He's turning a key in the door. I bet it's wooden. One he's crafted in his workshop. The door opens and he slips inside. The black mane of the boy swishes across his shoulders as Dad drags him inside. I race forward. 'Come on Jim! Let's go!'

I push through the door. Dad's not closed it properly. He's made a mistake. It's not like him. He's usually so careful. The detail on the key is incredible. His best work. I stroke the wood and then my face... such skill... but the muffled cries of the boy snap me from my trance.

'The stairs, Jim!' I say, and we race across the carpet and through the double doors.

The place is deserted, so no-one hears the footsteps of the serial killer or the cries of his victim. Mowgli's coming round though.

Dad has fucked up.

Maybe tonight is the night he fails. For my sake I hope so.

We track Dad up and up until we reach another door. Another key. It's open. He's leaving an escape route. He means to come back the way he came in.

Through door after door we follow. Me and Jim. Higher and higher, until we reach the biggest door I have ever seen.

And judging from all the signs on it, no fucker wants us in here:
KEEP OUT!!! DO NOT ENTER!!! WARNING!!!
'I think we get the message, eh, Jim?' I whisper.

Another wooden key sits in the final lock. The door ajar.

'Come on, Jim – in we go,' I say, and squeeze through the gap. Instantly, it hits me. The huge clock face. It's hard not to stare. 'What did you say, Jim?'

Jim tells me it's the back of the Guildhall clock. We are inside the clock tower. It is bloody massive!

I almost feel alive.

I mean, I don't feel anything inside. I'm not made that way. Dad has taught me things though and they're starting to sink in. I can't feel all this – not yet. But after tonight? After what the fairy told me –

who knows? (We're almost at the fairy bit, so stick with me.) Dad's chosen another landmark: the Guildhall. In all the cities across the world, he selects his killing ground carefully. He marks the locations on a map that he keeps in the workshop. He talks it over with me before he chooses. But now I can act on what I know. You see, I was visited by a shining star.

It's true! Don't laugh! A silhouette appeared at the window of Dad's workshop last night. The latch lifted and she drifted in on the breeze. A fairy! She spoke to me:

*'You have a wish, I can make come true.*
*But for that to happen it's all down to you.*
*Your father has a darkness inside him.*
*By day a man, a father, your kin.*
*By night a killer – drenched in sin.*
*To be a real boy you must stop him now.*
*For each life you save I will make a vow.*
*An arm, a leg, a body, a head.*
*A heart, a lung, a kidney, a tongue.*
*You will breathe and you will feel.*
*Stop him and you will be real!'*

I couldn't have remembered all that shit before, but now, it's like the words are engraved inside my wooden head. It's like she's improved me. Made me work. Dad doesn't know. He thinks I'm slumped down on the workbench, or propped up in that little chair he made for me. He'd be so happy, but I can't let him see me like this. Not now. Not here. Not tonight. None of us want that father-son moment just yet. It's dark in here. Like the workshop.

'What's that, Jim? It's like a dusty old attic.'

Jim is right. It is. Jim is very clever, but we're dealing with evil here. You need more than clever to stop that.

I creep further into the room, using the shadows to stay hidden. Then Mowgli screams like a tiger with its tail on fire. I do not feel his pain, but I know it's wrong for Dad to do what he's doing. I must stop him. Not just for my benefit, I mean what's that poor fucker ever done to Dad?

Dad is tying him up, binding his body against an old chair, in front of the clock face. A red spotted handkerchief is stuffed into Mowgli's gob to keep him quiet. I have to act. Dad's reaching into his backpack. He's pulling out a... a present? A present? WTF? A box with a pink bow?

This is some fucked up shit.

He places it at Mowgli's feet. The boy struggles, but he isn't going anywhere. He's not even allowed to open it. This seems cruel to me.

Dad cackles and tips his glasses. I duck behind an old clothes rack, full of dusty costumes. Dad does a little jig. He is sick. I guess this should make me sad or angry or disgusted, but I just stare.

'So, what do we do, Jim?' I ask. I nod in the silence. 'Great idea...' Jim does have great ideas.

Dad taps Mowgli on the head. He's leaving. He's heading straight for us.

'Get down, Jim!'

Dad whistles like it's Sunday. As if he's out for a stroll. But he's not. He's blowing up another boy. Twenty, at last count, the fairy told me.

Dad needs mending as much as I do.

When he reaches the door he stops. I panic and shuffle through the clothes. The hangers clink against the rail. He stares right at me. I freeze. He stares... He leaves.

I almost feel relief.

Taking one clumsy step after another, I move across the dusty boards. They remind me of what I may look like when I'm Dad's age. Mowgli looks even more horrified than when Dad was here. Thanks a lot you fucker! I'm only saving your life, here.

If the gag came out, his screams would shatter the clock face.

I try to act like a friend, but I'm not sure how to. I lower my arms to my side. I'm not used to moving without my strings. I untie the bow, which is a fucking miracle, with what I've got to work with, and the present falls apart.

There it is. Perfectly made. A small clockwork bomb.

He gasps. I stare.

On the little black ball that wants to go – Kaboom! – there is a small clock face, made from an old pocket watch. It is ticking. Both hands converging at midnight. But it is not midnight. It is not even nine o'clock. Trust me, I know, because I am standing in front of a great big fuck off clock.

Jim's trying to tell me something.

'What's that? The bomb will go off at midnight by the little clock. I see. You don't think it matters what the big clock says at this point. Hmm, I think you may be right, Jim.'

Mowgli looks at me as if I am crazy. Not everyone sees Jim the way I see him. Dad hasn't left me much time to save this boy.

'Less than twenty seconds, you say, Jim?'

I have no choice. I bend down and take the bomb in my wooden hands. Mowgli looks like he's shit his pants. Well, you can't blame him really.

'Don't worry. I am here to save you,' I say, and then I rush forward. 'Let's go, Jim,' I call, as I smash through the clock face.

Into the night, I clutch the device in my varnished palms. I am flying. I can almost feel the air around me running over my body. Is this what it's like to be a fairy?

It doesn't last. I fall fast.

Then comes the explosion, seconds before I hit the ground. Kaboom!!!

It's been a week since I stopped Dad.

He picked up what was left of me and Jim off the steps of the Guildhall and put us in a bin bag. He carried us over his shoulder. He cursed his rotten luck all the way back to Albert Road.

'The thieving little shits!'

'No-one puts their hands on my boy!'

He thought we'd been stolen and vandalised.

Back at the workshop he even questioned his sanity. Not a bad thing for him to do, I suppose.

He won't say so, but it's the way he looks at me... I reckon he thinks I'm possessed. Dad must still love me though, because he operated on me and Jim. I'm not moaning. I mean, I'm grateful, but my parts don't match like before. I've got nails pointing out of places I shouldn't. He might be trying to teach me a lesson.

One thing I've noticed about being here, in our new home town, is that the Canadians don't stare as long and as hard as the Brits. Don't get me wrong, I've had plenty of funny looks tracking Dad through the streets of Montreal – even in the dead of night. I guess Dad is taking no chances this time. The Montreal clock tower glistens like a ghost in the moonlight as I look on from the bridge. Dad's been tracking a group of lads in ice hockey shirts as they trudge home from practice. He's picked out the one on the left, but I'm going to stop him.

It's my destiny. I'm getting something out of it, too. The fairy returned, two nights after the Guildhall bombing, just before the taxi came to take us to the airport. She thanked me for saving the boy.

Beneath the illuminations of the Jacques Cartier bridge, I flex the skin on my new hand. Her gift to me.

Yeah, that's right.

I have an arm.

It's made of flesh and bone and juicy red blood and it works. It's on my right hand side, even though I'm certain I am left handed. That's a bit shit, but she's promised me another one to match. A set of arms. How brilliant is that?

Of course Dad can't see my new parts. The fairy has cloaked his vision. Fuck knows what that means.

Dad's in Canada on business and so therefore am I, I think? Not, I think, therefore I am, which was something Dad was trying to teach me last week. He's always read to me like I'm a real boy, but he's been stepping up the lessons recently. Shakespeare, Nietzsche, Marie Antoinette... I wanted to ask Dad if she invented puppets, but I have to remain dormant for now.

The fairy says that he kills these boys because he can't have one of his own. That makes no fucking sense in my mind. He's got me hasn't he?

Dad is obviously one chisel short of a toolbox.

I know I can't guarantee that I'll stop Dad and that I can keep on stopping him long enough to become a real boy. I mean that would be awesome, as they say round here, but who knows what's gonna happen.

I can dream, can't I?

After all, life may not be one big fairy tale, but good things can happen to people who do good things. I have to believe in that. Well, that's what my dad taught me anyway.

'Hey, Hoser! You dropped your cicada!' screams some guy behind me. He's dressed in a beaver suit, swigging from a can of Molson Beer. 'I must be howling at the moon!' he yells, then he shakes his head and waddles off, lost in his can.

I stop and reach down to pick up the fluffy green cricket with my new hand.

'Shit! Are you okay Jim?' I say.

## Freda
## Matt Wingett
*Map location: #7*


'She's sad, Mark,' she says to the man she is soon to marry. 'I can tell she is.' Impulsively, she lifts the wooden marionette from the table and eagerly turns it over in her hands, its silk dress shimmering in the sunlight. 'Shall we take her home?'

The man beside her bends closer to examine the carved figure; fine face, delicate features - so out of place among these paste tables heaped with domestic bric-a-brac. What a pretty little thing!

'We could keep her in the bedroom,' he grins, devilishly. 'She'll add a bit of oriental spice.' He leans close and whispers in her ear – 'As if we need any!'

Spontaneously, she hooks the back of his neck with her palm and kisses him passionately, ignoring the hagglers and bargain hunters jostling by in the cool spring air. Then she turns to the old bearded man hunched behind the table, who meets her questioning expression with a nod and raised eyebrows.

'What do you want for her?'

'What do I want for her?' he echoes, considering a moment. 'A pound?' he answers, almost with a question.

'Is she Indonesian, or something?' the young man asks, intrigued by her.

'Something like that,' the other says with a shrug.

'What's her name?' asks the woman, eagerly.

The trader looks dubious for a moment, then says:

'Freda.'

'Freda – doesn't sound very exotic,' she answers, screwing her face and lowering the doll a little in disappointment.

'Well, you asked,' he shrugs again.

Mark says: 'Do you have the other hand in the box somewhere? She's got one missing, see?'

The trader shakes his head and looks away. 'Sorry, no.'

Mark looks at the doll a moment more, and decides he can't resist. 'We'll take her,' he says, thrusting a pound coin towards the old man. 'Here,' he adds, so insistently that he takes even himself by surprise.


Sitting her by the little palm in the bedroom, Mark says: 'There you are Freda. How's that for you?'

His partner, Jo, claps her hands playfully at the entity gazing enigmatically from the palm fronds.

'She looks like she's waiting to ambush us!' she pronounces delighted. 'She's wonderful, isn't she?'

The young man's eyes sweep the doll up and down for a moment, alighting on the string attached to its one hand.

'Watch this.'

A tug and the puppet jumps to life, her playful wave bizarrely contradicting the severity of her face.

'Oh, that's weird,' Jo giggles with a thrill. 'Look at the way she moves - so natural. You know, she is weird!'

As she speaks, the puppet's balance shifts and the head snaps round to stare at her.

'Oh, don't!' Jo laughs at Mark. 'You could almost think I'd offended her!'


His tongue pressed against his lower lip, Mark examines the doll's face, the curving line of the body finely carved and painted, dressed in antique orange silks.

'Exquisitely done - her face... so beautiful,' he says, feeling as if he somehow knows her. 'And the wood. So unusual. Is it sandalwood?'

He lifts the marionette and holds her close to his face, sniffing the wood's heady scent and closing his eyes for a moment.

In his mind's eye a scene manifests from nowhere - *level dust-yellow exotic lands; a jagged, snow-capped horizon; a warm sun to bask and luxuriate in.* He opens his eyes, startled by the richness of the image. After a moment's thought, he closes them again and sniffs the elusive scent once more. Now he sees - *the flash of a girl dancing, her eyes fixed upon the watcher as she moves with fluid movements, gesturing him to come to her. Her eyes, bright and shining, her lips a beautiful red* - The image dissolves and he opens his eyes once more, looking around astonished. *It's so real!* He thinks he hears the girl calling to him, like an elusive memory from childhood.

Closing his eyes again, he starts his third deep draw of air into his lungs. Now Jo says with a puzzled stare: 'Stop it, you weirdo!'

He freezes for a half second, like a rabbit paralysed by a poacher's lamp. He exhales through his mouth, letting his lips vibrate together.

'She's great,' he says, shrugging off the compulsion he still feels. 'I wonder where her other hand is?'

A shadow flutters across Jo's heart.

'Leave her,' she orders, in a sharp tone she has never used with him before. 'A grown man playing with dolls! Come on, let's get some lunch. We've got plans to make. In case you've forgotten, you did ask for my hand in marriage - and I accepted. Remember?'

Reluctantly, he sets the doll down by the plant pot.

As he leaves, he looks back to appreciate her one more time; sullen, silent, exotic; contemplating her new foothold from the shelter of the palm fronds.

To him, her enigmatic face is the world.

After lunch and a plan-filled walk along the sea-scented shore, they step into the house from air that is cool with the approach of evening, and she makes her way upstairs to seek the warm hug of a jumper.

Stepping in to the half-lit bedroom, she gives a stifled scream and recoils, arms bent in front of her, palms outward as if to fight away danger.

'Shit!' she squeals. 'How did that get there?'

An interloper is lying on her bed. One arm by its side, the other behind its head, staring at the ceiling as if deep in thought. A nervous shock pulses through Jo's body and ends in a flush of sweat from her palms.

She turns to the sound of a footstep behind her and looks concernedly at Mark. He says airily: 'Everything okay?'

'What the bloody hell? You left her by the palm! I saw you,' she says, looking back over her shoulder.

'Didn't you move her?'

'No, I didn't bloody move her.'

'Well, somebody did...'

For a moment she contracts in on herself in a spasm of fear.

'Mark, I don't like it!'

He can't hold it any longer. His face broadens into a mischievous smile that spreads with vicious delight. 'It was a joke,' he laughs. 'I came back up - remember - when I said I'd forgotten my keys? I moved her then.'

'Well why the bloody hell did you do that?'

'I don't know. It just popped into my mind,' he shrugs. 'I suppose I thought it would give you a scare. I mean, you're so funny with your flights of fancy and fairytale worlds!'

'Fairytale worlds? How dare you!' She repeats melodramatically, withdrawing to her little dressing table in annoyance.

She glares at Mark a little longer for full dramatic effect, then admits with a contraction of the shoulder.

'You did give me a scare, though!'

Her face cracks into a smile. Then, with a lightning movement she reaches down and swings a pillow full in his face. She giggles as his surprised expression converts to one of mischief and he grabs a retaliatory pillow. Two more blows and counterblows and he launches himself at her, panting and kissing as they tumble onto the mattress.

'I hope this doesn't set a template for our wedding day,' he laughs, pinning her to the bed, his weight on her midriff.

'Which bit?' she asks with a wry grin, before pulling him in for another passionate kiss.

As they make giggling, joyous love, the doll lies beside them, its painted face turned to watch.

Later that night, Jo wakes. She is staring at the half-darkness of her bedroom; the Ikea wardrobe in beech effect, the double radiator on the wall that needs a lick of paint, the toy puppy she has owned from childhood with big soppy eyes.

Then she looks at Mark.

She notices in the soft glow of headlights from a car hissing by outside that his eyes are half-open, rolled up inside his head so only the whites show, his breath coming in quiet ghosts, little unseen movements stirring the air with their passing. Beside him she sees Freda on his bedside table. Her body is slumped forward, giving the uncanny impression of leaning in to confide. In her unfocused state Jo imagines the sweeping headlight beam animating the doll's wooden face. In this strange feral hour of the night when life doesn't obey the daylight rules, she fancies the doll has sensed her presence and turned its head ever so slightly. Jo stiffens on the bed in shock and the vibration sends the doll tumbling off the table with a wooden clatter, the fall forcing a yelp from Jo's lips.

Mark turns in the dark air and opens his eyes in a trance.

'I was in a dream,' he says. 'You woke me from a beautiful dream.'

He turns and pulls the duvet around his neck, putting his back to her as she lies on the bed, inexplicably trembling.

When morning comes, the fantasies of the dark creep into the recesses of night-forgetfulness and Jo wakes with nothing more than a sense of unease.

However, later that morning she insists that Mark takes the puppet downstairs.

The bright light of the spring days stretch increasingly long fingers toward summer, and the preparations for the wedding go on apace. Guest list, dress, stationery - the hustle and bustle of a couple in love planning for the future. A magical feeling that fleets the days carelessly - as if all the world is filled with gold and laughter. The special day draws nearer still.

There are times when Jo's mind runs ahead to meet the future. After the wedding, there will be the honeymoon, the settling in (even though they settled in with each other two years before), the kids. She watches their kids in her imagination, crawling, growing, tottering to their feet, the safe mundanity of the school run in the car. *We have so much to look forward to,* she thinks.

Freda is not completely forgotten, though. There are times when Mark seems tired by the whole business of arranging the wedding. At times he withdraws to the living room to sit and read in the big comfy armchair by the fireplace.

She catches him sometimes in there looking drawn, his head off to one side in a drowse.

When she approaches him at these times for opinions about a venue, a particular shade of tablecloth or a favour to adorn their guests' tables, he exhales heavily before labouring an answer - as if something is on his mind he won't tell her about. She wonders if all this preparation can really be dragging on his soul so badly.

Over coffee in one of the little coffee shops in Southsea she says to a friend, 'Yes, we're *engaged*, but he's just not *engaging* with the wedding.'

'He needs shaking. Get his interest. Sex him up,' her friend advises in a convincing tone, pretending she knows as much as the agony aunts whose pages her advice comes from.

Jo responds by spending a day at the Gunwharf shopping centre. She picks a tight, short dress, suspenders and stockings - enjoying the frisson of the apparatus of clips and hooks, feeling how it frames her sex, how it invites exploration. After a manicure and makeover, she arrives home, decked in new clothing, glitter and perfume, determined to bring back the sparkle to their lives.

She finds him in the hallway, bowing to the cup of tea in his hand while supping at its rim. He looks distant - about to close himself in the front room again.

'Put that down,' she says with a voice of command she didn't know she had. 'Come with me.'

She leads him by the hand to the bedroom where he responds to her sexual energy with his own; she plants hot kisses on him and their lips seek the soft places of the other.

It's an evening of long, sensual passion in which they become intently focused on pleasure, a mutual moment of giving. Just like the old days.

Afterwards, she falls asleep in his arms; he huddles close, spent and drowsing in post-coital warmth and Jo thinks: *All is right with the world.*

She wakes in the small hours to find he has gone.

She stands and looks around her, feeling a mixture of annoyance and bewilderment, before stepping from the room.

Downstairs, she finds an accusatory crack of light below the living room door and quietly pushes it open. He is asleep in there, with the doll next to his head, propped on the low table beside the armchair. It's almost funny, because it looks as if somehow the doll has climbed up there and fallen asleep with its head next to his.

But it isn't funny. Something inside her contracts with a cold dread, and she returns to the bedroom with a sickly sinking feeling in her stomach. She sits on the bed for ten minutes, inexplicably afraid before switching off the light and letting night creep back into the room.

She wakes the next morning to the sight of Mark lying next to her. Her anger and fear have burned away in her hallmark way - sudden moods and passions petering out like forest paths. All she has left is a dull resentment, but for what she is not sure exactly.

She heads down to the front room again. What was that crazy feeling she had the night before? Did she somehow imagine she had seen her man being unfaithful? *Unfaithful.* Yes that was the emotion!

She is standing by the door in the morning's cold light when the reality of the situation strikes her. He was sitting with a doll. *A doll!* A stupid little puppet that she herself spotted. Really, she needs to take charge of herself. *Unfaithful?!*

She pushes the door open and enters the room.

Before her is the doll on the table with its painted kohl eyes. She steps forward, sensing tension in the air. It's as if the doll is assessing her, watching, emanating waves of malevolence towards her. She is frozen to the spot with fear as the doll's painted eyes blindly take her in. It is going to do something terrible, something really awful, and her whole body tenses with foreboding.

She waits like this for an interminable few seconds, wondering what will happen next. Then she jumps with a sharp jolt and gasp. A car door slams outside. A couple are laughing.

The moment is gone. She is not looking at a malevolent entity. Of course not. It's just a doll. A little doll she found at a car boot sale.

Her shoulders slump forward and she lets out a breath. *What have I been so afraid of?*

Hesitantly at first she lifts the figure with a kind of careless indifference. She weighs it in her hand, feeling the lifeless wood. A childish grin crosses her face mixing with chagrin at her own stupidity.

*Afraid? Of this? I'm being ridiculous!*

With a flick, she throws the puppet in the air, giving it a spin as it launches. It flies up and tumbles down, clattering and flailing as it goes, its arms flying out as if trying to claw the air.

She catches it and hefts it again, its face whirring angrily by, a rush of silks flapping in the air.

*Why should I be afraid of this toy?* she thinks, catching the doll again, and with a giddy sense of malice spinning it up into the air once more, its arms flexing out with a chaotic *clack-clack-clack*.

She is exhilarated by the power she holds over this thing she imagined to have power over her.

When it comes down, she catches it awkwardly - a violent twist of the marionette nicking the little finger on her left hand as it lands.

'Oww! Bitch!' Jo hisses as she puts a little bubble of red to her mouth and sucks. 'Where did that come from?'

Her little finger stings and she looks at the doll with fresh eyes. Overcome with a desire for petty revenge, she considers dropping the figurine into the fireplace and being done with it. *But it would be far too much bother to light a fire*, she thinks. No, she will just tuck her away. In the shed in the back garden. *That'll show Mark* - a revenge for that first day when he put her on the bed and freaked her out. *He'll never find her*. She'll tell him she walked out on him!

With mischievous glee, she takes the doll into the garden shed. Here, she finds a little ice-cream container into which she roughly throws the doll before clipping the lid down with firm fingers. She hides it under the toolbox - a heavy old thing of pressed steel loaded with heavy-duty tools - a lump hammer, a monkey wrench and spanner set.

When it is done, she half runs back to the house with an exultant spring in her step.

Half an hour later she takes Mark a cup of tea.

He is in a drowse as she carries it to him. The room is still in darkness and she steps carefully over the tumble of clothes thrown on the floor the previous night. He sits up abruptly, pushing the cup away and spilling it on the bed.

'Something's wrong,' he says fiercely. 'There's something wrong.'

She watches him rush from the room; hears his bare feet thumping on the stairs. After a few seconds an enraged shout bellows from the front room.

He appears back at the doorway, face contorted with rage. She shrinks from him as he roughly takes hold of her shoulders and shouts in her face.

'Where is she? Where is she?!'

Jo freezes. A hole seems to open up beneath her. The solidity of their relationship, their love - everything is falling into the chasm below.

He continues to shout and shake her and she starts to cry. Her emotions whirl inside her - a crowd of spiteful children laughing and smashing the things she loves.

'The shed,' she blurts. 'In the shed.'

He runs from the room and the back door bangs open. Not sure what else to do, she follows him down, treading quietly in a bubble of shock that makes her notice the tiniest sounds in the house, the smallest play of light.

The everydayness of their home strikes her. Little motes of dust dancing in the summer light, the streaks on the rear window left by the previous night's rain, the milk carton with the lid off that she hasn't put back in the fridge (so unlike her). She sees it all in a detached dream, stepping out on to the concrete path from the kitchen door and hearing, at the little garden's far end, crashes coming from the shed. Above it all, her husband-to-be's voice.

'Where are you? Where are you?'

Then his own voice, higher-pitched: 'Here. Under the tool box. Here.'

The accent he is putting on has the half-formed consonants of the Far East.

'Ah, here you are. Under here.'

'I'm safe now. Thank you. Thank you.'

A high-pitched sobbing sound comes from the shed.

'I was so afraid, Mark. So afraid!'

Jo has heard enough. She turns on her heel, goes back into the house and gathers a few possessions in the bedroom, pushing - bizarrely - her favourite pair of stiletto shoes and a jumper into a cloth bag. She does it quickly, her breathing a chain of short gasps, tears pushing behind her eyes, the only thought in her mind: *he's losing it. God knows what he'll do.*

She hears him go into the living room and she rushes to dress and find her car keys. She pulls on her flat shoes, picks up her handbag and steps quietly down the stairs, aware that she must pass the living room doorway to get to the front door. *Slowly. Quietly. Don't disturb the nutter.*

It is silent in the house as she steps down. She visualises waves of fury emanating through the door ahead of her. There is a resentful silence more unnerving than his weird display of anger.

At the bottom of the stairs she steps across the living room towards the door and snatches at the handle. It doesn't move.

*Still locked from last night. Oh, how stupid!*

She scrabbles through her handbag for her key as the living room door quickly opens.

'Jo? Where are you going?'

His face is a mask of gentle composure.

'I need to pick up some breakfast, Mark,' she says, clutching her bag tight to her chest as she finally extracts her door key, pushes it in the lock and turns it with a frightened energy.

He looks at her levelly. 'And you're taking your stilettos shopping with you?' he says, looking at the heels poking from the shopping bag. He pats the door shut as she tries to open it, then rests his hand on it. 'People might call that a little strange.'

She takes a breath and considers him for a moment. She is afraid of him, she realises. This calm determination on his face is something she has not seen before. Like he's another man.

She looks over his shoulder. Behind him, the doll is on the table by the armchair, where she found it this morning. God how she hates it now. *That look on its face - it seems to be gloating,* she thinks, wondering how its face can now look so different from the gentle pretty painted one she saw at a car boot sale on a spring day. She shoots him a look of alarm.

'Mark, is she going to fall?' she asks, urgency in her voice. He turns quickly, dismay on his face, arms out ready to catch her - and sees the doll has not moved.

He turns back, an accusation on his face -

But his wife-to-be has slipped out of the door onto the streets of Southsea.

Half way up the street, the pressure in her head becomes unbearable. Her face flushes red. She has a tingling in her arm, spreading up from her hand. She raises it to her eyes. With shock she sees it swollen and pulsing with an angry redness. *That tiny little cut! That bubble of blood!* An explosion of nausea pulses through her body in one great quake. She tries to stand, gripped with deep shivers. She rocks on her feet for a second, her head filled with the loud beat of her heart. She doubles up as a spasm seizes her. Gastric acid fills her mouth and nose as vomit gushes from her. In another instant, she has collapsed on the street, the whole of reality disappearing in an onrush of kerbstones and paving slabs.

She feels a hand on her shoulder. Mark says:

'It's okay. I've got you.'

Mark comes into focus for a moment, standing above her.

'Can you hear me? Yes? Stay with us.'

She nods and closes her eyes. Silence takes her.

There is a sound in the darkness now. A low hum, it seems, but as she becomes more aware, the hum shatters into its component parts: consonants and shifting vowels. *Words.* Someone is speaking over and over, but she can't understand any of it. The sound continues on, droning through the night. She calls out -

'The radio. Switch off the radio.'

The motionless face of a doll floats above her.

*A dream*, she realises, closing her eyes.

The rhythmic speech drones on in a monotone.

'Please! Turn off the radio.'

She opens her eyes again and sees Mark, cold and detached, standing in a white-walled room. She vomits.

Darkness takes her a while. Then a nurse hovers at the end of her bed, a ghost in the darkness.

The nurse transforms into a human-sized doll with wooden-hinged limbs that float as it walks. The figure moves towards her through the night, reaching out a stump to her and rubbing the side of her face affectionately. She feels it and goes cold.

Mark appears beside the doll.

'Are you ready?'

The woman's voice: 'Now is the time.'

'Very good. Very good.'

Jo's eyes close and delirium overtakes her.

After a long, exhausting sleep, she finally wakes to see Mark standing above her.

He is looking at her with interested eyes, reading her face intently, a beam of sunlight striking across the upper half of his face, hiding the rest of his expression in shadow.

'And here you are,' he says flatly. 'Back with us. Welcome.'

Recognition rushes in on her. They are in her front room in Southsea. Instinctively she looks around her.

'The doll. Where is the doll?' she says to him.

He considers her with a straight face.

'You don't need to worry about the doll any more,' he says, reassuringly, sitting back on a low chair beside the sofa. 'It's all been sorted out. Everything has been tidied up and arranged.'

'Arranged?' she asks. 'What does that mean? What's been arranged?'

He is about to answer when there is a knock at the door. He looks up from her with bright welcoming eyes.

'Come in,' he says.

The door swings open and a woman walks in, her face hidden from Jo by a silk scarf over her head. She is slight, light of step, dressed in a shimmering orange and black silk dress.

The woman glides to the fireplace and stands by it, the scarf still masking her face. Jo watches her intently, dumbly fascinated as the woman looks around the room, appraising it proprietorially.

Finally, she turns her attention to Jo and pulls off her scarf.

Those fine features! Those kohl-painted eyes, the enigmatic look!

Jo tries to mouth something, but her body does not respond. Tears prickle behind her eyes.

The other woman turns back to the fireplace and looks along the mantle shelf. With a smile she lifts a little jewellery box. Turning toward the bright sunlight, she opens it and holds it up. A sparkling ring glitters in the light; a smile of delight spreads across her face.

Jo feels a flush of anger as she recognises it. *My engagement ring.* She lets out a low weak moan as she sees the other slip it onto her hand.

'A perfect fit!' the woman says with luxurious pleasure as her silks shimmer in the light. 'As if it were made for me!'

Jo's eyes go wide in horror. *That hand!*

There is the lurid line of a scar where it has been grafted on to her arm.

The woman looks to Mark. She reaches out to him and clasps the back of his neck, pulling him in for a passionate kiss. When it is done, she looks down at the figure of Jo on the sofa and says to him, 'We have a date set, huh, Baba?'

'Yes, my love. It's all going ahead,' he answers. 'It's been so good, having our little wedding planner do the work for us. I will miss her for that.'

The woman in silks looks down at the doll on the sofa. A little marionette of a modern Western woman, exquisitely crafted, its lifeless, painted face set in an expression of frozen horror. One hand is attached to a string. The other, the left hand, is missing.

The woman lifts the painted doll, eyeing it with cold hard eyes before turning to Mark with a carefree air.

'You know, I think it's time we got rid of this. Ugly little thing.'

'Do you think we need to... really?' he asks, a hint of guilt briefly crowding his face.

'Well of course we do,' she answers sharply. 'In case you've forgotten, it was *my* hand you asked for in marriage. Remember?'

### Porridge Guns and Croquet Balls
### Gareth Rees
Map location: #15


I was on my way to Morrison's to fetch a loaf of rye bread.
Actually, it wasn't just rye. There was wheat as well and a flour I'd
first heard about only a week or so ago on Hairy Bikers. I'm not sure
how it's spelt but I think it's spelt like spelt.

I had to cross a busy road to get to the supermarket and, while
waiting for a break in the flash flood of chariots, my eyes fell on a
billboard depicting a palatial lounge with furniture upholstered in a
gorgeous cowslip-yellow.

A photograph of a royal apartment did not feel like an assault on
my mind but advertising too often does. What an industry, bigger
than education I've heard it said, and yet it produces nothing as
useful as a single carrot. It's just an intimidating noise really. Well,
not all the time perhaps. Artists in need of the money for a pint of
milk or the rent may sometimes lend their skills to the squawker
hawkers and I'm thinking of a great piece of music that once
accompanied a Rice Krispies advertisement. It sounded like the
Rolling Stones and, as it turned out, it was the Rolling Stones.

'You can't buck the market,' boomed the oracle at Delphi. Or was
it Mrs Thatcher? But what does the advertising industry exist for
except to manipulate the market? It knows a human weakness, an
insecurity which sometimes produces a proneness to suggestion. My
conscious self praises myself for my reason and the power of my
mind to resist trespassers. But, isn't the subconscious the true
governor and who knows how outside forces may steal into that place

and become the puppeteer?

I suppose I'm taking a rather long time in telling you that I was manipulated by a billboard, not into buying a cowslip-yellow three piece suite, but into going to the Isle of Wight and paying a visit to Queen Victoria's home at Osborne House.

I was in the waiting room at the hovercraft terminal and a man sitting to my left said to a man sitting on his left, 'Well, the job in Newfoundland is finished now. I'll have a couple of days at home and then I'm off for a holiday and some diving in the Red Sea.'

My mind flashed back to childhood and being in a cinema on a ship in the middle of the Atlantic ocean. 'The Wind Cannot Read' was the title of the film. Of course the wind can't read, I thought. The wind never went to school. And then I was struck by sea-sickness and I rushed up on deck feeling that to actually see the heaving ocean lessened the nausea. The sea was grey. The sky was grey. It was cold. And then, looming out of the gloom, I was surprised to see a great landmass. It was Newfoundland. And it looked a very forbidding place.

Later, in mainland Canada, I discovered some of the people there looked down on

Newfoundlanders, called them 'Newfies' and made derogatory, screw-loose jokes about them as people used to do in England about the inhabitants of Scotland, Wales and especially Ireland. I don't know if the people of the Isle of Wight have suffered in this way but I did wonder about its intellectual eminence or rather the quality of its advertising people when, having arrived on the island, I noticed, emblazoned on the sides of buses, the words, 'Thinking Islanders Think Buses'. In my mind, the naming of the 'Cod Father' fish and chip shop on the esplanade scored higher on the scale of wit. I had a few minutes to wait for a bus to East Cowes so I walked towards a sign apparently indicating the location of a public toilet. The sign pointed down a deserted pier which stretched so far out to sea I could see no end. I started to think about eternity but decided it was more comforting to think buses and I ascended to the top deck of a double-decker where I sat in the front seat with my legs crossed and praying I wouldn't wet myself. I really was too grown-up for an outcome such as that.

How I see the world sometimes is, I think, a metaphor for my inner world. For example, I was falling prey to a view that the Isle of Wight was a bit of a dozy place when really it was me that was not quite in the here and now. But who wants to own the fault when you can blame it on someone or something else? Not quite being in the here and now may indicate depression and in a dozy state like that you hardly want to be woken up by bright colours. So, when the bus passed a yellow, blooming rape field, I nearly had a panic attack. I didn't panic though. Instead of hyperventilating, I did a few rounds of alternate nostril breathing and, having calmed down, I was able to listen to the conversation of two old guys sitting on the adjacent seat. 'I joined a ukulele band and a bloke turned up to play bass with one of those home-made instruments they used in the skiffle bands in the fifties. You remember, an old tea chest, a broom handle and a piece of string? I thought, I've got to have one of those and I went home and straightaway started to make my single string bass. I even put 'F' holes in the sound box. I felt at home with that instrument right from the start. It was... well, intuitive or something.'

'So, what made you join a ukulele band in the first place? They're really popular these days, ukuleles, aren't they?'

'Yes, well I think it's because it's supposed to be reasonably easy to play them. But I didn't find it so. I didn't just join the ukulele band though. I joined the local community choir as well and that's been wonderful. I've spent my life listening to music but I've never been a music-maker before. It's like a new life and, boy, did I need a new life.'

'Really?'

'Well yes, my wife died a couple of months ago. We were married in 1960. How can I begin to describe how it felt to lose her? You have someone to talk to, to pass on the little items of news in an average day, seeing a fox on the allotment as dawn was breaking, the car that nearly backed into me on the way to the shops. Yes, mundane stuff like that. And then, after she'd gone, I'd just have to store it all up and right now as I talk to you it's like I'm talking too much and over-flowing like an over-full water tub.'

'No, no, that's fine. So has the music helped you?'

'Oh yes, so so much. I used to be very matter of fact. You live and then you die. End of story. But since she died, well I can't accept that she isn't still around. Maybe wishful-thinking. But the music has helped me so much. It's like it takes me to a place that's bigger than death. It's a huge comfort.'

As I stood up to get off the bus, I looked at the man who'd joined the ukulele band. I knew he was old if he'd married in 1960 but his face shone with a new day. I alighted just outside the entrance to the grounds of Osborne House and, after the failure to locate the public toilet in Ryde, I needed to find an outlet quickly for what had been repressed. And I did so, a right royal relief it was amongst the blooms of a rhododendron tree.

Blessed now with a moment's peace of mind, I set off to explore the grounds. Being early summer, they were particularly beautiful. Huge cedar of Lebanon and horse-chestnut trees, newly in leaf dotted the parkland. In a copse, daffodils were still in bloom and there were violets and primroses. Also in the copse was a bunker-like building which had been used to store ice that had been cut from a lake in America.

The stroll round the house was more enjoyable than the stroll within it, a contrast between nature in a state of renewal and fading grandeur. The corridor walls were filled with oil paintings but they were hard to see because of the lighting which was deliberately subdued in order to conserve them. There was an alcove though with plenty of natural light and there was a picture with the title of 'An Anchorite Meditating on Death'. It showed a bald and bearded man with his head in his hands looking as depressed as hell.

I failed to be uplifted by the art and preferred the living art that was a party of French school children who were happy on their holiday and pirouetting rather than shuffling along in the queue in front of me. Behind me, I heard someone say, 'Bagpipes? No, I don't like them. Porridge guns I call them and I heard a thousand of them once in Edinburgh and, when they were joined by the army bagpipe band of the Hashemite Kingdom of Jordan who were playing in another key, I really began to seriously believe that torture and death by iron maiden would be a walk in the park compared to enduring that cacophony.'

We entered Queen Victoria's bedroom and, even though she'd died in that room a long time ago, it still seemed an invasion of privacy. Subjects may feel owned by the sovereign but I expect sovereigns often feel owned by their subjects?

The bedroom enjoyed a splendid view of parkland rolling down to the sea and then over the sea to Portsmouth. I wondered if the Queen, as she expired, might have confused Portsmouth with eternity.

And then we arrived in the room I'd seen on the English Heritage billboard. Yes it was gorgeous and yet, from a Buddhist perspective perhaps, it was dreadfully cluttered and, from an oriental sultan's point of view, it wasn't a room conducive to horizontal recline. The seating was designed for vertical posture and reflected therefore a demeanour disposed to be a bit stiff perhaps.

On the way home and boarding the hovercraft, I greeted a man I'd seen when I'd been looking at the miserable old anchorite in Osborne House and we sat next to each other for the crossing. He asked me if I'd enjoyed my visit and I said I had although I'd found some of the art work a bit gloomy. He told me that art for him was about fun. He said he worked as a freelance graphic artist and did a lot of work for the British library. But when he was at home he liked to have fun painting just what he fancied. Before going to bed at night, he'd look in on a work in progress as you'd look in on a sleeping child. He got grumpy when he finished a picture.

I said I'd like to see some of his work and he produced a glossy booklet which showed some of his paintings. One showed a naval officer from Nelson's time wearing a royal blue, gold-braided jacket which was undone and showed that he was wearing pink and white-striped pyjamas. He was sat in the bow of a boat and facing in the stern an ordinary seaman who was doing the rowing. The oars were garden hoes, the sea was a deep green lawn and scattered about were the hoops and balls of a croquet game.

### The Zeitgeist Chapters (Part 1)
### Tom Harris
Map location: #12

Through the pub window, Jacob Jacket peered into the night, drawn to the dark, foreboding Solent. The black harbour waters called to him: 'Jacob... Jacob... Oi! Jacob!' The voice finally found him. 'I hope the beer muse has been kind, my love, but sling yer hook will ya! It's time at the bar!'

The landlady smiled as she ushered him to the door.

'Okay, okay,' he said, pushing the unused notebook into his coat pocket. 'I'm going, but nothing is going in, you know?' He made a knocking sound and tapped at his head. 'Apart from the H.S.B. Lovely pint that, Sal...'

'Sorry to hear that, love, but it's almost midnight, so you best get home to your Irene. You're engaged now, remember? Ooh, when did you say her next book was out?' she asked, as she guided Jacob into the night.

'Next year, but we've both hit...'

The door slammed shut behind him.

'A second novel wall.' He blew a raspberry. 'Night, Sal.'

Jacob shivered, shrugging on his navy blue pea coat. The pub sign creaked in the wind that rushed in from the port mouth. 'And all was still in the west,' he whispered as he staggered into Rowes Alley, turning his ankle on the cobbles.

Pulling up his collar, he stumbled into the brick wall, shielding his eyes from the halogen security lights. 'Ow!' he moaned, dropping to the ground to tend to his ankle. 'Was I always such a useless fucker?

Why can't I bloody write?' he cursed, kicking out at a half eaten packet of crisps.

From the silence that followed a whisper of a voice, growing louder, found him.

'Well Jacob Jacket. I might just be able to help you with that.'

Jacob spun around to find a man in a wide brimmed hat and a cape, propped up against the wall. Smoke drifted out of the mouth of the stranger in the shape of paper and pen, but the man did not answer Jacob.

'Unless you've got any antipsychotics for this rather excellent hallucination, I don't see how you can help me?' he said, rubbing his eyes.

'You are quite sane, Jacob Jacket. I own ideas. They come to me. I store them and I trade them to people who need them.'

The security lights went out. The stranger was sucked into shadow until the dim bulb of an old fashioned lamppost flickered into life, casting a spotlight around the man.

'Now that's more like it,' said the stranger, removing his hat to reveal fluffy white hair and a child-like face. 'The name's Zeitgeist. Although children know me as The Midnight Man.'

'Ah, zeitgeist, a purveyor of trends, an understanding of the spirit of the age...' Jacob delivered the dictionary definition, still slumped on his arse in the dark.

The stranger bowed and opened his arms wide. 'Today's ideas – Today!'

'You need to work on the slogan, but I get it!' Jacob said, tugging his chinos down where they had ridden up. 'Look, fella, I know someone has set me up and it's a nice ruse all this, but I'm not quite pissed enough to believe in magical midnight men, well not quite... Was it Irene? Or Sal from the boozer? I bet it was. I could hear her cackling when she kicked me out the door.'

'You alone asked for my help, Jacob Jacket. You require an idea, do you not?' Zeitgeist dragged on a small cigar.

'Is that a café crème?' asked Jacob.

The stranger approached, the halo of light tracking him down the alley.

'What sort of bulbs do you use in that thing?' Zeitgeist whispered in his ear. Jacob's eyes widened and his mind sparked; a sudden sense of sobriety encapsulated him. When Zeitgeist finished talking, Jacob rocked back against the wall as if he'd been punched by a fist of inspiration.

'That's brilliant!' he said. 'I have to get back and write that down... Thank Sal for me, or that fiancé of mine. You know, you're not bad. You written anything I may have read?'

'That is not my domain. Do not worry. You won't forget a word. There is of course, a verbal contract. Some tiny rules to abide by. You must tell no-one about me and do not share these ideas, for they come at a price that you would not wish others to pay.'

'Great! Is that it?'

Zeitgeist nodded. 'I may call on you to grant me a simple favour should you seek my services again, but yes that's that. I wish you a good morning, Jacob Jacket. Until next time.'

Jacob spun around in the alley.

Daylight.

His legs almost gave way, as if he'd been standing on them for hours. He slumped against the wall. There was no sign of the lamppost or Zeitgeist.

'Oh, he's good. He's bloody good!' he said.

As he staggered down Rowes Alley, Jacob Jacket shielded his eyes from the intruding winter sun. Across the rippling water, the Spinnaker Tower, the new guardian of the port mouth, remained vigilant. Nothing had changed.

Had he imagined it? Dreamt an entire book from cover to cover? His head was bursting with a new story. There was only one answer.

'I'm a bloody genius!' he concluded. 'I knew it!'

Jacob Jacket raced to the end of the alley onto Broad Street, the ideas burning inside him, screaming to be written. A seaside potion of screeching gulls and the smell of seawater merged with bacon, cooking on the grill of The Spinnaker Cafe.

It was intoxicating.

'Good morning Bathing Lane! Good morning West Street!' he called, as he raced along the pavement. 'Morning!' he called to the bemused postie, as she pushed her bike along the cobbles. 'Good morning Old Portsmouth! It truly is a wonderful life!'

The sharp chill of the winter wind blew through the bedroom window as his frantic fingers flashed across the laptop keyboard. The words on the screen had been edited from brain to page. He was no more than a printer.

No coffee breaks. No procrastination on social media. This was a writer writing. A master of his craft.

It was perfection.

It brought goosebumps to his skin. The back of his neck fizzed as though he were being kissed by Irene for the very first time. When he pulled his hands from the keyboard, his fingers were bleeding. Jacob sat back and grinned. Breathing heavily, he tried to stand but his legs gave way and he slumped back into the old leather chair. He rubbed his thighs, as he shuffled to the window. The icy breeze stroked his bare arms, causing him to shiver.

He peered out into the pitch black. Stars. Moon. Headlights. Lampposts. Early Christmas lights strung along the promenade. It was beautiful, but nothing to match what he had created. He slammed the window shut on Jack Frost and turned to his laptop. In the right hand corner of the screen, the digital numbers flicked to 23:00.

'All day?' He scratched at his curly locks.

'Uh-hu,' groaned Irene from the bedroom doorway, in t-shirt and joggers. 'Are you ever coming to bed?'

'Er, yeah, I think I've finished,' he said, suddenly possessed by a yawn that almost stretched to midnight.

Irene padded off into the darkness. 'That's great. Well done you... '

'I'm starving! You eaten?' he called.

She grunted and he heard the bedroom door close behind her.

'Right, dinner for one then.'

Jacob yawned all the way into the kitchen and opened the fridge. Taking a swig of juice, he paused. He sprinted back to the laptop. 'Idiot!' he cursed, as he saved the document.

He sat back in his chair and with gritted teeth, he punched the air. Getting to his feet he danced around the desk, euphoria cruising through him, until the demons of doubt stopped him in the middle of a tango with the floor lamp.

He printed off the first page and read aloud whilst pacing around the flat. His head was spinning. 'Everything flows! It's perfect!' Jacob printed off two more random pages. 'It's brilliant! It's... It's him. Zeitgeist!' he said, glancing at the clock on the screen. 11:41. It took about half an hour to walk from his flat on Southsea seafront into Old Portsmouth.

He had time.

'Be back in a sec, my beautiful scribbler,' he called, pulling on his coat. 'Just got to see a man about a book.'


Jacob raced through the streets. A stitch burned in his side and sweat clasped his shirt to his back despite the chill of the night air.

Like the first moment he'd seen Irene, he was chasing something he could not do without.

Run Jacob Jacket. Run.

He'd downloaded Zeitgeist's idea somehow, but he craved more. The possibilities were endless. The perfect crime thriller. An ageless period crime novel with a poignant message. Maybe Zeitgeist could provide.

The ideas were free. No sleepless nights, no plotting, no characterisation, no editing, no proofreading, no brain freeze or fatigue – no anything – just writing and Jacob Jacket craved more.

He left Pembroke Road, onto High Street, past The Dolphin and The Duke of Wellington as the Pompey chimes from the Guildhall clock rang out across the city.

As the final chime faded into the ether, he arrived at the spot where he had first met the enigmatic stranger. There was no lamppost, but a wide brimmed hat lay on the cobbles beside a café crème butt. Inside the hat was a business card. It listed Zeitgeist's opening hours. Against every day of the week was a single word – Midnight.

'Shit!' cried Jacob. 'Shit! Shit! Shit!' Then he collapsed against the brick wall and laughed until his stomach hurt.


'I haven't seen you write like that for years. It was like you were possessed,' Irene mumbled, through the crunch of her morning toast.

He smiled, nodding through a mouthful of porridge.

'I wish I could get in the zone like that.' She swigged at the dregs of her breakfast tea and slammed the cup down. 'Wish me luck for the big meeting.' She reached across the table and kissed him on the cheek, away from the breakfast gunge on his lips. 'This new stuff I've been working on, it's got no soul, you know...?'

Jacob nodded. 'Remember, the ideas are all around us. You just got to reach up and grab the right one.'

'Oh, spare me that zeitgeist crap,' she grinned.

Jacob held up his hands and rose from the table to return the warming milk to the fridge. 'Don't knock it till you've tried it!'

'What does that mean? Anyway, the literary agent of death awaits. Why is everything I write so utterly shite? Love you!' she shouted, as she stormed out of the flat.

'You're only human!' he called back.

Jacob padded across the living room to the window. The coastal road was closed due to high winds; the crashing waves reaching out to the proud Portsmouth Naval Memorial, which marked old souls lost in conflict.

'Those who laid down their lives in defence of the empire and have no other grave than the sea.' Jacob recited the inscription from one of the plaques and saluted, as his fiancé crossed the road three floors down.

She waved as she skipped across the zebra, the wind battering her as she shrugged on her coat.

'You are so hot right now,' he chuckled, with his hand against the window, now specked with winter rain. 'I think I'd give up writing for you... well maybe short stories.' He smiled, catching his reflection in the glass.

Jacob Jacket stepped back.

For a moment he didn't recognise the man looking back.

Something was different. Something had changed.

'Who are you?' he asked. A vacant expression stared back.

He slumped down in the settee and turned on the TV.

It was going to be a long wait for midnight.

As Jacob headed down Rowes Alley, he checked the clock on his iPhone.

It was 23:59, but there was no lamppost. No hat. No Zeitgeist.

'Yep, you've really lost it this time, Jacob,' he said, pulling down his Portsmouth footie club beanie so it covered his ears.

'Lost? How can you be lost, when you've only just found yourself?' came the voice.

'You're real... '

'Keep your voice down, Jacob Jacket, let's not tarnish my supernatural aura shall we... So, how was it for you?' Zeitgeist turned to face him with a swoosh of his cape. Under the lamppost, from beneath his wide brimmed hat, he lit another cigar.

'It was incredible!'

'I knew you'd like it. So?'

'Are you really going to make me say it?' asked Jacob.

'Of course. I'm an ideas bank not a mind reader.'

'Please, sir. I want some more?' he quipped, hands stretched out.

'Step forward, Mr Twist. Come and get your gruel.'

Jacob approached, butterflies flitting inside his rib cage as Zeitgeist whispered his words. Dialogue and plot. Character arcs that would make Noah jealous. Conflict. Resolution. Motive. Voice.

'Perfection,' whispered Jacob, collapsing against the wall, as the cries of gulls welcomed the dawn.

'Before you depart, Jacob Jacket, there is something I'd ask of you.'

With his eyes closed, his head blistering with the joy of fiction, Jacob Jacket said... 'Anything!'

'All I ask is for you to deliver this before midnight.' Zeitgeist smiled, crouching to meet Jacob's gaze and handed him a brown paper package tied up with string.

'What's inside?' he asked.

'Just a few of my favourite things,' replied Zeitgeist, and with that... he was gone.

'Greetings from Midnight, Shinwell Johnson.'

Jacob Jacket stared at the writing on the parcel, checked the address and shrugged. Then he stuffed the lightweight package inside the letterbox. The parcel dropped. The letterbox clicked. A dog barked. Jacob turned and left the building.

Job Done.

The Spinnaker Quay apartments were so close to the alley, why had Zeitgeist not posted this himself? The question burned like the sun on this crisp Portsmouth morning, but desperate to write the new words tap dancing on his cerebrum, Jacob Jacket turned left down Feltham Row to head home.

The path wound its way alongside the Town Quay. The calm waters speckled with sunlight and the masts of moored boats clinked tunelessly in the wind like the percussion section of a school orchestra. Leaning against the iron railings, Jacob Jacket closed his eyes, absorbing the energy of this place, stretching his senses, before he headed home to write.

A noisy bevy of swans cruised the water beneath the path and he breathed it all in. Even the fish market smelled good this morning.

The pull of a pint of Fullers at the Bridge Tavern on the island across the quay, was not so strong when there was a novel to be written, and he marched on until his iPhone beeped reminders of missed calls and texts from Irene.

***Where r u?***

***Jacob! What is going on?***

***R u dead?***

As he typed his woeful response an explosion shook the ground beneath his feet. Jacob Jacket dropped to the floor as the debris rained down on the quayside. He covered his mouth with his beanie as the smoke engulfed him. Through the railings he stared down into the water. The leg of a Labrador bobbed on the surface.

Bile burned inside him and he turned to the blazing apartment block, as white feathers, fur and ash fell around him like confetti at a taxidermists' wedding.

*This is part 1 of The Zeitgeist Chapters – the story continues in part 2.*

**Ghost Ship**
**Lynne E Blackwood**
*Map location: #14*

'How did you do this? Wonderful photo!' an enthusiastic visitor
said admiring *The Ghost Ship*. That photograph had turned into the
focal point of my Square Tower exhibition. 'It could be the Mary
Rose,' he added, tugging at his shapeless jacket. 'I can just imagine
her sailing by as I stand on the defence wall and look out over the
harbour.' He smelt of wet dog.

'It's definitely not the Mary Rose,' I told him. 'She's down the road
in the museum and I doubt if you would see her sailing by.' My voice
came out sarcastic sounding, even though what I felt was frustration.
I couldn't explain how the sepia enlargement had turned out this
way. 'The photo was taken at the Tall Ship Race a few years back. Not
quite a Tudor galleon.' I had collected the proof prints and negatives
from Sam and he had asked the same question. How had I done it?

'How did I do what?' I'd asked him.

'This.' Sam handed me the photo.

It was one of the Tall Ships sailing past Spitbank Fort and into the
entry to Portsmouth Harbour. But the image was blurred. Not just
one shadow image as when the photographer moves the camera
inadvertently, but three. None were aligned either, but appeared on
both sides of the original image. They were neither up nor down, but
all around the original, as if enlarged, a series of superimposed
shadows. Encompassing the hull was a darker shadow with no detail.

'This is really weird.' I studied the print and tried to remember if I
had trembled or been jostled by the spectators when taking the

photo. 'No, I didn't move or do anything in particular.' Had the spooling slipped?

'But up and across at the same time? Show me the camera.' Sam opened the back of my precious vintage 35mm Leica.

We both examined it. There was nothing wrong with the winding mechanism. He took the strip of negatives and scrutinised them again.

'It's as I thought. Nothing wrong with your camera, but take a look at this.' He held the negatives up to the shop light.

The two other boats either side of the Ghost Ship were clear and precise. I had caught the 'perfect white' of bright sun reflecting off the hulls' wash. Great photos, I thought. But the Ghost Ship image was shrouded in mist, as if taken on a low-cloud winter day when the light isn't good.

'I don't get it. What a brilliant photo. Fascinating,' I clutched the print and tried to think how I could have inadvertently achieved the effect. No reasonable explanation was forthcoming.

The Tall Ship Race celebration in Portsmouth had been an exciting opportunity. I had loaded my favourite Leica with a sepia film and wandered through the throngs down along the seawalls to The Hard, following the tall-mast gathering's progress. Today, in the Square Tower, with my photos displayed around me, I felt that same enthusiasm from the crowds. It was almost as if those thirty high-masted ships from around the world were sailing into Portsmouth Harbour. The Ghost Ship especially generated excitement and since I was weary of the questions, I escaped into the November air to poison myself with a cigarette.

Sea fog rolled in from a dark Solent as I passed under the archway and onto the stone walkway of the high defences, where I had decided to grab a little shelter. A figure stood further down the seawall, gazing out over the harbour. What caught my eye was not so much the dark weather-beaten face but his clothes: a wide-brimmed hat, caped coat that met his ankles and hung loose on a massive frame. He was tall and burly. I couldn't distinguish his face. The light from the top of the defences was too poor and thick mist had rolled up to the stone bulwarks.

Foghorns boomed. I jumped at the haunting, desolate sound of watery graves from an ever-present maritime past. The Mary Rose had sunk in Portsmouth Harbour. Overloaded, the theory goes. More than six hundred dead, drowned only several yards off the Portsmouth shore. She now lay moist in her display museum under an eternal rain of chemicals designed to keep her timbers and shape intact. Most exhibition visitors likened my ghost ship photograph to the Mary Rose. I didn't quite know what to make of it all, couldn't remember the name of Tall Ship I had photographed, and it wasn't visible on the blurred photo. Friday night revellers making their way to Spice Island pubs and modern entertainment delights of Gunwharf Quays jerked me from my thoughts and I remembered the man. He had turned his gaze from the night harbour and was now staring directly at me through a break in the slow-motion fog that swirled around us both. His dark eyes caught my gaze.

'There you are, Jake. What the hell are you doing? You've got punters waiting inside,' Sam called. I allowed him to manage my affairs and he kept me in check where necessary. We were a good team, he with feet firmly planted in developing my career and keeping me from wandering into artistic vagueness.

'Alright, just taking a fag break,' I looked back, but the man had gone.

'Get a move on. I've got potential buyers waiting for the artist.'

'I'm coming...'

'The Ghost Ship is attracting a lot of attention. I think you could hang on and get a much better price,' Sam whispered as we entered the Square Tower and made our way across the gallery confines.

'I do love that photo, Sam. Not sure I want to sell it. It would have to be for a very good price.'

'Of course you want to sell it, mate. What are you talking about? You need the money. We'll set a higher price than the others. It's so popular, it'll sell quickly, so don't worry.'

I was reassured and images of what I could do with a hiked price cheered me up for the rest of the evening.

'This is wonderful. How much is it?'

Yet another visitor repeating the same question since I had taken the price tag away three days ago. I had followed Sam's advice and was now eagerly waiting what could eventually be an extravagant sum of money for the popular photo. Everyone was enthralled by the Ghost Ship. I was too. I was attracted to it more each time I looked at it and repeatedly told myself that I wasn't going to sell it. Then someone oohed, aahed and offered a decent price and I backed down as the offers began rising. But not high enough for me to let it go.

'Someone offered me four hundred pounds yesterday,' I lied.

'That's a little too high for me. I can do three hundred. I'll come back at the end of the exhibition. Perhaps you'll change your mind.'

He walked away disappointed, and I went outside for a break. I was looking for the mysterious man of the first night. Three consecutive evenings, three nicotine breaks later and each time he had moved closer to me along the defence wall, as if wishing to engage in conversation. But each time I attempted to approach him, he disappeared into the thick fog that had settled in Portsmouth Harbour. Fourth evening and the man stood in the archway. Another step closer to the Square Tower entrance. Blocking my way to the seawall. I saw him clearly under the lamplight. The intrigue and desire to approach him dissipated in an instant when I returned his stare and looked into the depth of his dark eyes. I rushed hastily inside.

'Are you alright, Jake?' Sam's reassuring voice and the gallery's bright lights shook me back into reality.

'It's nothing. I'm alright. Just needed some air.'

'What an amazing photo. No price marked. Is it for sale?'

'Maybe. I'm not sure yet.' The truth was that I really didn't want to sell the Ghost Ship. But I needed the money so was still holding out for the magical sum of eight hundred pounds. I had upped the ante and wanted more, in conflict with myself. I wanted to keep it, but also wanted more money. Yes, I knew I could get a lot more money for it.

'How much do you want for it?'

'It's very special.'

'Yes, I recognise that. It is quite something.'

'Nine hundred pounds.'

'That's pretty steep. I can offer you six hundred and eighty. There's something about this photo that I really like.' The man peered at the framed enlargement. 'What's the name of the ship? I can't make anything out because of the blur.'

I peered too. 'I don't know. Can't see anything either. Does it matter?'

'It reminds me of a famous ship, but no, that's not possible. It sunk well over a century ago. Are you certain you don't want to accept my offer?'

'No thank you. I'm sticking with nine hundred. Someone offered me more than that the other evening.'

'Why didn't you sell it, then?'

I had no specific answer. Was it because inwardly I didn't want to let go of this photo that gripped me with increasing fascination? Was that the true reason for putting up the price as the days passed? No, not really. I realised I was waiting for bigger money. I wanted more and thought I could obtain a heftier price by playing a waiting game. I was being greedy, but was it the right course to take? I could very well end up with the photo and no money. I needed a break to clear my thoughts.

He was standing outside, had moved several meters down the street, opposite the Square Tower entrance. Foghorns had continued booming for six straight days but I saw him clearly under the lamplight. The man grinned at me. Something glinted in his mouth.

A gold or silver tooth? It wasn't the fog clinging to my body that chilled my bones. It was an onslaught of irrational fear. What did he want? I nearly tripped down the entrance stairs in my haste to flee and made a beeline for the Ghost Ship.

It was once again under attack by prospective buyers:

'How much?'

'Wonderful!'

'Too expensive for me.'

'I'll give you a hundred pounds less than your asking price.'

The comments and questions continued along the same vein for most of the evening, then:

'Look at this. I can make out the sailors on board.'

Sailors? The photo was so blurred and I hadn't seen anything of the sort when examining the enlargement before framing it.

I moved my face closer to the print and searched what I presumed to be imagination on the part of the visitor next to me. There were faint outlines, but distinctive enough to make out the shape of a sailor clinging to one of the top masts. Another was in the crows nest. Several were dotted around the deck. I stepped back hastily. There had been nothing like this on the negative. Sweat trickled from my armpits and I felt ill, physically sick at the sight of the photo. Get rid of it. Something isn't right.

'Jake. This gentleman is trying to make you an offer.' Sam stood at my shoulder, nudging me back to the red brick room around me, to reality.

'Yes, I'll give you eight hundred for it.'

The exhibition was closing in a couple of days. It was an offer not far off the magical one thousand pounds I had now set my sights on, and a lot of money for one photo.

'No. There is someone else who has made a better offer. Increase yours and I'll sell it to you willingly.' Greed had spoken, despite the lingering chill as I looked at the photo and thought of the man outside. Waiting for me.

'Sorry, but that's really too high.' The visitor glanced at me quickly, hesitated before speaking as he moved away. 'I think you have made a mistake,' and turned to the mysterious man who was now hovering in the doorway.

My stalker from the fog seemed to want to come inside, but the bright lights appeared to affect him. He was waiting for me. I knew it.

'Jake, are you crazy? Let this thing go.'

Sam's indignant words washed over me. All my senses were focused on the man, his uncanny stare, the smell of the sea and burnt candle that now filled the Square Tower.

'Can you smell that?'

'Smell what, Jake?'

I turned to Sam. 'Candle or oil. Coming from that man over there.'

'What man?'

The doorway was empty. He had gone.

'You look really bad. What's going on?'

I didn't know what to say, so I walked out, bumping into the visitor who had offered eight hundred pounds. He grabbed my arm. 'Sell it. Don't be greedy. That photo is no good for you, so get rid of it.'

'I'll sell it to you now, if you still want it,' I had blurted out the words. Fear.

'Not now. Not after what I've seen. Throw it away, do anything, but get it out of your life.'

'What do you mean? What have you seen?' Panic now.

He turned back. 'I see things and I see that photo is no good for you.'

'What else did you see?' Fear tinged my words, but they did not reach the visitor who had hastened his exit and was now half way down the street, glancing nervously into the shadows thrown by the defence wall. I returned to Sam who was staring at me and frowning. 'Go home. You don't look well. I'll sell the damn photo if you wish.'

I said yes to the idea of going home and yes, sell the photo at a decent price. Just get rid of it.

I didn't attend the exhibition the next day, but the day after was the last night and closure of the exhibition so I reluctantly entered the Square Tower. I had hoped not to see the Ghost Ship. It still hung on the walls. No one had offered a penny for it. The usual excitement and admiration, but no offers to buy. I approached the image and peered, hoping the human images had been a product of my imagination. The sailors were still on the ship. In fact, I could have sworn there were more of them. Worst of all, and that was the point where I seriously thought I had lost my mind, the minute human forms appeared to be in motion with a delicate sway of the hull. One image drew me in further. Was it possible? The upper half of a man's body was thrust through a now distinct gunport. Was he waving at me? I stepped back and fell into Sam's arms.

'It hasn't sold.'

'I can see that!' I cried out. Panic. Am I going crazy?

'Get a grip. The exhibition is closing tonight. Let's try and sell the damn thing.' Sam thrust a wine glass into my hand. 'Permission given to drink tonight. I don't know what's going on but we'll get rid of the photo since you seem unsettled by it.'

Sam walked away to find a punter. I stood, transfixed, gazing at the gunport where a tiny arm gesticulated towards me. Yes, me. The human form definitely intended his waving at me. Why hadn't I sold it when the offers were made? Greed, I told myself. Sheer greed. Regret clutched at my gut as I stared at the Ghost Ship. None of this was right and I stood terrified.

'Goodness me. This looks exactly like HMS Eurydice!' A punter stood by my side, peering at the photo. 'How strange. This ship is named Eurydice as well. But that can't be. She sank off Shanklin in the storm of 1878. Bound for Portsmouth Harbour. Nearly made it too. Such a huge loss of life. Where did you take this photo?'

'The Tall Ship Race,' I whispered.

Silence. The visitor wore a pensive face. 'I was on the organising committee. There was no HMS Eurydice registered. In fact, the only ship of that name I know of is the one I mentioned that was sunk off the Isle of Wight over a hundred years ago.' He walked hastily away and I was left alone staring at the waving arm in the gunport and the human forms going about their nautical business. I should have sold it. Greed. I had smelt money and followed my nose to a place I was incapable of understanding. I was losing my mind.

Another punter's presence hung on my shoulder. The man. His grip of iron held my arm as he prised open my hand and placed an antique shilling into the palm. He closed my fingers around the icy coin.

'Hey Jake, I have someone who wants to buy *The Ghost Ship*.'

I watched as Sam introduced the visitor. But the person standing in front of the photo wasn't me because I wasn't there. He looked like me, spoke in the same tones, was dressed in the same clothes I had put on for the exhibition closure. He also appeared unusually cheerful.

A voice came from behind. 'I'll crack that bloody whip over your back, Jake, if you don't get back to cleaning the deck.'

I turned my bent body around. I was on HMS Eurydice's gun deck at the same gunport where I had seen a human form waving to me. The scream caught in my throat and I began waving frantically out of the gunport back at him, at me, my body, my face, my voice but now inhabited by the sailor at the gun port. Who was now me. Who had stolen my place in the real world. Who turned towards the photo with a satisfied smile, then continued talking with the potential buyer.

'Yes, I'll take five hundred pounds for The Ghost Ship. Where do you live? Gosport? That's good, this ship should never leave the harbour,' and he laughed. 'Press-gangs, you know. They could get you drunk, whisk you on board and then sail away before you realise a thing.' I, he laughed again. 'Taking the King's shilling was a guarantee of never seeing home for many years.' I, he, stared at my fearful face gazing out of the gunport. 'Greed. That was the downfall of many.'

'King's Shilling, Jake. You're signed up now, my lad and I'll ensure your time with us is rough.' The man who had haunted me, now towered over my hunched body, whip in hand.

### Mermaid & Chips
**Tessa Ditner**
*Map location: #10*


Dan met me at The Bridge Tavern for an emergency pint. I'd had a revelation, a life-changing thought this morning and Dan was the only one likely to get it.

'You want to become Dolly Parton?' He said, looking unimpressed.

'No!' I prodded the beer mat. 'Not *that* kind of doll.'

'What then? Like that bloke in *Kinki Boots* who can't decide whether to wear a polo neck or a dress?'

'Not a drag queen!'

'I need another drink,' he sighed.

I was on my own with this one.


'The city has a history of corset-making,' a saleswoman told me showing me leather and bridal corsets. *What am I doing here?* I thought. 'Once upon a time there were 9,000 of us, mostly sailor's wives. We do corsets for men too...' I mumbled something about the wife and hurried out of the shop. I tried to rationalise it. Since the accident, people see me differently. They'll tell you *you're not less of a man because you've got a missing leg*, but there's a distance, like I'm a victim and people are scared of hurting me more with the wrong words. I guess I was trying to not be a victim.


It was two weeks before I tried again. I took a train to Brighton. I buzzed the door, my earphones blaring to distract me from what I was doing. The shop smelt of rubber, it was overpowering, like being in a tyre factory. I couldn't tell if it was great or if it was too much. The owner wasn't wearing any of the rubber herself. She wore a cardigan and was reading *Homes&Gardens*.

'Have you ordered a face?' she asked.

'Ehm,' I said, and confessed I didn't want a mask, or whatever it was called. I wanted to be me. She nodded, like that made sense and then asked how many sugars I wanted in my tea.

'First time?' she handed me a mug that had written across the side *Best Mum in the World*. I nodded. 'Let's start small,' she said, 'this here is a culotte.'

'Culotte,' I repeated.

'French knickers,' she explained, pushing her glasses up the ridge of her nose.

'Right,' I said, trying not to feel nervous. I know how to weld steel and drive a tower crane. I ought to be able to handle a culotte.

Turns out culottes aren't such a big deal. They're like boxers, but rubbery and with a frill along the edge. I pulled them up my leg, they felt icy cold but they warmed up fast and then it felt like I was wearing butter.

'How about breasts?' she asked, squinting disapprovingly at my hairy chest. 'How big?' She strapped some samples across me, she inflated them.

'I can't see my feet,' I told her, grinning.

'This is a size F,' she ignored me. 'All my customers get carried away at first,' she warned, letting out a bit of air 'you don't want to look common.'

'No!' I said quickly.

'You've got big shoulders,' she said, 'so double Ds is proportionate.' I had double Ds. Which I prodded. Then she showed me how small my waist could go. It didn't get very small to be honest.

Was I really doing this? I followed her instructions wondering if perhaps I was bonkers. Maybe I was having a mid-life crisis? Or maybe I was suffering from some gender-bending psychosis? But I didn't want *real* breasts, this was something else.

'I only have two complete rubber doll outfits in your size,' she said, carrying over a heap of shiny colours. She laid it all out, like bits of a rubbery rainbow. 'Both have inbuilt corsets so you won't have to worry about that.'

'Oh good,' I said. I hoped that was the right response.

One outfit was black and purple, like some Gothy Beetlejuice getup. The other looked like a giant fish. 'So? Which one would you like?'

I pointed at the blue and green scales.

'Mermaid,' she nodded, 'goes well with your eyes.'

I got on the train with a plastic bag that contained a fish-themed skirt, a t-shirt with inbuilt waist puller-inner and inflatable breasts. On my face was a ridiculous grin. Why did this feel so fun? I would have to keep my rubber tail and breasts away from chlorine, which would damage it, the lady had explained with a straight face. With a straight face! As if I was planning to pop to The Pyramids swimming pool and have a go at the flume rides dressed like this.

'Fancy dress?' the train ticket guy caught me with my fingers in shiny scales.

'For the missus,' I lied handing over my ticket. He grinned, showing me his silver tooth and scribbled on the ticket. Did he know?

At Portsmouth Harbour I felt light and excited. Beside me were tired commuters grumbling about the rain. I wanted to burst my shopping bag open and stuff their noses in the rubber so they could feel this zingy too. I felt sparkling, like a firefly full of light. So despite the ache in my leg, I walked home, not caring that my walk wasn't quite as smooth as it should be.

When I was finally home, I had that first date feel. It was weird. I unpacked the rubber. Would it seem stupid now? Out of context? A waste of the compensation money I'd got from the accident? I spread each item across the bed. It looked like I was dating Barbie and she would walk in and get dressed any minute now.

I started with the top. I'd stopped bulking up in the gym after the accident. It seemed pointless to try and be a hunk with a missing leg. I didn't want to be patched up. I didn't want to be the same person but with a bit missing. I wanted to start again, see what this new me could be. I pulled on the long rubber fish tail with its blue shimmering scales. My artificial leg made it seem more realistic, actually. I turned to admire my new shape in the mirror. I looked like a very tall mermaid-Barbie. Well, a tall, hot and sweaty mermaid Barbie, but still. I didn't feel like a bloke in the wrong place at the wrong time.

I laughed. I probably should have shaved. I wasn't exactly oozing *The Little Mermaid*. The doorbell rang.

Dan was standing there with a takeaway. His eyes bulged.

'So?' I asked him and wiggled awkwardly. He stared at my bloke head sticking out of the top of this shiny, shimmering thing. He frowned. He coughed, like he'd got something stuck in his throat. He clutched the takeaway bag, his knuckles white.

He looked like he was thinking up an excuse to leave. *I forgot the ketchup to go with the chips.* Or: *I meant to get cod but bought haddock instead, silly me I'll have to go back and never come back.* That sort of thing.

He stepped towards me. Put a rough hand on mine.

It was the first time he kissed me since I came home from hospital.

## Asylum Night
### Christine Lawrence
Map location: #24

Late for night shift again, I hurried along Locksway Road. I was not looking forward to another long night at St. James' Hospital and would have loved to have been snuggled up in front of the TV for a mindless evening of soaps.

I stood at the foot of the tree-lined avenue. The night was bright - as bright as any day. I stared at the sky; the moon was full. I pulled my jacket closer to me, shivering, and found myself drawn towards the looming ancient building, its clock tower's face grinning menacingly at me as I approached.

The trees which overhung the avenue were still - no wind, not even the slightest breeze. Everything seemed unreal, no night-owls, no rustling of creatures in the undergrowth. Just me, the night and the gothic windows of the house at the end of the drive. I was about halfway along when I noticed a figure in one of the windows staring out at me. It was a woman dressed in the uniform of a nurse from the last century. Her long dark dress was covered in a white apron, the sleeves cuffed at the wrists and her hair caught up in a triangular white head-dress, like the caps nurses wore in the time of the First World War. As I moved a little closer I waved but she didn't seem to see me.

I reached the revolving doors and pushed my way through. I was curious to meet this figure but which room was she in? I looked about me at the wood-panelled walls, at the stern faces of past medical superintendents in ornately framed portraits, proudly displaying outrageous whiskers. Eyes appeared to follow me as I walked about the room which was familiar but strange in some way. I remembered passing through this room so many times on my way to take up my duties but those memories were slipping away somehow.

The wooden-framed glass doors swung open easily as I passed through to the bottom of a sweeping staircase. I trembled a little as I took the stairs one by one, trying hard not to let their creaks echo in the hallway. I looked up at the domed skylight high above me and in the light of the moon I swear I saw a figure again, leaning over the banister, silhouetted, staring down at me. I blinked and looked again - she was gone. I wondered if I'd imagined it, shook away the fear and continued to climb up towards my fate.

The heavy-looking doors on the first floor landing were all tightly closed. I hesitated to try any of them, never having been in this part of the building before - it had always seemed to be out of bounds. In fact, I wondered what had made me venture onto the staircase at all. I waited and listened but all was silent - uncannily so. 'Pull yourself together woman,' I scolded myself, trying not to think about the tales of past residents and the early treatments for the mentally ill. I was about to take to the stairs again, still curious to find the mysterious woman I'd seen, when I heard a faint scratching sound coming from behind the double doors set in the centre of the landing.

I stood before them for what seemed like a million heartbeats, the scratching sound persistently leading me on. I gripped the door knob, felt the cold metal in my hand for a moment, hesitated and stepped back, losing my nerve. As I was about to return to the staircase, a movement caught my eye. The door knob turned by itself. 'Someone must be on the other side of the door.' I felt myself sway slightly in fear with the knowledge that I was about to come face to face with - what? Or who?

Before I could bring myself to turn and run, the door swung open to reveal a sight that I found completely confusing. A man dressed in the costume of an Edwardian gentleman stood in front of me.

'Well, Mrs. Bennett,' he smiled. 'What are you doing, wandering about on the stairs, my dear?' he reached his hand out and gripped my wrist. I tried to pull myself away but he was too strong. He dragged me into the room.

'Please, let me go,' I protested. 'What the hell is going on? Who are you?'

The doors behind me closed with a bang. Another figure entered the room. It was a woman, the woman I'd seen at the window and later on the stairs. Her long apron was crisply white, as was the starched collar at her neck and the cuffs at her wrists. Her hair was hidden by the triangular headdress of her uniform. Her eyes bore into me as she crossed the room. I struggled again, laughing nervously. 'Please let me go.' I assumed I'd wandered in on some kind of party or film set, but I had to get to work. 'I'm due on duty in five minutes and I'll be late.'

The nurse looked at me with pity in her eyes, then past me at the man. 'You were right, Doctor,' she said. 'Mrs. Bennett is deluded. We will have to start the treatment again. The sooner the better.'

'What do you mean?' I was panicking now. 'Stop this messing about, please.' Realising he looked just like one of the men in the paintings downstairs, I hesitated, then went on. 'Come on, this is silly. Some sort of game.' My mind was racing. I was sure that they must be making a film about the old asylum and I'd walked in on a rehearsal. But where were the cameras? Maybe they hadn't arrived yet. I couldn't seem to think straight.

'Just give me a moment, Nurse.' The man was speaking over my head. He turned to me. 'Now, Mrs. Bennett, we have given you a lot of time with the new psycho-analytical treatment and yet you still seem no better than when you first arrived two years ago.'

'Two years!' I screamed. 'What on earth are you going on about? I work here. I've worked here for two years. I'm on my way to the ward for night duty. I have a family at home waiting for me.'

'It's alright Mrs. Bennett.' The nurse was speaking now, her voice soft and soothing. 'You're safe now, back at the asylum. We'll take good care of you.'

The doctor smiled as he spoke but what he said next sent a bolt of cold fear through me.

'I'm afraid we will have to start the hydrotherapy treatment again, Nurse. And I think some time in the padded cell in a straight-jacket, for her own good, you understand, just to calm her down.'

Of course I struggled. I screamed and kicked, thinking of my husband and children waiting at home in the morning. They would be wondering where I was and why I hadn't come home from work. The more I fought, the worse it got. At first I thought I could get away and I did break free from their grasp but before I reached the doors they flew open and there stood four more nurses, all dressed in the same old fashioned uniforms. One of them held a straight-jacket, just like the one in the museum in town. I still believed they were playing some kind of misguided and evil trick on me but here I am in this padded cell, trussed up with the promise of being forced into a bath of running water as soon as the day staff come on duty.

## Orpheus and the Spice Island Nymphs
**William Sutton**
*Map location: #9*

'Finding things as is missing something of a speciality,' said
Worm, 'with a sideline in unfinding things as may be better off lost.'

It was the Scotland Yard fellow, Lawless, who gave me my first
whiff of the Nymphs of the Underworld; but it was his little
messenger, Worm, who put me on the scent of my fantastical quest.
You see, since Eurydice vanished...

Ridiculous name, I know. But she was at least half-Greek; and
when first I saw her dance, I thought her the closest thing to a nymph
I had ever seen. When first I saw her dance, by Baffins Pond...

When Eurydice vanished, and the Gosport police proved useless, I
took the train to London and trudged across the snowy bridge to
Scotland Yard.

'Abducted, sir?' Sergeant Lawless tried to be gentle. 'She may have
been, sir. Smuggled away to a Turkish harem. Fanged by a serpent,
and gone to the nether world. She may have been, but it's most likely
she's gone wilfully. You scared her off with toil and drudgery; too
many beatings, or not beatings enough. People are free to do as they
wish, and the police shan't meddle in household affairs.'

'But Sergeant, that's simply not the scenario. We're intimates,
conjoined in art and love. Since first I saw her dance, that day upon
Hampstead Heath, willowy limbs, dark eyes, skin as lovely as can
be...' I stammer to describe my world, vanished with her strange
evanishment.

He raises a hand, sympathetical like. 'Mr O'Fahy, I cannot help you.'

I should have no help to find Eurydice. I had already stomped and stamped, shrieked and wailed, wrecked my home, rent my cheeks, torn my clothes, shorn my hair, kissed her portrait, blest her eyes, missed her, cursed her, missed her.

Of this operatic grief, the Sergeant heard only the pale echoes, yet he shivered as if the shades had trailed their fingers down his neck. 'I can't. But I may know someone who can.'

'Worm, sir, of the Euston Square Worms, public company as yet unlimited. Finding things as is missing something of a speciality, with a sideline et cetera et cetera.'

I met Worm by Seven Dials, a filthy spot for dirty business. As the snow fell faintly down, I told him my woes.

'Mr O'Fahy,' said the urchin most sympathetical like, notwithstanding the whiff of sewer life he exuded. 'Indeed Maestro, if I am not mistaken, for I seen you in the military band down Wilton's Music Hall. Your troubles stir the old heart, common though they be in these days of abductions, garottings, knifings, beheadings, rape, pillage, plunder and politic collusion. My Worms are a dab hand at finding what is missing et cetera. But for this, I'll need to invoke the very gods of the earth. Advance us five quid, and I'll make enquiries among my Pompey associates. See you next week at the Gosport dock.'

My hearth lay bare and cheerless. I raged. I raved. Bit my nails, tore my hair. Such hopes I had, retiring from the naval band, to make my Gosport home a haven of creative endeavour, alongside my Eurydice. Since first I saw her dance by Baffins Pond—

'Maestro O'Fahy?' Worm took me by surprise. 'It's a poser you've posed, and no mistaking.'

'But can you do it?'

He gazed at me, his eyes a brilliant blue 'No, old cove.' He wiped his nose pleasantly on his sleeve. 'But I'll tell you who can.'

Worm led me down to the ferryman by the Stygian water. 'You wouldn't have a couple of shekels, old cove?'

Two obols, perhaps he meant. I would gladly have paid but I had brought only my instrument. So I played.

The ferryman's pockmarked face was stern as a skull. Yet at the first notes he yielded. The oars plashed rhythmically over, ever nearer Eurydice.

Three guard dogs fought at the gates of that shadowy underworld. I struck up my song. Straightway, they lay becalmed, and we passed by, toward the palaces of the lost and debased.

The king stared in wonder. 'Are you still alive? Only we don't normally get your type down here, my friend.' Hades glared at Worm. 'Call yourself a psychopomp? You're meant to bring those so far ruined I may leach the final vestiges of life from them.'

I told my tale: evanishment, torn clothes, finding things as is et cetera.

Hades was unmoved.

I told how we met, when first I saw her dance. Even he, even here, could not be immune to love. He laughed: actually laughed. Still no help to find Eurydice.

I comforted myself the only way I know how. The song of love escapes unbidden from my fingers. And his queen, Persephone—the grimmest bawd you ever saw—gripped her black husband's arm, as my music melted her icy heart.

'Maestro O'Fahy, stop, I beg you.' She asked for a daguerreotype; I sketched Eurydice dancing. She asked of her accents; I played in out the sweet music of Eurydice's voice. They asked for five quid; I wrote a cheque. 'Give us a moment.'

Amid those degraded spirits, fallen bodies, these nymphs of the underworld, I lost myself in a haze of whisky and laudanum. A minute, an hour, a week. I knew not, nor cared, if I might find my Eurydice.

Worm shook me to my senses. He led me to the balcony to view the bawd house floor. My heart leapt. And there, among the lost spirits, the dead souls, I saw—the tangled hair, the dark eyes, the skin as lovely as can be—Eurydice.

I felt upon my shoulder Hades' icy hand.

'Two conditions, my friend, consequent upon a further payment of fifty guineas—and we'll have no more infernal plucking. If you take her, she is yours, and you must do with her as you please. Only I warn you, do not look too close, lest the nymph of your heart melt back to the underworld.'

Back to the river, footsteps behind me, my heart singing. Worm showed us discreetly to our boat. And there, in the shadows, I took her in my arms, and I held her, and I had her.

Then, as the mist cleared arose, I looked... I saw... this was not my Eurydice. This hateful creature? This? This was a pitiful, hateful, painted creature, a ruined imitation of my Eurydice.

What happened I cannot quite tell.

As I came to my senses, the boy Worm was looking at me. The oars plashed through the ice, the boat otherwise empty. Had I thrust her from me, back to that underworld which had consumed her? Or did I toss that mocking shadow into the river of forgetfulness, thinking to throw with it my love? Worm handed me my instrument. And ever since, I play, and forever play, for Eurydice.

## Old Harry and the King of the Sea People
## Matt Wingett
*Map location: #11*

Old Harry was a drinker, that's for sure. From early in the hungover morning till late in the legless night, booze gripped him as tight as he gripped his bottle.

In the venerable institution called The Coal Exchange at Portsmouth Point, where once the young Nelson (alongside other heroes innumerable) had stumbled out to give its walls a watering, he sat each day and watched the big ships.

The sea. *Lifeblood of the Empire* he called it as the afternoon light seeped through the window and the booze hoisted a limp pennant of nostalgia in his soul. 'God Save the King.'

'What's that, you old soak?' Angus, the ginger-haired landlord called affably across the bar at the Salt, who had just that moment ranged an expectant pay parade of big copper pennies and tiny silver sixpences on the table.

All to no avail, as it turned out. With a glance at the clock, Angus lifted the hinged bar and announced to the tobacco-and-sweat-smelling saloon: 'Time, gentlemen, please. Drink up, now!'

Old Harry flinched and glared at his coins. *Five bells! Damn it! I lost track! Three and a half hours till evening opening.*

Most days when he stumbled three sheets to the wind into the diesel-sweet sea air, he nipped a worn hip flask from his pocket for a plug of Nelson's Blood, smacked his lips and laughed at bamboozling the beak and all his idiot licensing laws. On this particular day, however, his rum ration was dry.

'Bugger,' he said and marched back to the pub for a quick off sale - *on the Q.T.*, so to speak. But no. Angus, always a stickler for King's Regulations, signalled no through the frosted glass door.

'Oh come on,' Old Harry cajoled, pushing the handle as the Landlord slid the bolt home.

'Half two,' Angus called cheerily through the door. 'Go on. On your way, Harry. I've got to go out.'

Harry kicked the frame and came about to face the unpleasant truth that today reality might just slip a torpedo through the submarine net. That meant facing the wife sober with the swelling shiner he'd dispensed last night, and meeting his grown-up kids straight, something he hadn't done for three years. *Pub closing time. It's not civilised. This is 1951, after all!*

A Destroyer, two tugs in attendance, black smoke pluming from her stack, served to remind him of his Navy years.

'God I miss those days,' he said to a vision of native girls waving from the wharf as he made port somewhere exotic, his wallet bulging. 'That's what life's about. Loose women and drink - both at a fair rate of exchange.'

He wheeled to glare at The Coal Exchange and to his sudden pleasure, saw red-headed Angus bump through the front door encumbered with a bicycle and a flat cap. With a quick push and swing of the leg, Angus launched himself up Broad Street.

Now, Old Harry had been through that door so many times he knew it better than his own. He also knew that Smudge Smith had strained the lock while he and two doxies swung on it while offering to the world a boisterous rendition of *All The Nice Girls Love A Sailor, And I've Got Two Right Here* just the night previous.

He listened closely to the breeze with the growing conviction that he could hear his name upon it.

'Come to us, come to us, Harry!' A chorus of siren voices called him. *Yes!* The bottles inside were crooning his name.

After a quick push and a kick at the bottom of the door, a drunken survey of the saloon bar confirmed every soak's dream: alone in a boozer!

Licking his lips and rubbing his hands he grinned gleefully at the spiritual delights before him. He placed his trembling hand on the hinged counter, his personal gateway to oblivion, then...

'Good afternoon,' said a sing-song Scottish voice from nowhere.

Old Harry spun on his heel to see, seated by the window a small, powerfully-built fellow who might have been a boy had it not been for the thick red mutton chops framing his delicate face. He appraised Old Harry with girlish eyes.

'Who the Devil are you?' Old Harry blurted.

'A visitor,' the other replied. 'Doon from the Highland and Islands. Dull at hame. - Bonny, nae doobt. But droochit. Glabber everywhere!'

'What?' Harry said, his face contorted in confusion.

'Glabber. Mud, you call it.'

'Oh.'

Harry lifted the counter and stepped behind the bar, staring all the while at the newcomer.

'Pour me a drink!' the Little Man called.

'That's the ticket!' Old Harry called back with relief, slapping his palms together. 'A man after my own heart.'

'Couldn't do it, mysel',' the other explained. 'Iron strip on the bar. Allergic to iron. All my folk are.'

'Well, I'm here, now, little fellah,' Harry answered absently as he surveyed the lines of bottles, serried like sailors on parade. 'Don't you worry 'bout no allergies.'

He brought his sights to bear on the single malts: Laphraoig, Talisker, Dalmore, Glenfarclas, Macallan. Liquid gold glittering behind glass. He ran his finger along the bottles with childish delight as his tongue licked his lower lip.

'Here's the rule,' said the midget, annoyed at the interloper's poor manners. 'Seniority. I drink first. It's just polite. Do that, then good luck to ye.'

The words washed past Old Harry as he lifted down the '42

Macallan, poured himself a hefty slug, then tucked the bottle under his arm.

'Bring it here!' Yelled the Little Man with growing impatience. As an afterthought he added: 'Bring yourself a glass, too,'

Harry put the bottle, his brimming glass and the Little Man's empty tumbler on the table.

'Very good,' said the other, grabbing Harry's full measure.

'Hey!'

The Little Man raised an arresting palm. 'Smoke before we drink.'

Harry glared and dispensed a hefty slug into the second tumbler then lifted it to his lips. The Little Man shot him a black look.

'Seniority, remember? Not impressed with English manners. No, no. There's far more respect for royalty in Scotland.'

Old Harry slammed the glass down and roared with laughter. 'Royalty?' he said, slapping his leg heartily. 'Scotch mist more like!'

Something in the Little Man's expression made his laughter choke in his throat. He watched with puzzled eyes as the other stuffed his pipe with leaf, struck a match indignantly and filled the room with sweet-smelling smoke.

'What do you mean, royalty?' the Englishman asked, sceptically.

'Exactly that. Ancient royalty. From a line that lives in the secret places of the North. On desolate shores. Where rocky bays roar. My people come ashore to meet in fairy rings in the woods and speak of old times together.' He lifted a bushy red eyebrow and said pointedly. 'Where the bee sucks, there lurk I. We bring fortune to your sort. Good and bad. We favour some. Others... we curse.'

'Hahahaha! Curse? Curse!' Old Harry roared. 'Where's your bundle of heather, eh, Gypsy Joe?' He wheezed at his own joke.

'Not a gypsy. Crógach, King of the Seonaidh - the Sea People.'

'King of the seven dwarves, more like! Where's Snow White, then, Grumpy?' He howled again, mighty pleased with his own line in humour.

Crógach's eyes narrowed and his body shook. He gazed furiously upon the Englishman, who just before sinking his first glass of golden fluid toasted him with a mocking - 'Splice the mainbrace, Sneezy!'

The Little Man fumed as Old Harry poured another and knocked that one back, too, this time with 'Down the hatch, Dopey!'

He poured another and said, 'Absent friends, eh Bashf -'

The Little Man, seeing where this was going, cut him off:

'Don't say I didn't warn ye.' Then with an ironic 'Slainte Mha!' he knocked back his own glass, glowering all the while. 'Remember, I drink first and good luck to ye. Works roundwise, too. Ye drink first - and bad luck to ye!'

Harry sneered and wafted his hand, as if the Little Man had just made a very bad smell. 'That's one dwarf who's not Happy!'

'Right! That's it! I'll grant ye three wishes...' the Little Man said, a threatening edge in his voice. He snatched the bottle from the old sailor and emptied the last of it into his glass and muttered under his breath, 'Ye'll see.'

Old Harry glowered for a second, then laughing, tottered to the bar and brought over the Glenfarclas.

'Three wishes,' the Little Man insisted.

'That's easy, Doc,' Old Harry slurred. 'There's only three things I want in life. The first is to be back aboard ship!' His eyes defocused in a dream of imperial glory for 20 seconds. Then he muttered - 'Oh, now look who's Sleepy' and started to nod and snore a little.

The Little Man poked him angrily in the ribs with a bony finger. 'What else?'

'What else what?' Old Harry twitched back to wakefulness.

'Second wish.'

'Always to have a whisky bottle nearby!' He lifted the Glenfarclas to the light and kissed it.

'Your third?'

'My third. Hahaha. I know. That's easy! Never to leave this pub ever again!'

And with those words, just as if a press gang had blackjacked him, he dropped into unconsciousness.

When he woke, he was lying on a wooden floor. In the walls were neat ornate windows. A desk nearby had a chart and sextant on it and some ship's biscuits on a plate. A picture on the wall showed a Little Man in a wooded clearing sitting on a toadstool. *Strangely familiar, that figure in a Tam O'Shanter*, Old Harry thought after he'd groaned back to full consciousness.

He was in a ship's cabin. Indeed, there above his pounding head was the hammock he'd just fallen out of.

Dragging himself off the floor, he looked out at the weird foggy air and saw land in the far distance. Pushing the window open and poking his head out, he realised he was aboard an old tall ship, its wooden walls painted in black and tan. How he'd got here he had no idea, but he was reassured to see, through the strangely distorting air, they were just sailing into - yes - Portsmouth Harbour.

A shadow filled the sky. The ship rocked so violently he was forced to grip the window frame to prevent being hurtled across the cabin. Then the whole structure lurched on its side!

'All hands to the pumps,' he shouted instinctively to an imagined crew. 'Prepare to broach!'

A massive orb moved along the outside of the ship, white with a black circle inside a blue one and shot with reds. It disappeared. Then with a jolt and slide the ship righted and came to rest.

Old Harry scurried above decks to assess the damage.

'I should have fixed that lock!' Angus said the moment he walked in. Two empty glasses on the table bore witness to the crime. 'Ach! Thieves, breaking in and drinking my best whisky!'

Whoever they were, he decided, they weren't so bad. In fact, he was more puzzled than angry - because they'd left him a gift.

'Now that is queer,' he thought, as he hefted it in his hands and turned it on its side to examine the extraordinary workmanship, bringing his eye close up to it. 'Beautiful! I'll keep it safe, up here,' he thought, and placed it on a high shelf over the bar.

It was a whisky bottle, and far more than that, too. For in that whisky bottle was the most uncannily wrought model of a tall ship he'd ever seen, the sails billowing as if it were racing across the ocean, white capped waves overtopping the bowsprit while seagulls wheeled above. The model was painted startlingly realistically and fashioned with minute precision, even down to the brightwork. A thing of almost magical wonder.

'I wonder where Old Harry is?' he thought, placing the old boy's pint of Brickwoods on the bar, ready for him to breeze in. 'I mean, he almost lives here.'

Then, as if from afar off, he thought for a moment he could hear a high-pitched voice, frantically calling.

'Angus! Angus!'

But no, he shook his head and greeted the funny-looking compatriot of his, who the previous night had rented a room from him for a few days.

'What'll it be?' Angus asked.

'Whisky, always whisky,' said the other with his peculiar curt way of talking. Then, with a wry look, he glanced up at the bottle on the high shelf and chuckled to himself.

Above, in that tiny ship-in-a-bottle, Old Harry's desperate shouts were drowned by vengeful laughter echoing all around.

## A Pear Fell to Earth
## Gareth Rees

Jeremy arrived in class still wearing his black motorcycle leathers. His forehead was shiny with sweat and he said he'd only left Lyme Regis an hour ago. You'd think he'd run all the way rather than sitting on a saddle and letting his big Harley do all the work.

'Greetings, Revered Teacher,' said Anne the Fan, making an elaborate curtsy at the same time. She was teasing him, of course. He'd often had a go at us for referring to him as our teacher. 'Teaching is a great job,' he said, 'but it's sometimes more about being a government screw than an agent of enlightenment.' He knew a lot of us had issues with authority and saw it as another word for making you feel small and bad about yourself. He knew we wouldn't get much done if he was seen as yet another social worker or a police officer trying to be chummy.

He said that, if we had to give him a title, we could call him a facilitator. He explained the heuristic method to us, a way of discovering answers for ourselves instead of somebody sitting in front of the class and dishing them out. His job was to maybe offer hints or clues which we'd chew over until maybe some light bulb inside would light up and there'd be understanding.

Usually, the class started with him writing down some strange stuff on the board and then asking us to ruminate for a while and see what thoughts might be triggered by what he'd written. I say the stuff he wrote was strange but usually it was related to what we'd been discussing the week before.

Here is what he wrote down at the class yesterday evening in the room we used at the school for children with Down's Syndrome: The Ongoing Chemical Reformation Company. Theatrical Melancholy. A Pear Fell to Earth.

The Chemical Reformation Company? Was this connected to what Benny had been saying the week before. Benny's not his real name. Benny's short for **B**enzedrine. But now he's Benny the Boffin because he knows about science. He used to watch Open University when he couldn't get to sleep.

We'd been talking about death and about whether it was the foundation stone of being bothered about stuff, the great worry upon which all lesser worries hang. Jeremy suggested the bother might be a waste of time because we don't actually know that death is bad news. We don't know that life doesn't carry on after the body stops breathing.

'I bloody hope it doesn't,' said Dismal Donna from Merthyr Tydfil.

Anyway, Benny said about how nature doesn't divide the world into black and white, right and wrong or life and death. 'There's no death in nature,' he said. 'It's just an ongoing chemical rearrangement process. We can get upset if we want by a rotten, stinking corpse. But, in nature, rot and death are just a bacterial rock and roll show.'

'Theatrical melancholy?'

Well, we'd been talking about depression, not wanting to get out of bed in the morning or the afternoon even. Most of us had experience of this but nobody competed with Mike the Artist. He said he lost heart when he lost his job as a technical drawer at the Ministry of Defence and hardly got out of bed for two years.

'So depression is a problem?' said Jeremy. 'They called it melancholy in the old days. It was something that happened. These days it's not supposed to happen. It's a problem. And maybe this makes it worse. Maybe the problem's the problem. What do you think?'

Typical Jeremy. Once he asked how we knew a letter box was red. It does your head in thinking about questions like that.

'Yeah, depression, that's what doctors call it. It's like it's not normal to be depressed. But it is.' So said Barmy the Bishop and, as he spoke, he rose from his chair and waved his arms about. His eyes flashed like a light-bulb on the blink. He's a bit alarming sometimes, like a scarecrow that's come alive. He told us in a coffee break he needed to go to a church in Kentucky so he could test his faith in the Lord by shoving his hands in a box full of writhing rattlesnakes. If his faith was solid, he wouldn't be harmed. If he was bitten, well he'd know he'd been fooling himself.

Barmy's voice got louder. 'It's not like a few people have got the pox and most people haven't. Everybody's sick. It's in the beginning of the Bible Book of Genesis, the human race got chucked out of Paradise. It's a bad condition to be in. The human race said no to the Lord's command and finished up like Cain in the Land of Nod. People call it depression but it's not like something just for oddballs. The whole human race inherited trouble from Adam and Eve. No, don't let them send you to the doctor. Only one way out. Speak to the Lord. Tell him you've strayed but you wanna go home now.'

The Bishop whirled his arms to complete his point and, in doing so, knocked Anne the Fan's bag off an empty chair. Bottles of tablets fell out of it, enough to stock a chemist, and scattered across the floor. Anne, as she scooped them up, was heard to mutter, 'Gor blimey, love a duck'. Her restraint was commendable. In spite of the provocation, she abided by the group decision to avoid swearing.

Barmy sat down and covered his face with his hands as though he was in despair. I looked outside the window where I could see the pink of a cherry blossom tree swaying slightly in the evening breeze. The sky was blue. And then my little holiday in this other world was ended when I heard another voice. It was opposite to Barmy's which was as good on the ears as finger nails scratching a blackboard. This voice was soft as silk and belonged to the normally quiet Toper Tom. He raised his chin from his chest and said, 'May I say something?'

Flipping through TV channels the other night, I paused at the sight of a man conducting an orchestra. The man turned out to be

Simon Rattle and he looked just like Toper Tom. He has long, wavy, ash blond hair and wears drainpipe tartan trousers, a cream white shirt and a charcoal waistcoat. He's only an occasional member of the group because Jeremy won't let him in if he's got alcohol on his breath. Some of us reckon it's partly because it opens up Jeremy's own box of snakes.

Anyway, Toper Tom who studied the Dark Ages or Persian at Oxford University and then joined the army began to tell us about Fred the Centurian tank-driver. 'A lovely man,' he said, 'never had an ill word for anyone and always made you laugh. We were out on an exercise in the middle of the night in Germany. It could have been boring and uncomfortable but Fred had us all in giggles. But it wasn't funny when he drove the tank through a garden wall and crushed someone's vegetable garden. When we got back to the depot, I told Fred that what happened in the village didn't really happen and that it would be best to paint over the scratches on the tank before higher authority woke up. Well, he not only painted over the scratches, he painted the entire tank. The only problem was that he used pink paint instead of camouflage green. Higher authority when it did wake up was not amused and Fred eventually found himself locked up in the military prison at Colchester. I did see Fred again. By chance, I bumped into him in a pub about a year ago. It was a shock. The experience of prison had changed him and after prison he'd gone to a psychiatric hospital. When I met him in the pub, I hardly recognised the man I once knew. His love of life, his humour had vanished. He had dead-dog eyes, was suspicious and seemed not to want to communicate.' Tom finished his story and said to Jeremy, 'My friend didn't have a problem, not to begin with. He was foolish maybe, not understanding how vicious serious people can be sometimes. It was other people saying he had a problem, calling him a criminal or a nutter, which was the problem. Is this what you had in mind, Jeremy, when you said calling something a problem makes the problem?'

But it wasn't Jeremy's voice that came next. Wolfy Lopez decided to have a say. 'You saying my mother doesn't have a problem? It's her doctor who's got the problem because he told her the cancer had spread too far and she'd better sort out her affairs. You saying it's the doctor who's got the problem and my mother doesn't. And settling her affairs doesn't come into it 'cause she's got no affairs to settle, that's if 'affairs' means money.'

Well, the group went silent after this and the subject of theatrical melancholia evaporated like a stream in the desert.

But why was melancholy theatrical?

When we were talking about depression, everybody agreed you only add to the grief by bottling it up. But if you spill it, people walk away because listening to moaning is like subjecting yourself to Chinese drip torture.

We decided there were two types of people. Some people express their grief and then it's like they've laid down a heavy load. Feeling lighter, they're ready to get back aboard the life train. Other people, the moaners, they want to keep the heavy load and add to it so they can stay in the sick bed. These, I think, are what Jeremy called the theatrical melancholics. Jeremy should write for 'The Daily Mail'.

A Pear Fell to Earth? The only time I remember the subject of pears coming up was when Mike the Artist told me about the wonderful pear juice he drank when he was in Florence. Oh yes, and then Jeremy said about falling asleep underneath a fig tree in the same part of the world and being woken up when a fig landed on his head.

Anyway, we were heading off to the pub after last week's session and Jeremy, noticing a big bunch of keys hanging off Benny's belt, said to him, 'Do you guard what you say with the same care as you guard your things? Do you make sure that everything you say has psycho-dynamic significance and lightens the load of the world?'

Benny said, 'What's that psycho word you used?' And Jeremy who can be quite lordly at times, said, 'Psych-dynamic. Look it up when you get home.'

Well, I obviously I did otherwise I wouldn't be able to say that the words he wrote about the pear were, for me, quite psych-dynamic.

Have I actually experienced this, I asked myself, hearing a pear fall to earth with a little thud? Well, maybe not a pear.

It was an away-day from the city village and the terrorising of the petty tyrannies. Well, that's the beauty of getting away. Very bad stuff becomes petty bad stuff. How could it not be so in the beauty of the Hampshire countryside in the magical light of a sunny, late summer day? We were laying on the warm grass in a pub garden when there was a little thud. It was an apple that had fallen to earth just next to my head. It felt like being firmly but quite gently woken up to life and it was like happiness in a moment.

## Dribble
## Diana Bretherick
*Map location: #17*

Have you noticed that whenever horror strikes there is always a before and an after? In Jack's case the before was nothing special - a placid normality that required no thought for its progression. But his after, though dark and terrifying, was still a delicate little thing, always hungry and always needing to be fed.

That night when his before was so brutally transformed, he was walking along the beach in the crisp, cold darkness breathing in the solitude with the salt and the seaweed. As was so often the case these days he had been tossing and turning on his own sea of crumpled sheets and disarrayed blankets. It had seemed an excellent idea to calm himself with a stroll by the Solent. When he looked back of course, the source of his discomfort seemed so trivial. It was after all merely a matter of love. But then the fact of his rejection by the young woman he had thought of as his soul mate was overwhelming him to the extent that he could think of nothing else. Fresh sea air was exactly what he needed to clear his head, or so he thought.

When he first caught sight of the bundle of rags on the beach Jack had thought it was a piece of flotsam and jetsam washed up by the tide, but as he drew closer he could see that it was the body of a young man, probably of an age similar to his own. He was lying half in and half out of the sea with the waves creeping gently around his legs. Jack pulled him out of the water and up onto a ridge of pebbles and set about seeing if there was any life left in his find. He knew what to do. His grandfather had shown him often enough. The sea was a dangerous place even for the most experienced of fishermen. There weren't many of them left it was true, but for those that remained it was as well to know how to bring a drowning man back from the dead.

This time he did not have to do much. As he lay the body on its side the man began to choke up the salty water he had evidently swallowed. After a while, with a little help he sat up but was still shivering with cold and damp. Jack removed his jacket and placed it around the man's shoulders.

'Thanks,' he said, his voice trembling slightly. He looked straight at Jack. 'But you shouldn't have saved me.'

'Oh come now. It can't be as bad as that, can it?' Jack said.

'You do not know what you have done.'

Jack stared at him. His skin had a greenish tinge as if he belonged in the water.

'Are you saying that you tried to drown yourself?'

There was no answer. The young man merely continued to look out to sea, his eyes full of yearning, as if he longed to be back amongst the waves. Jack followed his line of sight. It was a clear night here on the mainland but he could see that the Isle of Wight was shrouded in mist. A few lights were visible but nothing more. The sea itself was strangely calm. The waves, such as they were, lapped rather than broke onto the shore and the moonlight was reflected in the water almost as surely as a mirror. All was silent except for the sound of breathing.

'I don't know what has made you do this but whatever it is, you should put it behind you and start again,' Jack said.

The young man laughed but there was no humour in it, just bitterness. 'Even if I did, nothing would change. My affliction would still be with me. The only cure for it is death.'

'Explain yourself,' Jack said.

'Why should I? It will not help.'

'I saved your life. You owe me something.'

The young man roared with despair and misery. 'I owe you

nothing!'

'At least tell me your name.' Jack said.

'I am Friday.'

'And I am Thursday,' came another voice. Jack stared at the young man. The second voice seemed to have come from inside him. His lips had not moved at all.

'How did you do that?' Jack asked in wonder.

'Well he ain't no ventriloquist!' said the inside voice, harsh and nasal, like a sharp nail on a blackboard. Then there was a cackle of laughter, as if the nail had gone right through Jack's ear and was piercing his brain.

Jack looked at Friday who had started to cry in huge racking sobs that seemed to engulf him.

'Cry baby, cry baby,' the second voice taunted. On and on it went, over and over again, slashing into the silence. 'Cry baby, cry baby...'

'Shut up! It's horrible!' Jack grabbed hold of Friday and started to shake him, desperate to stop the ghastly voice coming from inside him. 'Cry baby, cry baby.' In the struggle Friday's shirt began to gape and the voice seemed to get louder and louder. 'CRY BABY, CRY BABY...'

Friday stood up and threw Jack to the ground. The voice stopped.

Jack looked up and what he saw would stay with him for the rest of his days. Friday's shirt had come adrift revealing his torso. On his chest, roughly over where his heart should be, was a face. It was small and wrinkled like a goblin in a fairy tale. Its mouth wore a wide smile revealing sharp little teeth of varying lengths like needles and pins.

'Now do you see what you have done?' Friday cried.

'Oh stop whinging, you useless lump of shit,' Thursday said. 'It's your fault I'm here and that's a fact.'

'What did I do?' Jack asked.

'You saved my life, that's what,' Friday said.

'Till death do us part...' Thursday intoned.

'Exactly,' Friday said.

'Don't say any more, or you know what comes next,' Thursday said.

'You tried to kill yourself because of him?' Jack said. 'Is there no other way?'

Friday shook his head. 'Not unless I want to live the rest of my life with his voice in my ear... and it isn't just that.' Suddenly he cried out in pain.

'Feed me!' Thursday said.

Jack looked at Thursday whose face was contorted. Dribble ran down his sharp little chin onto Friday's chest. It ran down in rivulets leaving bright red welts in its place as if he had been lashed by a whip.

'Tell tale, tell tale, tell tale...' Thursday shouted.

'How did this happen?' Jack asked.

Friday was silent.

'It's all right, you can tell him...' Thursday said.

'I was cursed...'

'Who cursed you?'

'My brother...my twin brother.'

'Go on.'

'Yes, go on. Tell him how you wronged me...' Thursday said.

'It was an accident!' Friday said.

'Talk about brotherly love!' Thursday said.

''That's your brother?' Jack asked.

'Yes, or rather it is what is left of my brother once all that was good was eaten away,' Friday said. 'I pushed him, that was all. We were playing a game and I pushed him. He fell and hit his head. I ran over to him but he was dead, or so I thought. I picked him up in my arms and hugged him. All I wanted was for him to wake up.'

'So was he dead, or not?' Jack asked, puzzled.

'It depends what is meant by death, I suppose, but his body was no longer alive, that was for sure.'

'What happened then?'

'I lied and told my parents that he had slipped. No one questioned

207

it. We buried him and that was that...or at least I thought so.'

'You didn't get rid me of me that easily though, did you?'
Thursday said.

Friday looked down at him and sighed. 'A few weeks later I
started to feel an itching in my chest. When I looked it seemed like a
pimple...but then it grew and grew, first into a boil and then, as it got
bigger and bigger, it began to develop features...until it turned into
this.'

Jack stared at him. 'Didn't you try to find help?'

'I was too ashamed. Every time I tried to talk to someone he
would say something insulting and make it seem as if it was coming
from me. I can control him up to a point, as you have seen...but not
for long. So I became a recluse. And then finally I decided I could not
take it anymore.'

There was a long silence as they all sat on the ridge and
contemplated the future.

'What do you want me to do?' Jack asked finally.

'Kill me,' Friday said.

It was a simple statement but somehow it required no elaboration
or even a response. Still Jack felt that he had to offer something. 'I
can't!' he said. 'There must be another way!'

But he knew even as he protested that in order to right the wrong
he had done Friday, albeit unwittingly, he had to this for him.

'Oh no you don't! Feed me!' Thursday said. 'He screwed up his
face once more and again the acid dribble poured out of his mouth
making Friday cry out in pain.

Jack backed away. All he wanted was to turn and run away from
this nightmare, back to his before where the only thing on his mind
was his poor broken heart. But as he looked down at Friday hunched
over in agony, he knew that there was no choice. 'Tell me what to do!'
he said.

Friday managed to point towards a large rock. 'Use that, but do it
quickly!'

Jack went over and picked it up.

'I really wouldn't if I were you...' Thursday said.

'I'm sorry...'Jack said and lifted the great rock high above his shoulders. He paused for a moment but then brought it crashing down on Friday's head. The young man fell back. Jack went over to him and saw that he was still alive but only just.

'Hold me,' Friday moaned softly. Jack took him in his arms, hugging him tightly until he felt his body go limp. For a few moments he stayed there until he realised that all was strangely quiet. Quickly he pulled his friend's shirt aside. He gasped. All he could see was a chest. There were no blemishes at all. The ghastly little face had gone.

He sat there on the beach, next to Friday's body staring out to sea until he heard the frantic blowing of a whistle and some shouting. He looked round and saw a group of uniformed men running towards him. As he did so he felt a curious itching on his chest. He opened his shirt and looked down to see a small and familiar face.

'I'm hungry...' it said. Then it began to dribble.

## The Lonely Planet
## Tessa Ditner
*Map location: #21*


Angelica bashed her fist into the mattress and chucked a pillow across the hotel room. A quick mission to Earth, they had said. A few days, a month at most. They had promised. Then we'll put you onto something really challenging: celestial engineering, divine archaeology... she shrieked at the Laura Ashley headboard.

"Angelica?" Her boss appeared at the doorway. He was carrying a bag of recycling. She jumped down from the bed and straightened her cleaner's uniform.

"Hello Mr Jenkins," she said. "I was making the bed," she smoothed over a fist mark she'd left on the bedding. "It's a new exercise. You blend cleaning with a workout. It's called... piloxing."

"Nah," came a voice from behind Mr Jenkins, "you're doing it wrong."

Kate, the second hotel cleaner, had been into fitness fads at some point last year. "Piloxing is Pilates and boxing, not pillows."

"Maybe it's the other one," Angelica shrugged.

"Listen," Mr Jenkins said, "seeing as we're all here. A quick staff meeting..."

"Evening class!" Kate shouted and left.

"Since when?" Mr Jenkins called out but didn't try to stop her. He'd just re-tweeted an article called *Relax! You'll Be More Productive* and was trying not to be a twittocrite, if that was a thing. Even though Mr Jenkins was only 34, he often felt like a dinosaur.

Angelica leaned over to take the bag of recycling he was holding.

"It's not what it looks like," he told her. He untied the rubber band and showed her its content. Inside were hundreds of empty bottles of guest shampoo, conditioner and body wash.

"Evidence," he whispered. "It's in my blood."

"Shampoo?"

"Criminal investigation. Had I not taken over the running of this place, I was on my way to becoming a pretty good constable, and this, Angelica, is evidence of your colleague's kleptomania."

Angelica didn't like the sound of that. Kate was her friend, sort of.

"Maybe she was framed," she suggested. Marc took out a mini bottle of nettle-infused body wash.

"Oh sure, maybe Barbie set up a hair salon in her garage?"

"Yes!" Angelica nodded.

They didn't have sarcasm in heaven. She had been posted to Earth six months ago on a specific mission to protect a portal to heaven. Six months wasn't a long time for a typical posting, but it was her first and she wasn't used to spending long periods of time in human form. It still felt like she was wearing full body armour made of heat packs. And everyone felt horribly close, like being pressed up against bodies in a fart-filled lift. And of course she missed her wings. Not having wings to get around felt like driving up the M1 in a shopping trolley.

The portal she was protecting lay hidden under the fitted sheet of the hotel's biggest double bed. It looked like an extra layer of foam, but when the chosen one lay on it, the whole platform would activate and turn into an intergalactic flume ride. The hotel, and frankly the city, was quite run down. Angelica was disappointed by this. She'd expected 'the island city' of her first ever mission to be Hong Kong or New York. They'd seen documentaries about human behaviour such as *Sex and the City* and it looked sort of fun. The fact that she did the same thing every day in the same disguise felt rather... well, it was better for the portal, something about tall buildings having bigger roots.

Angelica's first shopping trip on Earth had been the hardest. She didn't need to eat, but she wanted to blend in, so she went to Waitrose. Copying the other shoppers, she picked out vegetables and dropped them into her trolley. She had no idea what anything was. Not being able to see colour didn't help, but she made up for it in enthusiasm. She walked up to the fish counter and took a large salmon from the chipped ice, rubbed its lovely scales and was about to drop it in her trolley when the lady behind the counter squealed. It made no sense, but people were staring, so she dropped the fish back on the ice and walked off towards a wall of shiny pillow-shapes. They contained chips, she discovered later, when she sat on the packet and it popped open.

Angelica, despite her initial disappointment, soon found that she was intrigued by the people who stayed at the hotel. A few days in the building had a magical effect on some couples. They'd go from riddled with tension (veins pulsating, twitching eyes, stress-wrinkles, fingers tapping phones...) to smiling, almost woozy. In heaven you didn't have off days, love was love, like a consistent pulse running through everyone. When Angelica asked Kate to elucidate, Kate, ever the reductivist, explained it was due to: "Loads of shagging, obvs."

Mr Moore was another regular who fascinated Angelica. He was lazy, but saw himself as a Herculean demi-god. Kate joked that Mr Moore would rather starve than reach for the room service menu on his bedside table. This didn't make sense to Angelica. She didn't understand that human sight was made of rainbows. On his latest visit, Mr Moore, who had been told of Angelica's 'quirkiness' from Kate, had claimed not only to believe the pale-looking cleaner, but that he would be the ideal candidate for the portal.

"I'd do a fabulous job!" he ranted, producing a box of Thorntons from under the duvet. "Divorced," he munched, "no strings attached. I've always fancied myself a travel journalist. Sipping cocktails in Honolulu..."

"They're not looking for that sort," Angelica explained folding fresh towels for his en suite. "They need the sort who will lean into volcanoes."

"I've leaned into loads of volcanoes," he pointed a chocolate at her accusingly. "Just last week I leaned into a volcano. Then there was the other volcano the other week. Just because I've put on a bit of weight... it's always the Bear Grylls of this world..."

"Did he try and lure you into his bed?" Kate asked Angelica later.

"No."

"It must be so relaxing being plain," Kate mused, fiddling with a huge, glittering necklace. "I, on the other hand, am like fly tape to perverts."

"Where did you get that?"

"A guest didn't trust the safe," Kate pouted innocently. "Asked me to wear it until the end of her stay."

"How long is that?"

"She left yesterday. Probably wants me to keep it as a tip."

Angelica was as intrigued by Kate's kleptomania as she was by Mr Moore's Thornton lock-ins.

Later that month, when Kate had completed just over half of her *Therapy for Beginners* evening classes, she decided to confront Angelica. Kate thought Angelica was nuts, which was fantastic as she would be able to use her as a case study. The problem was working out *which* mental illness applied to Angelica.

"Okay, so if you're an angel explain this," Kate asked, finding Angelica mid-bath scrub. "What's up with those confession sex lines in churches?"

"Confessionals," Angelica corrected her, spraying Mr Muscle into the grime. "And they're not just for conversations about sex. You can confess other sins too."

"Like what?"

"Like bumping into someone and forgetting their name. Or stealing. Stealing's a good one."

"Yeah but why go to a church? You can put it on Facebook. And why do they sit in the dark and wear dog collars?"

"Yes, well... that's not my department. I'm here on a specific mission to keep the portal safe."

"I reckon you have delusions of grandeur," Kate said trying to see her wisdom teeth in the mirror. "Learnt it in class. Means you think you're an angel, but you're just a cleaner and you've done nothing with your life. So you invent another version of yourself, as a coping mechanism."

"So why can't I see colours?" Angelica asked. "And why can't I swear? And why do I look like this when I've been alive for three hundred years? And why don't I have a belly button?"

"You don't have a belly button?"

Angelica made to unbutton her uniform but Kate quickly stopped her. "I don't do horror films," she said. "Anyway what do they know? My cousin has a place in Magaluf, he says the locals don't age neither. There's something in the olive oil." She examined her manicure and then told Angelica. "You know he's afraid of you. That's why he hasn't sold the hotel. It's because he believes you about being an angel. Or maybe he thinks you're fit. Or maybe he's religious. Or maybe..."

"You know what," Angelica interrupted. "I don't give a hoot what Mr Jenkins thinks. I trained in 17 forms of martial arts to take this mission. I've made omelettes out of dragon eggs, slaughtered slughorns and termite grits and took a thrickstrong prisoner using mind games. And if Mr Jenkins' constable career is thwarted by my presence, he can bloody well not moan about it!" Angelica surprised herself at that outburst.

"Yeah," Kate nodded, "but it's different for him. You live forever, but he's only got twenty or thirty years and then he's dead. And if he doesn't try for constable now, then that's it. And it's all your fault."

The Mr Muscle slipped out of Angelica's hand. Her body hummed as if the heat packs were being microwaved inside her. She squealed as she got a flashback from her training. What were those classes called? Moral Dilemmas, that was it. The one module she repeatedly failed. Kate must have seen her reaction because she added. "He'd probably be a shit constable. Honest, Angie, I didn't mean it!"

"They've done it on purpose," Angelica told her friend. This had never been an ordinary work placement. They knew how hard she'd worked. It wasn't her fault if she found no logic in the Moral Dilemmas module. She sat back in the bath and tried to think. What was she supposed to do? Was there no human chosen one? Had the portal just been a puzzle or final exam? "You know that question where you have to choose who to lie across the train track?" Angelica asked Kate. "It's either a family of twelve or a suicidal murder on morphine?"

"Yeah, you put the murderer, obvs. Shove him down, chain him up! Easy."

"Why's is it obvious?"

"It just is," Kate shrugged. "You need to chill out, live a little. Men like strong women. Like Mr Jenkins. I bet he thinks I'm dead hot but 'cause he's trying to be all gentlemanly he's not going to say." *Maybe Kate isn't just a cleaner?* Angelica wondered. *Maybe Kate is part of the test.* "Go on," Kate was saying, "swear a little."

"I can't. You know I can't swear. Especially the H word."

"Just try, go ahead, say -bloody hell-."

"Bloody heeeeaaaaaaaaaa!" But try as she might, Angelica couldn't say the word 'hell'.

Instead a protective shield of choir voices filled the bath. "Did you hear that?" Angelica asked once the choir had faded.

"How's my hair?" Kate asked spotting Mr Jenkins approach.

"Clean."

"Hey, Marc," Kate said. "Is it alright if we call you Marc? Mr Jenkins is a bit..."

"Of course, Kate," he nodded efficiently. "Angelica, do you have a minute?"

"Angie's been slagging you off," Kate said, giving Angelica a wink. Angelica looked up at her teacher hopeful. *What kind of test is this?*

"Thank you for that enlightening analysis Kate," Marc sighed.

"Angelica, what are you doing in the bath?"

"Confession booth," Kate carried on. "We're doing a séance. With all this training I'm like a priest. Soon I'll have to charge for a natter. Rakin' it." Kate walked off down the corridor pausing now and then to lean against the walls in supposedly seductive ways. Angelica stood up in the bath, which was clean by now anyway. She felt what she had to say couldn't wait.

"Mr Jenkins," she said.

"Please call me Marc..."

"If you want to become a constable then you should become a constable. Because you'll be dead in twenty years."

"It's very precise," Marc laughed awkwardly. Angelica remembered too late that human beings were funny about death. "Angelica, would you..." he said. He was fiddling with a small cross around his neck. "I find you frightening, but not in a bad way. Your directness is sort of... nice. Would you like to go for a drink some time?"

Angelica concentrated on the greys that made up his face. She was trying to work out which of the two meanings of that sentence he was using.

"I don't drink liquids," she said eventually, but he was already half way out the door. She wished she didn't make people feel uncomfortable. That's why she liked Kate, Kate never felt uncomfortable.

The next guest to sleep on the portal was another regular, so Angelica didn't get her hopes up. Instead she tidied around him as he typed, knowing that he was writing the same chapter as last time. She wondered if repetition was an essential part of the human experience. She pulled out the magazine Kate had given her. Kate had explained that *Closer* was a highly psychological publication that featured the very latest in moral dilemmas and she was hoping to find some clues.

After the writer came a new guest. He had a lot of luggage. Angelica was hoovering the corridor when he reached the third floor,

*Closer* propped up. Angelica gave him a brief glance and once he'd stepped into the room it was Kate who pointed out he might be the chosen one.

"Stamp collector," Angelica said dismissively, she'd seen the big book he was carrying under his arm.

"Who even does that?" Kate mumbled.

"Not the chosen one!"

"Did you manage a little sarcasm?" Kate nudged her.

"Did I?" she grinned and then she didn't. She felt... strange. Angelica's nose stung. She could smell cooking, bacon and eggs and fresh towels. She could smell Kate's perfume and deodorant. She hurried to the room, opened the door and her eyes filled with salty water. The previously grey wallpaper was now a mural of pink petals and green thorns. The carpet and the curtains blotched with colours. She had to take a deep breath for the reds, blues and yellows to settle. And then she saw the bed. Or rather, the space where the bed had been. There was nothing but a black hole and a few stamps floating daintily towards the carpet. Angelica rushed to the portal, but it was covered in thick magma that barely budged as she bashed her fist into it. She wanted to dive through the tar-like door, go home, *be* home, instead she shrieked helplessly.

"It's okay, Love," Kate tried to hold her back, thinking *she's lost it! You move the furniture around a bit...*

"They've taken him!" Angelica bashed the floor.

"Maybe it's a sign that you're getting better?" Kate suggested. "Try to swear, Angie..."

"I can't! I can't swear!"

"Try, Love," Kate insisted.

"What's going on?" Marc rushed in.

"Hell. HELL. Shit.... SHIT!" Angelica shouted and there was no choir sound protecting her from the words. She covered her mouth and felt a growling in her stomach. She had the strange desire to rush down to the hotel kitchen and eat. She stood up and once again colours whirled. Her skin turned cold and arms wrapped around her, warm. The colours settled on Marc's face and she saw that his eyes weren't grey like before. They were worried and frightened and hopeful and green.

### The Zeitgeist Chapters (Part 2)
### Tom Harris

*This is part 2 of The Zeitgeist Chapters – the story begins in The Zeitgeist Chapters part 1.*

The door slammed behind him. He staggered across the flat into the bathroom and threw up in the sink. His hands trembled as he turned on the tap. He rinsed his mouth under the cold water and stared at the stranger in the reflection.

'What have you done? Who are you?'

This time the mirror image whispered: 'Write Jacob Jacket! Write!'

He nodded and stormed into the living room, straight for the bottle of single malt on the cabinet.

He poured a large measure in a tumbler and necked the peaty, golden liquid in one gulp. Slapping his face, he marched to the laptop and sat down at the desk in front of the window.

The word document booted up and he was calm.

As if detached from the world, his fingers raced over the keyboard as the prose flashed across the screen in a blur of perfection. In the zone, pulse steady, heart pumping, Jacob was in the eye of a perfect storm.

The cursor flashed to the right of a capital D.

It was done; but there was blood on his hands figuratively and literally.

Rising from the chair, flashing headlights drew him to the window. Wailing sirens screamed through the night, sparking images from the quayside: the parcel... the swans... the dog...

He raced across the living room and shot into the bathroom. He saw the walk-in shower first and on all fours he retched, but there was little left. Tracks of bile dripped from his chin and ran down his top as he reached up to turn on the shower. Once the water warmed he sat under the stream. The shaving mirror caught his reflection. He didn't feel his lips move, but the man looking back whispered...

'Murderer.'

Jacob watched Irene from the door. She sat at the breakfast table, drawing red-pen lines through a stick man inside her notebook. Jacob smirked at the initials of her agent that were scrawled beside the figure.

'Play nicely, or I'll tell T.J,' he whispered behind her, kissing her neck. She shot up from the chair and screamed. Her pen veered across the page and marked the table.

'You idiot, you scared the shit out of me!' She slapped his arm.

'Whoa, looks like you hit an artery,' he said. 'You could always be an illustrator if everything goes tits up.'

He turned from her but caught his repulsive reflection in the mirror. 'Murderer, murderer,' came the whisper again and again.

'Where are you, J.J?' she asked.

'I'm right here.' A corny reply. A lie. But the truth was impossible. Jacob sat down and helped himself to coffee from the cafetiere.

Irene reached out across the table as he sipped from the mug. 'I'm really pleased you are writing again, but you were a bit-'

'Intense?' he smirked, placing his coffee on a bamboo coaster he'd never seen before.

'Scary, more like,' she said softly. 'I tried to talk to you last night, but you didn't even see me. Missed calls, voicemails, I can deal with that, but I was right there, next to you and I didn't exist.'

'It's complicated.'

'So tell me!'

'I'm just in the zone, like you said. That's all. You know me. It won't last.'

'And that's your answer?' She rose from her chair and pulled on her scarf. 'Well, that's great, but in case you'd missed it, I'm screwed, J.J! I have nothing. No ideas. No time. No career!' She ripped out her squalid sketches, screwed up the page and hurled it across the room. 'If I don't come up with something in the next few days, I'm back to unsolicited submissions, back to agent one-to-ones at conferences. Begging *them* to read *my* stuff! *They* should be begging *me*! I am pleased for *you*, but I need *you* to be *here*. Not wherever it is you've been over the last two days, okay?'

Jacob nodded. Irene grabbed his hand. 'I don't want to end up like that writer on the telly. All that potential – unfulfilled. There was a real buzz about her new trilogy. Her agent said the final draft was ready and then... well we all know what happened next.'

'What?' he asked, sipping at the black, bitter broth.

'You haven't heard? That Lola Montez, local writer I follow on Twitter. You know the one. Remember that thriller she wrote about the Irish dancer involved with the I.R.A. A Dance of erm...'

'A Dance of Rivers.'

'Yeah. Well she died this morning, gas leak or something. I didn't even know she lived in Old Portsmouth. You do know her, she writes under that pseudonym from the Sherlock Holmes' books. Minor character that Conan Doyle used... Oh, what the pissing hell is wrong with my brain today? Her poor doggy, Toby... it was all pretty gross... Ah, Johnson. That's it. Shinwell Johnson.'

Irene continued but her words did not get through.

There was a dark side of him that enjoyed seeing other writers fail, but not this!

Irene's words burned like verbal shrapnel inside his heart. He forgot he was holding the coffee cup and the black liquid pooled across the table like blood at midnight.

In his dark glasses and beanie, he returned to the alley.

'Well, well, welcome back. You are one serious writer, Jacob

Jacket,' said Zeitgeist, surprising him from behind the pop-up lamppost. 'Not many cold-hearted bastards come back for a third crack. Nice disguise, but you don't have to worry about The Fuzz. They can't tie that package to you - gas leak, end of story. All those old pipes and rusty fittings - such a terrible business.' Zeitgeist took a long drag on his cigar and grinned. 'Thank you for your loyalty. I do hate it when they break the contract. *I* applaud *you* Jacob Jacket.'

'I shouldn't be here,' said Jacob, softly, broken.

'Oh come now, of course you should. Your passion for writing has brought you back to me. Deep down you've always known that writing is more important than anything or anyone. That has just taken you time to understand. Congratulations, Jacob Jacket, you've discovered the real you.'

Zeitgeist was right. He craved the whisperings; the rush of a perfect story. He'd tasted it and wanted more. A perfect addiction. He could not stop.

And so, for the third time, Zeitgeist delivered.


At dawn, Zeitgeist handed him the next brown package. 'As before,' said The Midnight Man, who at once disappeared into shadow.

'I understand,' said Jacob, the lightweight parcel tucked beneath his arm. His brain buzzed with Zeitgeist's whisperings.

As he turned onto Broad Street, a shiver ran down his back. The sensation of being watched overwhelmed him. Car windows, glass shop fronts and even the mirror of a chained-up push bike. From all sides, the face staring back cackled like a working class Doctor Moreau. He was truly lost, unable to control temptation, unable to stop the hunger.

The reflections murmured. 'Look at it! Look at it!'

They were pointing to the package.

Jacob glanced down and his heart almost stopped: the address was his own.

The name on the brown paper packaging... was not.

The third book was complete.

Another day had flown by.

There were no lights on in his flat, but why would there be? It was late. Irene would be asleep.

He sat cross-legged on the common, beneath a streetlamp; the damp winter grass oozed into his chinos. Jacob Jacket turned the package around in his hands and glared at the name scrawled upon the brown paper: Irene Norton.

'Irene, goodnight, Irene, lah, dah, de, dum... ' he hummed, as he climbed to his feet and paced across the grass. Jacob crossed the road and unlocked the main door to the building. He headed up the stairs and at the door of their flat, he lifted the letterbox.

Then Jacob Jacket made his choice.

Rain dripped down the back of his neck as he stood on the steps of the Guildhall.

Jacob placed the package between the stone lions that guarded the mighty clock tower and sat down next to it.

Further up the concrete staircase, homeless drunks swigged from plastic bottles, drowning in alcohol and melancholy. Their misery would soon be over. There were always going to be casualties and there would be further consequences for Jacob Jacket for what he was about to do. But he was willing to pay the price of guilt and self-destruction, to save his Irene.

On the cold, wet concrete, he wrote a note.

As the rain flattened his hair against his head, he pushed the message into his pocket to keep it dry. Lost in the rhythm of drumming water, he closed his eyes and waited.

The alarm on his phone went off at 23:58.

Jacob Jacket got to his feet and headed down the steps.

He'd made it to the council offices opposite Central Library when the first chime triggered the bomb.

The clock tower exploded in the night.

He didn't look back.

'Without time, there can be no midnight,' he said. 'Without midnight, there can be no Midnight Man.'

Tears merged with the rain, trickling down his face as he headed home.

The printer whirred away into the morning and at the end of the third ink cartridge it shuddered to a halt. Jacob retrieved the Zeitgeist Chapters from the machine and piled them high.

On the table in the living room was Irene's journal, a faded hazel colour, that matched her eyes. Inside the cover was her notepad, open at more sketches. This time she'd signed the drawing and called it – Dismembered Newspaper Critic.

Jacob grinned and placed the soggy note from his pocket on top of the folder.

***My future is nothing without yours. J.J***

As he turned his back on the Zeitgeist Chapters he caught his reflection. Recognising the smiling face, he nodded. The man in the mirror returned the gesture. 'Welcome back, stranger,' he whispered.

He woke the next morning, with a large yellow post-it note stuck on his forehead.

***Wow J.J! This is the best stuff you have EVER written. I'll own up once it's published. Love you loads today xxx***

A smiley face rounded off the message.

Jacob stuck the note to his chest and pottered to the bathroom. He grinned at the mirror.

It was over...

The lady on the radio spoke of the devastation. The city had not only lost nine innocent people to the blast, but its identity – a beloved landmark lost forever. They took loads of callers on the show. It seemed more people mourned the clock tower than the homeless drunks who had been blasted into the afterlife. Jacob shook his head at society's flaws as he typed The Zeitgeist Chapters on his keyboard.

'No time. No midnight,' he recanted, suddenly frowning at the screen.

The words he'd typed had vanished.

The cursor flashed on the blank page.

Jacob tried again.

He hit the keys harder but no writing appeared. He tried again and again, but nothing. He checked the connections, turned the laptop on and off. No matter what he did, Jacob could not write.

Breathing heavily, he cursed the name that circled his brain. 'Zeitgeist!'

Hours later, a woman's voice droned like an irritating wasp. She laughed at her own jingle and wished her listeners well. He hurled her across the room, shattering the radio against the wall. The laptop was next – a silver Frisbee, that smashed into the skirting boards.

'Useless piece of shit!' He grinned madly and picked up a biro and a small notepad. He tried to scribe the letter **Z** on the page, but it was as if there was no ink inside the pen.

He tried a pencil - nothing.

Jacob could not write.

Whatever he tried – chalk, felt tips, butter, ketchup, jam or blood from a pricked finger, no words formed on any surface.

He had betrayed Zeitgeist and this was his punishment.

Slumped against the wall, his head in his hands, the letterbox slapped, followed by a thud on the carpet. Jacob raced to the door and gasped at the package on the mat: Brown paper tied up with string.

'Greetings from Midnight, Jacob Jacket,' he read aloud.

As he turned the package, a piece of folded paper drifted to the floor.

The handwriting that scribed his initials belonged to Irene.

***It wasn't right to take your beautiful writing. So, I***

*found someone who can help me write. I can't talk about him, but he said he knew you and to give you this package. He said you'd understand. Aren't you lucky to have me xxx*

Jacob stared at the smiley face at the bottom of the note and picked up the package. 'No!' he cried, scrambling to his feet.

He flung open the door and raced down the stairs.

Irene was already across the road, climbing into her car, when he reached the main door, but it was the figure in the cape on the common that caught his attention.

The Midnight Man doffed his wide brimmed hat and smiled.

The package in Jacob's hand ticked and tocked and then it stopped...

## Acknowledgements

With thanks to the true editors of this collection, six brilliant Portsmouth University students who kindly gave us their time and expertise and edited three stories each. They are: Madeleine Watson, Michael Kelliher, Robyn Omahony, Tayla Osborne, Jessica Matthews and Esther Migueliz Obanos.

Thank you Jon Everitt, Danielle Shaw, Tracy and Kate of Port&Lemon, Nick Ingamells, Richard Stride, David Percival, Lindy Elliott and Julie Duffy. A huge thank you to Arts Council England for believing in us and supporting our workshops, readings and promenade.

Tessa Ditner: thank you Ric Amorosi. No one but you could have dragged me away from London, I'm so glad you did. Thank you to my mother, Dolores Ditner, for always 'throwing ideas out there' (even when it is annoying) and to David Stafford for saying 'Why are you waiting for a gold star?'

For help with the Lawless stories, William Sutton thanks Caroline Sutton, Tom Harris, Matt Wingett, Zella Compton, the Portsmouth City Museum, and Caroline Morrison at the Victory Museum in the Historic Dockyard.

Sarah Cheverton: I would like to thank Martin, Angela, Ron, Matt, Amy and Adele – for everything that I am and for our story as a family. May ours be a tale without an ending.

Lynne E Blackwood: To my father who gave me the education and strength to become who I am today.

Matt Wingett: Thank you, Portsmouth. Every day I find out new things about you and your people, both past and present - and think how amazing you are.

Lightning Source UK Ltd.
Milton Keynes UK
UKHW02f0841181217
314679UK00011B/647/P